Strange Little Girls

Belladonna Publishing
belladonnapublishing.com

Strange Little Girls

Edited by
Camilla Bruce and Liv Lingborn

Belladonna
Publishing
belladonnapublishing.com

belladonnapublishing.com

978-82-999548-3-9 ISBN

Contents

Fairy Tale Ending
Terra LeMay

You're made of sticks and bones and greasy feathers, as are all changelings.

You didn't always know this, but now that you do, it's easy to imagine how it went down.

Your mother's baby – not you, the real one – cried all the time. Night and day, every minute, without cease. You know this because your mother told you. "God, you were such an awful baby."

Not *you*, the other kid.

Your mother never suspected you were a changeling. She doesn't know, even now, and not knowing the other baby wasn't you, she says things like, "You wouldn't suck, you wouldn't sleep, but you sure knew how to scream. Sometimes I wanted to put a pillow over your face."

Your mother didn't have the means to experiment with brands of formula or the latest in special diapers for babies with sensitive skin. No magic balm guaranteed to make any baby sleep. There was a wind-up swing, and sometimes she sang lullabies, but those things never worked. The baby – who was not you – wouldn't stop crying.

"Put her car seat on top of the dryer," said a few people, but your parents didn't own a car, a car seat, or a dryer.

Your mother told them she'd tried it already.

"At least hire a babysitter for a few hours," they said, as if it were an easy, straightforward thing to do. "You need to get some rest."

But how? Babysitters aren't free. And people who talk about welfare mothers have obviously never tried to pay for daycare on fast food service wages. After rent and utilities, baby blankets and binkies, there's no money left for a sitter. Not even for an hour. Not even when your mother's baby cried for three days straight.

But what about your father? Couldn't he watch the baby for a few hours? Just to give your mother a break? Where's your father in all this?

Your father's working longer hours to make up the shifts your mother can no longer work. There were no extra hours available at the Glad bag factory, but he found vacant slots he could fill at Maytag. It's not enough to get the phone bill in on time, but it keeps the baby in diapers so she can run your mother ragged. Until one day, it's just too much and your mother says the magic words that brought you into the world.

Your mother lifts her wailing infant into the air, just as a cute teenage girl on a television a few feet away does the same with her baby brother: Your mother is watching The Labyrinth.

"Goblin king, goblin king," she whispers, along with the actress on the screen. "Take this child of mine far away from me!" Stupid, ill-thought words spoken in a moment of weakness, but the desire that fuels them is, for those few seconds, genuine and heartfelt.

Miles and miles away in faerie, bored, surrounded by muppets, a goblin king hears your mother's heartfelt wish: "What about it, boys?" He snatches a chicken drumstick from the mouth of a nearby muppet, and says, "Shall we go and fetch the babe?"

The muppets shriek and bounce with the kind of enthusiasm only muppets are capable of, heads bobbing and limbs flailing. This king cleans the meat from the drumstick, then gives the bone to another muppet to carry it for him. It will make a good femur for a baby.

Ten minutes later, your mother would have taken her words back, if she understood what she'd started. If she'd been reading fairy tales instead of watching them on TV, she might have had reason to suspect. Instead, your mother's real daughter is in faerie being pampered like a fairy princess while you have the displeasure of living her sad little life.

Life is never fair, is it?

On the way to your mother's apartment, the goblin king collects the rest of what he needs.

Sticks and bones and feathers until he hits the highway, where he finds a discarded wife-beater with food and oil stains on it, an athletic shoe, and a dead opossum. A perfect windfall, for his purposes. The opossum's skull and jawbone are ruined, crushed by the weight of whatever automobile struck and killed it, but its decaying organs will become your stomach, your liver, your kidneys, your bowels. Your undersized lungs.

Its heart he discards, thankfully, in a sudden surprising moment of compassion. In the off-chance you survived, the opossum's half-rotted fleshy heart would be tender, easily bruised. Weak. He picks out a chunk of broken asphalt to use in its place. Granite would have been better, but there's no time to be choosy. Anyway, the odds are not in your favor. Most changelings don't live but a scant handful of days.

At your parents' apartment, the baby's eerily quiet. He lifts her gently from her basinet and cradles her against his chest, cooing. She's too warm, probably coming down with a cold or a virus. He'll have to call upon the herbalist on the way home. His little princess needs medicine.

The muppets deposit the collection of sticks and feathers and putrid roadkill they've gathered into the dirty wife-beater, which he ties up at the bottom to make a sack. Once they're finished, he looks at you, then at the baby, then at you again. He opens the window and tosses the baby out into the air, toward the swollen, yellow moon above. Before she can fall to her death, he claps his hands and turns her into a bubble. A gentle breeze blows her toward his castle. Easy peasy.

You, on the other hand, are a problem child. You smell atrocious and do not much resemble any baby, much less his new little goblin princess. He ties a shoelace around the shirt sack, just below the arm-holes, then knots the top so it's roughly spheroid like a baby's head.

When he's satisfied, he drops the makeshift baby – you – in the basinet and considers. The stains on the wife-beater almost make a face, especially once he tears a hole for your mouth, but you're still not quite there.

What to do? he ponders, *what to do.* Then decides he must give up something of his own to bring you to life. He picks his teeth, withdraws a bit of gristle from some earlier meal, and plunks it down for a nose. It's still not enough. Almost, almost, but what is missing?

Oh, that's right, your mother's baby likes to cry.

He pinches your cheek hard, to make you scream and, obediently, you howl to wake the dead. Perfect. Your mother will never know the difference.

Changelings are meant to be temporary. If you last thirteen hours, you're a success. But even if you don't last a minute, as long as your corpse fools your parents for thirteen hours, you'll have done your job. The goblin king doesn't linger to see if you'll become a rare survivor. At home he has a real, live human child to nurture, and she's sick. He must get back to his castle as soon as possible. What becomes of you is of no consequence.

A few minutes after he disappears, your new mother wanders blearily into the room and scoops you up. If she notices anything amiss, it's only that you're too warm and your breath rattles. By morning, you're limp, almost lifeless. Your parents borrow money from their neighbor to pay for a cab to the emergency room.

It takes weeks of feeding tubes and intravenous fluids to get you stable enough to take home again, and forever after you suffer from a weak constitution. After all, there's only so much you can do with sticks and bones and roadkill. But you do not die.

Maybe it was the chunk of asphalt for a heart that did it for you.

You're not exactly certain when you began to suspect your origins. All little girls grow up believing they're lost princesses, right? You have vague memories of seeing Disney's Cinderella at the theater – but it must have been a rerelease. You're too young to have seen the original.

Scratch that, maybe it was Disney Princesses on Ice. Your mother's boss's wife, DeAnna, took you to see it when you were seven, because you were near the same age as her own daughter. Though, even at seven, you were able to recognize the signs that DeAnna regretted inviting you as soon as she came to pick you up. The wrinkled nose. The forced affectionate gestures. It was near that time in your life – early elementary school – when you began to recognize you were different from other children. Poor people smell funny, but with you, it was something deeper. Indefinable, but intrinsic to your identity. Your roadkill internal organs, perhaps, though it's really hard to say. In any case, the other children recognized it too and steered clear of you.

Ever after, you identified with the Disney princesses because most of them were outcasts just like you. Best of all, they gave you the secret handshake: *Wish for a better life.*

So simple! So intuitive. All you needed to do was make the right wish, at the right time, in the right way, and the whole world would be made right, just for you.

Never one to waste time, you began wishing on stars, chicken wishbones, four-leaf clovers and rabbits' feet.

You wished every night before bed, and first thing when you woke up in the morning. You wished for a fairy godmother, a fairy godfather, and talking mice.

You wished your mother would stop crying. You wished your parents would stop fighting.

You wished your father's unemployment wouldn't run out next week.

You wished the car (they finally bought a car when you were three – a piece of shit that left your family stranded on the side of the road more times than you can recall) would get more miles to a gallon.

Most of all, you wished Prince Charming would rescue you and take you away to live with your real parents, the King and Queen. You didn't understand romance back then, but you understood the purpose of heroes and wish-fulfillment fantasies.

By the fifth grade, you'd gained siblings, attended half a dozen elementary schools, and lived in at least nine different houses. Possibly more. Somewhere you lost count, probably before you were old enough to properly keep track anyway.

Your parents never meant to provide such an unstable home, but economic circumstances forced your family to move again and again while your mother and father chased vainly after employment and educational opportunities. Faerie lights, most of them, disappearing just as hope that they were real seemed plausible and near.

Your earliest memories are as blurry as any human child's, but you remember how hard things were. Do you remember living in a mobile home out on route 40? No air in summer, no heat in winter, and you slept under scratchy wool army blankets to keep from freezing. You were only five or six, then, but you remember.

Soon after, your parents rented a farmhouse that had rats bigger than the biggest cat you'd ever seen, and your mother said it was because they were eating corn from the grain elevator on the other side of the barn. They were nothing like the mice in Cinderella, but you kept wishing they would talk, that they would tell you when your fairy godmother would show up, because there was never any food in that particular house. Nevermind the corn in the grain elevator, which was feed for cattle and belonged to the landlord who owned the house anyway.

You remember watching Disney's Pinocchio at your babysitter's, then going home and staring out your bedroom window, breath frosting the glass. Which star? Which star could you wish upon to get your fairy tale ending? Always wishing for that. Always wishing.

You can hardly recall a memory that doesn't contain a wish in it, truth be told.

Then your family moved to the city, into a small townhouse, and you remember... what? Nothing. Who am I kidding? You don't remember any of this, do you? No, of course not.

This isn't really your story. It's mine. And you, you little bitch, I bet you don't even know how good you have it. Stolen away as a babe – plucked from your cradle before you'd even learned to smile and raised in the lap of luxury by the Goblin King himself.

Surely you must have guessed something was amiss. All that glitter, those shining baubles and golden fruit?

You've stopped to examine your privileges from time to time, haven't you? You've asked yourself, "How did I get to be so lucky?" at least once?

No?

No.

Happily Ever After is never enough, is it? You want to know where you came from, what you lost. You want to know who your real parents are.

Well, screw you, princess. No matter what happens to you – dragons, trolls, locked away in a tower, pricked fingers and a thousand years of sleeping – it doesn't matter. You get your happily ever ending no matter what.

Me?

There are no fairy tale endings in real life, and besides, nobody cares what happens to a changeling. We're nothing but trash to be discarded when we've served our purpose.

Just like the family you left behind.

Deep Down
Tim Jeffreys

Lucy was five years old when she first realised she'd been born in the wrong skin. In truth, of course, she'd always known – deep in her heart, in some dim, disregarded way. To all appearances she was – outwardly at least – a normal five-year old girl with straight blonde hair, watchful grey eyes, two chubby pink arms and two chubby pink legs. But on the inside she was, she knew, a fish. As a matter of fact she was a black sea bass.

She knew this despite having been born and raised inland, in the middle of a noisy crowded city, and never having set eyes on the sea. The nearest she got to water was the inflatable paddling pool she'd drag out on to the lawn every summer. She would fill the pool using a hose, then loll about in it for most of the day, kicking and flapping about in frustration. Her mother used to take her to the local pool but this had stopped one day when Lucy was three. That day she'd waited until her mother's back was turned, pulled off her armbands, dived down to the bottom of the deep-end and rested there, head-down, as happy as she'd ever been in her life. Happy, that is, until her mother plunged into the water beside her and yanked her back to the surface.

Lucy knew better than to ask her mother to take her to the pool again. If she did ask, she would always get the same lecture.

"You were down there for more than five-minutes!" her mother would say, "I was frantic, searching all over for you. In the end they had to get everyone out of the pool and it was only then that I saw you floating near the bottom. What were you trying to do? Drown yourself?"

"I wasn't going to drown, mother," Lucy would say, though she knew it was useless to try to explain. For the time being she had to make do with the outgrown paddling pool and the dreams she had almost every night of skimming along in the near dark on the ocean floor.

At school she had a weird compulsion to find large groups of children and closely follow them around. These were usually children she didn't know, since she had no real friends of her own. The children were sometimes amused by her following, and would taunt her and laugh; or they would find it strange, frightening even, and throw stones to scare her away, or they would run fast to escape her. Lucy always ran with them as much as she could, snaking paths around the school yard, even when she knew they didn't want her. Questioned about this by her teacher, she said she didn't know why she did it. She just had to. It made her feel safe.

"Why don't you just find a nice couple of children and make friends with them," her exasperated mother said.

"I can't," Lucy told her. "They're not like me."

"What do you mean? Of course they are!"

"No," said Lucy, thoughtful. "No, they're not."

Aged seven she found her way into the learning library and checked out a book on fish. A few days later she said to her mother:

"I was born a girl, but I might not be a girl forever." This caused her mother to drop her crochet set.

"What?"

"What I mean is: you needn't worry if one day I change and become a boy. It's perfectly normal. For my kind."

"What on earth are you talking about?"

"We all start out female, but some of us change. I read it in the book."

"What book? What book have you been reading? Bring it to me right now."

When Lucy returned from her room and presented her mother with the book on fish, the poor woman was even more confounded. An appointment was made with a child psychologist.

Lucy told the psychologist, whose name – much to her amusement – was Doctor Fligglestone, about her dreams of swimming along the ocean floor, and of how she sometimes stood in front of the mirror making O-shapes with her mouth, how following the groups of children around at school made her feel safe, and even about how she might become a boy one day, but Doctor Fligglestone seemed not to understand. He was an old grey man and had hair growing out of his nose.

"Do you feel you *are* a boy, underneath?" Doctor Fligglestone asked, sitting up in his chair.

"No," Lucy said. "Not really."

"So you want to *be* a boy?"

"I don't want to be a boy," Lucy said, with a little laugh which she hid behind her hand "Boys are rough and dirty."

"But you think you might *become* a boy?"

"I might," Lucy said. "I don't *want* to really, but I might."

"Hmmm." Doctor Fligglestone scribbled something on his desk pad. "What is it you think you are then?

Lucy paused a moment, biting her lip. Then she leaned forward and said in a whisper: "You won't tell my mother? Promise."

"I can't promise that, Lucy."

"She wouldn't understand."

"Why don't you just tell me for now, and we can think about whether or not to tell your mother later."

"Well," Lucy said. "What I am is a…" She closed her eyes and made a great effort to pronounce the words as she had read them in the book: "Centro-pri-stis stri-a-ta."

Opening her eyes again, she sat back, pleased with herself.

Doctor Fligglestone looked at her for a long moment. His pen hovered over the pad. "What?"

"Centropristis striata," she said, and smiled.

"What is that?"

"It's a black sea bass."

"A…" Doctor Fligglestone gazed at her. Lucy noticed again the tufts of white hair in his nostrils. She felt a great desire to pull them.

There was a hushed conversation between Doctor Fligglestone and Lucy's mother as Lucy sat on a chair outside the room, swinging her legs. Her mother looked angry when she finally emerged.

"What is it?" Lucy asked.

"Come on," her mother said. "We're going home. You don't have to come back here again. You know sometimes you're too clever for your own good, madam."

Lucy couldn't understand this, or why her mother was angry and calling her madam.

All she'd done was tell the truth.

"Can we go to the seaside in summer?" she asked.

"No," her mother said. "Absolutely not."

"But I want to see the sea. I want to swim."

"Well… you can't. So there."

She had to wait another eight years until a boy she became friendly with – Jason was his name, three years older and in possession of a driving licence – borrowed his father's car and took her on the long journey to the coast. The first time she saw the sea, she was mesmerised. She couldn't stop smiling. How it shimmered. How the waves crashed and turned. How it called to her.

Turning to Jason who stood beside her on the beach, she said: "I want to go in."

"Shouldn't we get a drink first?"

"No, I'm going in right now."

She began to peel off her clothes. Underneath, she already wore her swimming costume. Jason seemed surprised.

"I didn't bring mine," he said. "I didn't think…"

"Wear what you've got on. No one'll notice."

Leaving him, she raced down the beach and leapt into the water. The sea grabbed her like a cold embrace. At first she swam about the surface, laughing. Then she began to duck below the waves and swim along the sand with her eyes open, examining everything. Jason appeared in only his underwear, looking sheepish. He caught hold of her as she broke the surface.

"Why're you so happy?"

"It's the water. Isn't it wonderful?"

"It's alright. Listen, I think I want to kiss you."

Lucy laughed, assuming he was joking. He drew back with a hurt expression. Seeing this, and feeling that she owed him something for bringing her there, she straightened her face and said, "Alright." His mouth tasted of cigarettes, and she couldn't stop the giggles. *He doesn't know,* she thought. *He doesn't know what I am. He doesn't know that he's actually smooching with a fish!* And imagining this in her mind, Jason and the sea bass, mouths locked together, she giggled all the more.

Put out by her amusement, he drew away again and gave her a dark look. "Is there something wrong with you?"

"Don't you know?" she said. "Can't you see?"

"I don't know what you're on about."

"No." She turned away from him. "I just want to swim," she said, and dived again.

There were other boys after Jason, but whenever one tried to kiss her she got the same image in her mind of him, lips locked with a fish, and she couldn't help but laugh. After a while, the boys left her alone. She was unconcerned. Her passion was the sea. She had learnt to dive.

She was eighteen and had passed the driving test too, and acquired an old car, and since her mother could no longer stand in her way, she would pack the boot every weekend and head for the coast. Inadvertently, she met a man – Cam – who shared her passion. He too, was so happy in the water that she wondered if he too was secretly a black sea bass. When he kissed her, it felt right. There were no fits of giggles.

Those hours she spent down in the dark ocean with Cam where the happiest she had so far known. But still, she felt, there was something wrong. Unsure what it was, she returned to the books, and found the answer.

Not only am I in the wrong skin, she realised, *but I'm in the wrong place too*.

When, the next time she saw Cam, he surprised her by getting down on one knee and proposing marriage, she realised this was her chance.

"Yes," she said. "On one condition. That we honeymoon in Mexico."

Cam looked puzzled, but said he had no problem with this.

The day came. Lucy stood up in the church and repeated what they told her to repeat. She wanted to get it over with so they could set off for the Gulf of Mexico where all the books agreed she would find her kind. Her mother was overjoyed to see that her odd daughter had succeeded in finding a husband. But then, when Lucy lay with Cam in bed that night – after all the pushing and grunting was over with – she said to him:

"This isn't the right way at all. Our kind normally lay eggs of course." She heard his soft laughter. "What's that?"

"Do you think you'll still love me if I change sex?" Cam sat up in bed and stared at her.

"Change... change *sex*?"

"It could happen. It happened to you... didn't it?"

"To me? What do you mean?"

"Yes, you..." She stared into his face. "You mean...you're not...are you...just a man?"

"Of course I'm just a man. What did you think I was?"

"Well, I... well." She examined his face for a long moment. "Well, it doesn't matter. I was just being silly."

Cam looked relieved and started to laugh. He bent to kiss her but she turned her face away.

"What is it?" he asked.

"If only you could see what I see, inside my mind."

Mexico was hot and crowded and dusty. Not long after they arrived, Lucy insisted they take a boat out on the gulf coast.

"Shall I pack the diving gear," he asked her.

"No. Leave it here."

So they hired a small yacht and set out, just the two of them. When Lucy could no longer see land and all about her was blue and tranquil, she climbed up on to the prow of the yacht whilst Cam was busy at the helm.

"What're you doing?" he casually asked, glancing up at her.

Lucy sighed. "I know you won't understand, but I've no choice. None of us have any choice, really. We just have to be what we are, or – that is – what we're not but know we are underneath."

He smiled. "What're you talking about? Get down from there, you might slip."

"I need to find the others. The ones like me."

"Oh," he said, still smiling. "There's absolutely no one else like you, hon." Lucy wasn't smiling. "Tell my mother I'm sorry, will you?"

"Sorry for what...?" Cam began, but before he'd finished speaking Lucy turned and dived into the sea.

"Lucy!" He ran to the rail and scanned the water. There was no sign of her. "Lucy!"

The Cottage of Curiosities

Annie Neugebauer

Patty could never decide which way to face when she got on the tree swing.

She looked across the lawn at the house. It was small and white with a pointy roof with dipped sides and pretty green trim. The stone chimney crooked like a kindly old man, and the curtains were open to let in the evening sunlight. If she faced the house, she felt more cheerful, but then she always felt the urge to turn and look behind her at the woods.

Things lived in the woods, and most of them weren't bad, but sometimes, Patty was sure, they got hungry in there. Mama said if you walked too far in you could get turned around.

Through the two ropes that held up the swing's wooden seat, Patty looked at the woods, studying the narrow limbs of saplings and the ground where the first of the dying leaves collected in puddles of burgundy and gold.

A little beyond where the yard met the forest, something shiny glinted under the last touch of the setting sun, winking at her once before it disappeared.

Patty stepped around the swing and took a few steps forward, ignoring the fretful squirrel that chattered at her from the tree. The sparkle flashed again.

Distantly, she heard the cuckoo clock go off inside the house. The little bird cried six – seven times before falling silent, which meant it was time for Patty to go back in. Mama didn't like it when Patty pretended not to hear it, and Mama hadn't been feeling well for several days now, so she wouldn't want to get out of bed to ring the big brass bell that could be heard from even farther away than the cuckoo.

But Patty wanted to know what the shiny thing was. Maybe it was something neat that would make Mama feel better! Mama loved neat things; she collected them.

With that settled, Patty mustered her courage and tromped into the brush. She kept her eyes trained on the spot where the glint came from, and even though her heart was pounding, she got there quickly and squatted to pick it up.

It was some special type of rock, about the size of her small palm. She flexed her wrist and tossed it into the air. It made a satisfying smack when she caught it. The surface was rough and angular, mostly black and gray with a little bit of brown on it, but parts of it gleamed silver. It was perfect.

The deep, full tolls of the bell rang out. Mama wanted her to come inside. With an eager bounce in her step, Patty ran back to the house.

Mama's room was the only room where Patty didn't need to shut the curtains for the night. They were already closed, and the air was very dim. Several candles were melted almost down to their bases, and the room was smoky.

When Patty walked in she saw Mama's silhouette under the covers. She must be very tired to get back in bed after ringing the bell. Patty tried to be quiet, but the old wooden floors creaked beneath her feet, even when she walked across the woven rug, as she always did, to look at the shelves.

They were full of Mama's collection. There were pale seashells – one with a pearl inside it – and tusks with carvings on them, paintings and sketches that hung from ribbons, and the skull of a critter with horns. There was a stuffed bird in a big fancy cage, and a globe in its own stand. There were bugs of all different kinds pinned to a board, but Patty didn't like to look at those. Instead she looked at the little clay pot full of brightly-colored feathers.

In the center of it all hung the dark, fancy cuckoo clock with its mysterious chains and weights dangling from it like necklaces. The center piece swung back and forth, back and forth. Its ticking filled the room with familiar, incessant rhythm. Patty stared at the door the little bird lived in, then looked away.

It had been just her and Mama for as long as Patty could remember, but people used to travel through the woods to see the house sometimes. They called it the cottage of curiosities. Mama liked to show them her treasures, but she never sold them, so eventually people stopped coming.

The special rock felt heavy in Patty's hand, so she left the shelves and sat on the edge of the bed.

"How do you feel, Mama?"

Mama rolled onto her back with a soft groan, peering up at Patty. Her face almost looked like a stranger's in the gloom. "Hi baby. I'm a little cold."

Patty tilted her head to the side. The breeze outside was crisp and chilly, but inside the house it was almost too warm. She reached out and put a hand on Mama's forehead, like Mama did to her when she was sick. The gilded mirror on the nightstand on the other side of the bed reflected Mama's profile.

"You're very warm," Patty said.

"I don't feel warm," said Mama. Then she pulled the blankets in tighter around her chin and rolled back onto her side. "Will you blow out the candles when you leave, sweetheart? Mama's very tired."

Patty frowned. Mama wasn't going to scold her for making her ring the bell? Or ask her what it was she was holding in her hand? She really must be feeling bad.

Patty stood, blew out all of the candles but one, and set the chunk of silver on the tray next to the bed. Maybe it would cheer Mama up in the morning. Then she kissed Mama on the cheek, took the last candle, and left her to sleep.

Patty brought Mama breakfast, but she didn't want any. The silver rock was gone though, so she must have gotten up during the night and seen it, maybe put it on the shelves somewhere. Patty hoped it made her smile.

Patty stayed inside all morning and afternoon, just in case Mama needed her. She walked around their small home and studied every single shelf and all their curiosities. She'd seen them before, but every time she looked she noticed something new.

This time she spotted several dark, oval medallions hanging high on one wall, but she couldn't read what they said. In one cabinet she saw a whole bird's nest with four eggs in it, next to some arrowheads and a piece of strangely shaped coral. There was a section of wood that felt like stone and a stone with the skeleton of a fish in it. Then there were her old favorites, like the knight's helmet and the stuffed fox with his long whiskers and glass eyes.

As fascinating as these things were – for Patty loved to make up stories about each object and where it came from – by the time the cuckoo's cries grew short and began to grow long again, Patty was twitchy with extra energy. It was still a couple of hours until she'd have to be inside for the night, so she decided to go outside and swing.

This time she faced the woods, but for the first time, she didn't feel the need to watch them just in case something came out. She wanted to go back in. What if there was more silver in there? Or something better, like gold? Or something Patty couldn't even imagine? If she could find something really good, it would make Mama feel better for sure. Only babies were afraid of the woods.

The cries of the cuckoo came from inside – six of them. She still had an hour before Mama would ring the bell.

Patty didn't even stop swinging. She jumped forward when the ropes were stretched all the way, and she hit the ground running. She'd have to search fast.

Patty's fingers trembled as she picked it up. She could hardly even believe it.

Nestled among old brown leaves was a short stick completely covered in bright orange moss. She'd never seen moss that color before – only greens and grays – but it got better. There was a little black crow's foot still attached, grasping one side. What had happened to the rest of the crow she didn't like to wonder, but there was no doubt Mama would love this curiosity.

Patty straightened back up, gripping the stick by the end furthest away from the foot, and turned to leave. Then turned again. And again.

Which way had she come from?

A twig snapped to her side, and she whirled. Nothing moved, but it had gotten darker beneath the leaves. What time was it? Was Mama worried about her? Had she already rung the bell?

A crunch, this time from farther away. "Hello?" Patty called softly.

There was a waiting silence. "Who's there?" Patty asked.

For some reason, Patty thought she might get an answer, and she desperately didn't want to.

She ran.

She clutched the stick with the crow's foot to her chest and bolted, sprinting through the trees like a wild doe. Twigs scraped the soft puffs of her cheeks, and once she tripped on a vine, but she never looked back. She didn't know if she was going the right way until she heard the bell ring. She adjusted her direction toward it.

She didn't hear anything chasing her, but still she ran. Finally Patty burst through the trees into the soft sunlight slanting from behind the house, and she didn't stop. She ran up to front door, twisted the knob, and skittered inside, shoving it closed behind her. She stood leaning on it, panting.

"You're such a baby," she muttered.

Just to prove how silly she'd been, she went to the window and looked outside. The grass stretched wide and green and empty beyond the flowers next to the house. The woods were still.

Her tree swing swayed gently. Patty held her breath, but then she forced herself to laugh. She'd probably bumped it when she ran through the yard. She shut the curtains for the night.

Only then did she remember her prize: the moss-covered stick clutched in her hand, the little crow's foot perched on the end.

Mama was lying on her side again, and the room was still smoky and dark. Patty was surprised Mama had bothered to get up to ring the bell at all.

Patty crossed over the creaky floors and the thick rug to look at the curiosities. She scanned the shelves for where Mama might have put her silver rock, but she couldn't find it. She spent a few moments studying the pretty miniature town on the far side. There was snow on some of the roofs but not all of them. Mama said Patty could put them in her room when she got a little older.

From the cuckoo came an odd, strangled cry, and Patty stared at the wooden door the bird lived in, but it wasn't time for it to come out. The clock's tick hiccupped, then kept going. Patty turned away.

"Mama?" she said softly, walking over to the bed. Mama groaned.

Patty put a hand on Mama's shoulder, but she wouldn't roll over onto her back. Patty peered into the mirror on the other side of the bed, but it wasn't turned at quite the right angle to see her face.

"Mama, are you okay?"

Mama mumbled something Patty couldn't hear. Patty reached over to feel her forehead, but her hand hovered. She knew Mama was sick. Really sick. Patty didn't know what to do.

She lightly brushed Mama's hair back, then set the stick on the tray next to the bed. "I'm sorry the silver didn't make you feel better," she whispered. "But you'll like this one. I can tell."

When Mama's only reply was the deep breathing of heavy sleep, Patty took the last candle and left, dragging her feet behind her.

Patty had to do something to help Mama. The stick with the crow's foot was gone in the morning, which meant Mama had gotten up at least once overnight, but she refused breakfast again.

She had to go back into the woods. She had to find something really good so Mama would get better. Maybe she'd even meet a person – a grown-up who would know what to do.

As Patty headed into the green shade, her swing hung still and silent under the tree, and the squirrel watched her, holding his tail. Patty marched with purpose, heading in as straight a line as she could.

But it was impossible to walk in a straight line with all the trees in the way, and before Patty knew it she wasn't sure which way she'd come from. The first tear had started down her cheek when she spotted something white.

Sniffling a little, Patty eased toward the small fluffy lump. She nudged it with the toe of her shoe, but it didn't move. She knelt, reaching out to touch the soft fur with her hand. It was a rabbit.

Patty gently picked it up, but it flopped limply. It had two big ears so tall she could see the veins running through the insides of them. Its eyes were open but a dull, blank black. It was dead, but Patty didn't see anything wrong with it.

"You poor thing," she said. "What happened to you?" The rabbit didn't answer.

Then Patty got an idea. Maybe this could be a curiosity. Its fur was perfectly white and pretty and it didn't have any injuries. Mama could have it stuffed like the fox and the bird, and she could add it to her other treasures. Patty was sorry the bunny had died, but she was very happy to have found the best curiosity so far. This was certain to make Mama feel better!

Patty stood, but something was wrong. The woods were silent. She looked around, holding the rabbit to her torso, but nothing moved. She felt like someone was watching her. Was there someone here? Could they help?

"Hel—hello?" Patty asked softly.

There weren't any sounds. No one was there, but the hairs on Patty's arms prickled and danced.

She wouldn't be a baby like last time, though. Clenching her teeth together, Patty turned and headed in the direction she was pretty sure was home.

She forced herself to walk slowly. She felt like something was behind her, but every time she looked nothing was there. Her pace gradually increased until she was shoving her way through branches and striding with stiff legs.

Patty thought maybe she saw the yard ahead. If only the bell would ring so she could be sure. A twig snapped behind her, but she knew it must be her imagination. Or another squirrel. She refused to look. "I'm not a baby," she said.

She could see her swing. Something scraped behind her, and Patty couldn't stand it anymore.

She ran across the lawn as fast as she could – past the trees, past the swing, over the grass, and into the house. Even as she slammed the door shut, she couldn't bring herself to see if anyone was there. She ran to the window and closed the curtains without looking outside.

Patty stood clutching the white rabbit to her chest, where her heart pounded so hard it made her skin pulse all over.

"You're a stupid baby," she told herself, but there wasn't any punch to it.

She stood there until her breathing slowed down, and then she went to check on Mama.

This time Patty set her treasure on the tray by the bed right away. She propped the pretty rabbit where the moss-covered stick had been, then went to the shelves to try to find the latter. The cuckoo ticked like an echo of her heartbeat as she searched, but Patty couldn't spot where Mama had placed the stick with the crow's foot.

The floors creaked as Patty walked over to the bed and sat down on the edge. Mama was on her side again, and for a moment, she seemed so still that Patty froze too. Then she saw the covers moving with Mama's breath, and her shoulders sank with relief.

"Mama," she said. "Are you awake?" Mama didn't answer.

"Mama?" she said a little louder. Mama let out a strange, tiny groan.

Patty reached out a hand to rest on Mama's shoulder, but for some reason she hesitated.

Her hand dropped back to her lap.

"Mama, I'm scared. Are you okay?" Heavy breathing was the only reply.

Patty shifted, leaning over to peer into the mirror on the other side of the bed and see Mama's face. But Mama had the covers pulled up all the way around her head like a cape, so her face was hidden in shadows by the blanket.

Patty lifted up the candle nearby, holding it over Mama's body so she could see into the mirror. The flame made the glass glint and wink, and the glow only dimly reached it. Patty moved her arm around until the light reflected just right, stretching barely within the shadows of Mama's covers.

Patty saw a face that only half looked like Mama's. Patty raised the candle, and eyes glinted within the blankets. They were open, staring at her. They looked solid black.

The cuckoo cried out. Patty shrieked, leaping back.

Mama didn't move. Patty whirled to face the clock, where the strange little bird burst madly in and out of the door where he lived. Something was wrong with the chime. He made a gurgling sound as he thrust forward, over and over.

Patty didn't wait for him to get to seven. She ran out of the room and shut the door.

She hid in her bedroom until morning.

By the time sun came through Patty's window, she felt silly but still very worried. She had been a baby last night and let her imagination get the best of her, but she knew she had to go get help. Today a new curiosity wouldn't be enough. She'd have to go not just into the woods but through them, all the way out the other side where other people lived.

Before she left, she cracked open Mama's bedroom door and peeked inside. The rabbit on the tray was gone, and Mama looked like an unmoving lump under her blankets. Patty stood in the doorway and watched long enough to see her breathing, then shut the door again.

The woods were very dark, even though the sun hadn't gone all the way down yet. The trees overhead made a roof of jagged leaves, and all of the shadows looked long and green.

Patty had been walking all day and she still hadn't gotten out of the woods. She was tired and hungry and anxious about Mama. She passed a large tree with a misshapen knot in its belly.

Hadn't she already seen that tree?

Patty stopped, looking around.

Had she already been there?

In the distance, Patty heard the cuckoo begin its mottled cry. Her throat felt tight as she turned toward the sound. It wasn't very far away. It sounded like it came from the side of the cottage.

She'd been walking in circles.

The little bird kept crying, although the sound was slow and warbled. She counted to seven, then eight. It kept going. Nine, ten. But it wasn't dark yet, so it couldn't be that late, could it? Eleven, twelve. Patty looked around, hugging her arms tight.

Thirteen. Fourteen. Fifteen. The cuckoo kept going.

Patty bounced on her heels, hugging herself. She was supposed to help Mama, but she got lost all day. The thought of going back to the house made her start breathing heavy. "What should I do?" she whispered.

The little bird cried and cried.

Something to the side caught her eye. Patty took a few steps toward it, deeper into the woods. As she began to see around a tree trunk, she realized it was the bottom of a shoe. Above it was white fabric, over an ankle.

Patty stopped.

Her heart pounded.

"Who's there?" Patty asked.

The only answer was the cuckoo's deranged call.

Patty felt tears trail down her cheeks, warm compared to the nip in the air.

"I don't want any more curiosities," she said, but the shoe stayed.

Her chest began to shake with sobs, but Patty wouldn't let them out. She wasn't a baby, and whether or not she looked, the shoe was there.

She continued walking around the tree, bringing into sight the matching shoe and ankle. Then a long skirt, spread askew and dotted with crimson leaves. Next to it, two hands that looked familiar.

Patty's whole body shook, but she stepped the rest of the way around the tree that blocked her view.

Mama lay dead in the leaves, facing up, her pale blue eyes open and staring listlessly at the trees. Her skin was gray from being outside for days, and ants trailed into the corners of her mouth.

Patty screamed.

If Mama had been here, what was in her room?

Inside the cottage the cuckoo stopped, burbling into a silence that ticked through the woods like a clock too strange to tell time any longer. The silence tocked and dangled and swayed, waiting.

Then the bell rang.

Black Flower Butterfly

Rich Hawkins

The storm woke him into the dark that filled the silent room as rain pattered at the windows and the old walls. Roland wheezed through dusty lungs and put his hands to his chest as brief detonations of thunder crackled overhead. The cottage creaked and sighed in the downpour.

He sat up in bed, his body of rusted knots and tired bone protesting at the sudden movement under the thin sheets. He rubbed his eyes, cleared his throat, and as he looked around, he thought he heard a scream upon the wind.

In the soft glow of the bedside lamp, he dressed into boots and the old overcoat that came down to his calves and swaddled his fragile form. He grabbed the torch from the cupboard under the sink. In the distance, in the storm, another scream erupted from raw lungs. Then he was at the front door, pawing and panicked, heat in his chest. He gathered his thoughts enough to coordinate the actions of his hands and pull the bolt back from the front door. When he stepped outside, the rain pelted him for having the gall to enter the storm.

Darkness, save for the meagre torchlight sweeping the ground in one trembling hand. The wind pulled and pushed at him, stole his breath as he staggered down the pathway that cleaved the sodden lawn to the end of the garden and onto the dirt lane flanked by pitch black fields. Mud and gravel churned under his boots. A sheet of lightning turned the horizon white for a second and left a dancing imprint on his vision. Trees wilted and waned, limbs thrashing, and there was no shadow to be cast. He blinked rain from his eyes and bowed his head against the storm.

The next scream sounded closer, and female. Then it became a frightful sobbing. Who would be out in this weather apart from a foolish old man flailing and drenched to his bones?

Up the lane, stumbling on divots and holes. He flinched from the roaring sky. The sound of rain on his overcoat was blunt and flat. He spat water from his mouth, wiped his face and scanned the fields with the torch.

Ahead, a pale form was in the middle of the lane, prone upon the ground. Something with limbs. It screamed. It cried. It wailed to the sky. Roland halted. Ran the torchlight over it as his mouth fell open and he tasted the rain.

A naked girl stared at him from behind a soaked fringe of hair plastered to her face. She was lying in a foetal ball, limbs withdrawn and trembling. Her skin was like marble. Eyes the colour of wood smoke. A baby bird fallen from its nest.

The girl reached out to him as he approached on shivering legs and cringed at the low whimpering in her throat. She did not shrink from him, even as his hands found her freezing flesh.

"It's okay," he said, but his words were lost to the storm. He took off his overcoat and placed it over her shoulders as he raised her to a sitting position. Then he pulled the girl to her feet and held her upright despite the thinness of her legs. She looked at him with doleful, bovine-like eyes. He couldn't help but touch her face.

In the terrible storm and beneath the crashing heavens, she was beautiful.

The girl was asleep in the guest bedroom, the first guest in all the years he'd been here, and he'd been alone among the silent walls, dusty floors and grey photos for a long time, lost in the memories of his old life.

A tap dripped into the kitchen sink. The old radio on the dining table hissed frail voices. The storm had broken and the first light brightened the eastern horizon below the clear sky. The kettle boiled in the kitchen while he stood at the foot of her bed and watched her sleep. Roland hadn't seen such rich red hair since one of his old girlfriends during the Sixties.

The girl looked to be about eleven or twelve, so what had she been doing out there? He remembered watching French horror films where female protagonists escaped from the cellars and dungeons of sadistic killers and fled into the countryside in nothing but rags and the skin on their bones. Had she escaped from such a place? For the first time in years, he wished he had a mobile phone or a landline to call the police.

He could have walked to the nearest village, but he didn't want to leave the girl alone in case she awoke while he was out. He didn't want her to be scared. The nearest village was seven miles away, as the crow flew.

The morning dwindled into midday, then early afternoon. Clocks ticked and the sun crossed the sky. The girl didn't wake, and Roland watched over her, drinking sweet tea and eating biscuits from a tin that used to contain wrapped chocolates. He made her a bowl of vegetable soup and buttered three slices of bread, then left them on a tray by her bedside.

Roland left the room in silence and went to the kitchen to listen to the afternoon news on the radio. An African country had fallen into civil war; a politician had been caught with a high class prostitute; an accident on the M5 had killed a young family. It was all bad news.

He turned off the radio.

This was the month of the shortest days of the year, when dusk arrived early and eager. Roland looked out over the greying fields before he switched on the lights and closed the curtains. He ate a small dinner of sausages and boiled pasta, and had hoped the smell of grilled meat would have woken the girl, but when he entered her room with a cup of tea and one of his old science-fiction paperbacks she was still asleep.

He pulled up a chair and sat by her bedside. Put on his glasses and began his vigil. The clock above the bed ticked away hours. The soup had congealed into cold paste and the bread had hardened into sharp crusts. No storms tonight. He was grateful for the silence.

The paperback's pages started to blur, the words melting together. He took off his glasses and rubbed the bridge of his nose, and when he replaced them he saw the girl staring at him. His heart twinged.

The girl sat up slowly, the sheet up to her neck, and her careful eyes didn't leave him.

There was no fear in her face. Roland opened his mouth and made a mammalian-like murmuring while his face became hot and flushed with blood.

The girl said nothing.

Roland closed his mouth and offered her the glass of water from the bedside table. She looked at the glass, then Roland, and then back to the glass. Roland's hand was shaking slightly.

"Please," he managed to say through the parting of dry lips.

She took the water and downed most of it in two mouthfuls then wiped her mouth with the back of one thin wrist.

"Take it easy," Roland said. "We're not going to run out of it."

If she got the joke she didn't let it show. Her lips were as pale as her face. "How are you feeling? What happened to you?"

She held the sheet to her small body. "Where are you from? What's your name?" No answer.

"Don't be afraid. I'm not going to hurt you. You're safe here."

Her dark eyes regarded him, and her long red hair caught the light and seemed to glow. Christ, she's beautiful.

"My name's Roland," he said.

The girl reached out with her left hand and placed it on his arm. Her small mouth formed a delicate smile.

He smiled too, and the shifting of muscles in his face felt like cracks in barren earth.

The girl dressed in a woollen jumper and a pair of old jeans too small for Roland's burgeoning waistline. He had to turn up the hems so they wouldn't drag on the floor as she walked. When he offered her some old shoes he'd last worn in the previous decade, she shook her head and frowned. They were too big anyway, and he felt foolish for considering it. Her feet were small, ivory white and smooth. Stunted toes. Little piggies. The feet of a princess.

She drank more water until she was sated. Roland offered her the pick of what she wanted from the fridge and the kitchen cupboards, but she declined all food. He asked her more questions and she gave him no answers. He watched her and she watched him. Was she deaf or mute? Maybe she was foreign; there was a slight Nordic thinness to her face and the nose upon it. Maybe she was lost or mentally ill. Did that explain how she had ended up naked and alone in the previous night's storm?

Was she simply choosing not to answer?

Roland stood in the kitchen and eyed her through the doorway as she sat in the living room watching television. Some turgid romantic drama full of grinning faces and shrieking laughter. She watched it without emotion, staring blankly at the screen.

Just before nine o'clock she rose from the armchair and walked to the spare bedroom through the opposite doorway. Roland let her go and opened the bottle of whiskey he kept in the cupboard above the sink. He sat at the dining table and drank into the early hours.

Roland awoke in twisted bed sheets. A noise had pulled him out of sleep. He was trying to convince himself he'd dreamt that long keening wail, when he heard it again from outside the house. He slipped on his boots, shrugged on his coat, swallowing the wet crawl of his heart trying to climb his throat. His mouth smelled of whiskey and tasted like peat, and the cold air outside turned his breath to mist. His feet crunched on hard frost.

He found the girl in the front garden, staring at the glowing full moon. She was a slight figure in his old clothes, bare-footed on the frosted grass.

He stood alongside her and asked if something was wrong, but she didn't answer. Her face was stretched with wonder, and her little mouth opened with a meek smile full of tiny white teeth. A vision in porcelain.

"Please talk to me," he said. "Why won't you talk to me?"

Something moved in her face; a twitch, an involuntary spasm, and her smile faded. There was worry in her eyes.

Roland followed her gaze to the moon, the silent and pallid satellite. And when he turned back to ask her what was wrong, she went to him and hugged his chest tightly before he could work his mouth to form words.

The next morning Roland found a black flower growing in the front lawn. It looked like a poppy, with six curved petals reaching up to his knees, and it was in full bloom despite the cold of winter. The centre of the flower, its heart, was the colour of coal. Roland crouched to smell the intruder, and wrinkled his nose at its acrid scent. Like formaldehyde in a glass jar.

The flower quivered, and he wasn't sure if it was because of the breeze.

He gripped the flower by its thin black stalk, which felt oily and slippery on his fingers.

He struggled to take purchase of it, but kept pulling until the flower escaped from the ground in his gnarled hands, dirt crumbling from its long roots, sickly pale and damply dripping. He was sure that the roots twitched, like needling appendages, as though they were desperate for the touch of his skin.

He threw the flower in a bin bag that contained grass clippings from the previous summer, and when he turned back to the cottage, the girl was watching him from the window.

Roland slumped in his armchair, aching and faint. Tired and sagging. A flawed construction of brittle bone and skin filled with jellied insides slowly winding down like the damaged workings of a grandfather clock.

The girl watched him from across the living room. He offered her a tired smile, but the little muscles of his mouth were stiff and trembling.

He dozed, falling in and out of dreams that he couldn't wholly remember when he woke.

A vision in his mind of a black flower.

When he woke, the light was on and the curtains drawn against the dusk. The girl had laid a dusty blanket over him while he slept. Steam rose from a cup of tea next to the armchair. The girl sat on the floor, legs crossed, and she turned to the cardboard box by her side.

Roland's heart quickened and he was annoyed at the girl for taking the box from under the stairs where he kept it. But when he saw that she was handling the contents with care, the bloom of heat in his chest faded and his limbs relaxed.

The girl took out a sheaf of old photos and several scrapbooks secured in twine. She studied the photos in silence. She was too young to recognise the people in the photos and, most probably, the younger Roland with them all.

He smiled at bittersweet memories. His old heart wept.

There were photos of Roland with William Hartnell and Peter Cushing on film sets; Britt Ekland at a party in London. Christopher Lee and Diana Rigg. Old memories and stills from films and television shows featuring Roland in various costumes and roles: a vampire hunter's assistant; a back alley brawler; a soldier in red fighting the French at Waterloo; a police constable attacked by a man in a rubber monster suit.

The girl leafed through newspaper clippings and reviews of plays in a scrapbook. A reel of film from the 1972 movie *Scarlet Eyes*. A silver locket given to him by a female starlet he'd had a fling with while filming *The General's Daughter*.

The girl glanced at Roland and smiled. Maybe she did recognise him.

"I used to be someone once," he said. "But that someone wasn't who I really was. I couldn't stay around people. Had to get away. Better to be alone."

The girl nodded, as though she understood. In that moment he thought of her as a kindred spirit, a soul dismayed by the faults and follies of the human race.

She raised her face towards the ceiling and her eyes sharpened; a tremor in her jaw. Her throat worked.

"What's wrong?" Roland said.

She shook her head while she stared at the ceiling – beyond the ceiling – then returned her attention to the box and replaced Roland's memories inside.

He rose unsteadily from the armchair and plodded to the window, parting the curtains so he could look outside.

The land was painted grey and silver by the moon that filled the eastern horizon. The scars of craters and canyons. It emanated a deep coldness he could feel through the thin glass of the window.

When he turned back to the girl, she was trembling and would not rest her eyes on the window filled with ghost-light.

When he looked out the window during the morning, he counted twenty-three more black flowers growing on the lawn. He imagined their roots coiling and spreading in the earth. Spreading ever outwards.

Roland began teaching the girl how to play chess with the set his father had given him back in 1975. The year before he had died alone in his car somewhere in a country lane during the depths of that particular winter.

The girl learned quickly, displaying aptitude and skill beyond her years.

Roland felt drained and lethargic, his limbs like heavy burdens. He couldn't eat food without feeling sick. He was merely so much air wheezing through chambers of meat and bone, connected to a beating muscle that waned and withered. His eyes were tired and the lids above them heavy.

Attempts to make the girl eat were futile and often ended with Roland emptying the fridge's contents upon the dining table in an effort to coerce her. Hunger never seemed to pain her, unless she was sneaking food from the kitchen during the night.

In the evening Roland found a black flower growing through a crack in the kitchen linoleum. He plucked it, threw it in the bin, and tried not to consider its implications.

They spent the night watching old episodes of *Lost in Space*, and just before ten o'clock the girl fell asleep with her head resting on his chest. He looked down at her sleeping form and the weaves of red hair about her face. Freckles under her eyes. Her mouth partly open. He wondered if she dreamed.

He put her to bed then retired to his room, where he slept fitfully and was plagued by dreams of flittering things in the darkness.

They made a sound like busy butterflies.

In the morning Roland waited at the kitchen table for the girl to emerge from her room. The sun rose, pushed away shadows and filled the sky. Dark clouds approached from the west.

He waited for hours, drinking tea and picking at buttered toast he couldn't stomach, glancing towards the girl's room and expecting the door to open and her pale face to appear with the sun shining through the window behind her.

By midday she hadn't appeared. Cold tea swilled in his mouth. The toast was soggy and limp in his hands. He padded over to the door and placed one ear against it. Silence inside. No stirrings or even the sound of breathing.

He opened the door.

The bed was empty and the sheets muddled. The room smelled of damp and the window was shut. The clothes he had given her were strewn on the floor.

There was something on the ceiling. Hanging from the ceiling. A cocoon or chrysalis of some kind, melded to the ceiling by resin and just large enough to contain a small child. A little girl. It was coloured like jaundice and appeared to have the texture of spiders' webs and dusty things. Inside, a shape wallowed in fluid and membranes, sloshing and sucking in wetness. Roland stared at it in fascination and awe and confusion. His open mouth caught dust motes. He realised he made a low murmuring sound.

He sat on the edge of the bed and wept at the beautiful creation above him.

Despite growing tiredness and failing concentration, he kept a vigil throughout the day and into the night. He didn't touch the chrysalis for fear of damaging it. The low beat of her heart dwelled in his mind, strong and keen in amniotic fluid. She dreamed inside the womb.

During the dark hours he sensed the moon rise and silently pulse. He didn't look out the window.

Exhaustion pulled at his eyes and blurred his hands when he held them before his face.

Dulled his thoughts. He would not break the vigil by falling asleep.

He yawned. Swallowed sour spit. He reached for his cup of coffee but it was empty.

His eyes closed for a moment before he snapped them open again. His heart was slowing into echoes of falling rocks.

He fell back on the bed and felt his eyes shut despite the silent screaming of his brain begging him to keep them open. And he dreamed of the girl as his daughter in another life.

In his dreams the girl sat by him and cooed into his ear. She kissed his forehead and smiled, and thanked him for being her father and keeper.

Roland woke face down on the bed. He sat up, his back cracking, and rubbed his eyes with gnarled hands. He wanted to sleep again. He felt shrunken, wasted, used up.

Black flowers were growing from the bedroom floor through the thin carpet. He looked at the ceiling and saw that the chrysalis was open down its middle, empty, split from the emergence of its former occupant. It sagged from the ceiling and dripped pale fluid to the floor.

There were sounds of mewling and high-pitched hoots from outside. Something shrieked from the sky.

He stumbled along the hallway, crushing and snapping the black flowers sprouting from the floor. The ones left intact quivered as he passed.

The walls shivered. The front door was open and moonlight pooled on the kitchen floor.

The world outside the house seemed unmoving and silent.

Roland went outside into the glowing night. There was no wind, and the trees and fields were like painted depictions from a fragile mind. A silent land.

The creature crouched on the lawn, hunched and trembling, glistening from the fluid in which it had been born. The ground around the house was filled with black flowers. Roland flattened them with his feet and they leaked dark fluid from their stems.

The winged thing met Roland's eyes. It was humanoid, with thin arms and legs and skin like liquid that was almost translucent, revealing ticking organs and working chambers. A heart of slick black. A hairless body. Membranous wings six feet wide. Roland shied from its face, the scraping of mandibles and its wet mouth. Eyes the same colour as the girl's.

He stepped towards the thing before his strength failed, and his reflection in the window was something of emaciation and illness.

The thing mewled to him through its fearful mouth, and as he halted, it raised one hand to his face and touched his cheek so gently that he barely felt it.

The thing took away its hand. Roland slumped to his knees. He couldn't help a slack smile forming on his lips. He felt giddy, able to take to the air with the flying things, even though he knew it would never happen.

Wings flittered, growing faster as they worked. Butterfly noises. A sound like playing cards being shuffled.

The winged creatures called.

The thing took to the air and joined the others. Heaven cracked. The moon swelled and filled the sky.

Roland collapsed among the black flowers.

He woke as stars appeared, one at a time, in the fading sky until there was more light than dark. He was pinned to the ground by the flowers growing from inside his shivering body just as they did from the uncaring earth.

The moon looked down at him and swelled as the last thing in his eyes. Cold light swept over the contortion of his limbs, and he wept to the moon with silver tears as he became nutrients and sustenance for the things that prospered and wrapped spindly roots around his bones. His heart was slowing, failing, winding down. And when he opened his mouth to say a prayer, a slick black flower bloomed from between his lips and took the last of his breath.

Beehive Heart

Angela Rega

Paulina was born coated in a film of creamed honey and a swarm of bees. When they flew out of her mother's womb whirring like little clockwork toys; one stung the midwife's upper lip but she didn't complain. The last time she had seen a totem birth, she'd said to Paulina's mother, was in 1972. It had been a terrible year for geese. A goose herder girl gave birth to a feathered gosling of a baby that was apparently kidnapped and made into pate.

Rather than bathing Paulina in the common way, they scraped the honey from the crevices and soft folds from the infant's skin.

Her mother wasn't surprised her daughter was born amidst a swarm of bees. She'd had the most desperate cravings for honey during her pregnancy. She'd sucked the little open wombs of honeycomb as afternoon tea. Perhaps she had swallowed bee larvae and they had grown inside her, too. She kissed the honey dripping off her daughter's eyelids.

"A totem girl," was all the midwife said, a look of worry between her long cameo earrings; she left Paulina in her mother's arms, her wheezing breath like the tiny buzzings of winged insects.

At forty years of age, Paulina still smelled sticky and sweet. A gummy substance exuded from her pores, and it was strongest when she gardened, sweat or made love. A smell that was both cloying and tart.

It was at the onset of puberty, she first had longings her mother called 'unusual.' They had been on a picnic with family friends in the Botanical Gardens. It was the third week of spring. While others tucked into cheese and relish sandwiches, Paulina's body throbbed at the sight of the red bottle brushes that looked like they would tickle, the tall stalks of pussy willow that looked downy and soft. An urge pulsed through her. She wanted to stick her tingling fingertips into open flowers and feel the tacky and velvety texture; she wanted to taste them, breath them in, stand naked in the sun, her arms outstretched like a scarecrow and let the pollens of wildflowers dust her naked body. She stripped off her clothes, leaving them in a puddle by the picnic rug and ran towards the bushes. Her mother had run across to where Paulina stood, clutching at an old rug to use it to cover her daughter's body. The two teenage boys present at the picnic giggled; it was the first time they had seen a naked girl. But Paulina didn't mind. She had the buzz of the bees in her mind, the ecstasy of sticking those pulsating fingertips inside flowers, of pollens coating her skin.

If that hadn't caused enough stir, it was the school outing at the hobby farm that had made Paulina's mother know that her daughter was truly different. Paulina had trembled in fear that first time she stood naked next to Old Mackenzie's beehive but the urge was too strong.

At first, the stings were pinching and hot. The heat and itch expanded, pinkish like enlarged areola around the sting, but she taught herself to not resist. There was pleasure in that stinging, throbbing pain, then a gentle tickling at the gauzy texture of those little bee legs crawling up her forearms, behind her earlobes and under her chin. She thought about the gosling child. No doubt the feathered baby would have grown to peck at the ground and preen her feathered hair if she had lived. Maybe she still did. It was only hearsay, after all, that she was turned into pate. Paulina was lucky nobody had wanted to eat her; unlike geese, honeybees weren't yet scarce. She knew the truth about human nature; people always wanted to devour what they couldn't have.

When Paulina left school and her mother realized she wasn't hers to keep or worry over, she wished her well and bade her adieu. They held each other for what seemed a long time, Paulina's tears sticking to her mother's short curled hair. Her mother knew who she was.

"Listen to the beehive in your heart," she said "my sweet daughter."

"You will leave us soon," Zeinab looked at Paulina with her kohl-lined eyes and Paulina laughed out loud.

"No chance."

She was happy. She'd worked her wonders at Ibrahim's Lebanese Pastry store for over fifteen years now. She had grown to love the brightly lit shop with towers of pastries stacked like pyramids and sprinkled with pistachio nuts. A pastry chef of Middle Eastern desserts was a perfect profession for a girl who loved all things of bees and honey. Her batches of baklava made people queue at the door.

"Yes, yes. You will." Zeinab said shaking her head from side to side as if she was saying no.

"She cannot leave." Ibrahim brought a large silver tray from the kitchen to the bench and shook it so the pastries didn't stick. "I hired her for her yellow eyes and her magic in making sweet pastry."

"Told you!" She poked Zeinab in the arm, but Zeinab just kept shaking her head. It was in the coffee cup, she said, and she was a mystic just as Paulina was a woman born of bees.

"I mean, look at these!" Ibrahim grabbed a pair of tongs and stacked the ladyfingers, birds' nests and baklava on the large silver platters, arranging them with architectural precision into pyramids. The sweets were baked with flaky pastry, butter, honey, and rosewater, then coated in more honey and sprinkled with ground pistachio or walnuts. Paulina's honey made them glistening wonders to behold.

"She can't leave when she makes them as good as these."

"You will leave us soon," Zeinab's beautifully manicured red nails pointed to the coffee grounds that formed a mountain. "You will stay here," she said touching the mountain peak.

"I'm happy here," Paulina said, but Zeinab shook her head. "You will leave us soon." And she kissed her on the cheek as if to say goodbye. "You will not come back."

He was sitting at the corner table next to the shop front window reading a newspaper and ordered three ladyfingers.

"Table three wants more honey," Zeinab called out over the sound of the milk she frothed at the coffee machine. Paulina looked up to where Zeinab's free hand pointed. It was the man that had ordered the ladyfingers. She took the honey jug and went to the table.

"More honey mix?" she asked, tilting the jug in accordance with the question.

"Yes please."

She poured the rosewater and honey mixture over his sweets. Leaning over the table, she felt his warm breath on her forearm as the sticky liquid gushed from the little jug. Their eyes met and an undulating wave unfurled in her abdomen. It was like every pore of her skin was an antenna prickling to attention. The sound of the buzzing in her heart boxed her eardrums; the beehive in her heart had been thrummed.

Only once before had someone moved her to awaken the hive heart. Ibrahim had a brother, Mustapha. She fell into an impulsive love with this musical man who recited Rumi's poetry, played the oud and worked as a car park attendant. But he did not love honey and didn't understand her beehive heart. Said it gave him a headache. They separated a long time ago, no longer even friends.

This time the buzzing was so loud Paulina wondered if the man at the table could hear it. He stared at her for such long a time, she wondered if it had offended him.

"You sound lovely," he said.

"You can hear it? You like it?"

"Yes," he said and put out his hand to shake. "Gustav."

"Paulina." She put the jug down and lightly shook his hand. "I have a beehive in my heart."

He let out a gentle laugh. From the way it came out, Paulina could tell he didn't laugh easily. He stopped and his face became serious. He squeezed her hand and said nothing.

Paulina's face reddened. Her palm was sweating and secreting the honey her body perspired.

"I'm sorry. My hands are sticky." She wiped her hand on her apron.

And now he laughed out loud, and the humming in her heart grew so loud that even old Mr. Bartok looked up from his daily crossword and coffee. A flush of embarrassment burned her cheeks. Paulina looked down at the table to the newspaper Gustav was reading.

In bold letters it said: *Colony Collapse Crisis. Why are our bees disappearing?*

"Do you know what that is?" He tapped at the heading with a long finger, his other hand still holding hers.

"I know that bees just disappear from their hives."

"Yes. And so you don't, here is my card." On the front it said *Gustav _____ Entomologist.* Then he scribbled his address and a date. It was for two days' time.

Zeinab was right. The next day Paulina departed. Gustav had left her with that same desire to stick her fingers into blooming flowers and stand naked letting the pollens dust her body.

"Not forever, Zeinab," Paulina wiped Zeinab's tears with the flat of her index finger. "Ibrahim has given me a week's holiday. I'll be back in a week." And she took a train into the bowels of the inner city where he lived.

He met her at a busy intersection outside the train terminal. He took her hand, and she noted how small her hand was compared to his large one, how well it fit inside his. They did not speak. There was so much noise between them. Her buzzing, the traffic, the commuters. He leaned into her, and a sensation crawled up her arms. It was as if there were thousands of silken fine hairs on her skin unfurling and making her ignite. She leaned closer into him.

He led her up seven flights of stairs, past his abode to the communal rooftop gardens of the apartment block.

Paulina looked around and delight tingled through her body. He kept a rooftop honey sanctuary! She was high above the city, in a garden overgrown with sunflowers and lavender, sage, oregano, mint, wild daisies, apples, almond trees and cucumber.

"I feel like I've come home," she said.

"It started with my concern about Colony Collapse Syndrome. That and mid- life crisis," he said. "I wanted to do something positive with my life. Keep the honeybees from dying out."

"Honey is pure," Paulina said as if speaking her thoughts aloud. She knew this. She was born with this knowledge. For a moment, she thought of the poor goose girl. She would have understood the pure essence of things, too, if she hadn't been devoured. She dismissed the thought with a flick of her hand. That was just a story. Then, she thought of Zeinab's prophecy, and wondered what had compelled her to pack a bag and come to see a man that she barely knew – she, a totem girl. A girl who could have been eaten for her sweat and bled for honey. But she was compelled; the urge was too strong. And her beehive heart had not been silent since they had met.

"The body corporate approved me keeping the bees here," he said, stretching his arm out towards the hives proudly.

"Usually they approve the keeping of a dog or cat," she said "but bees...I would have given approval for the originality of the request."

"You would have approved it for you are an enchantress of honey bees," he said.

Paulina smiled.

"I think more than allowing the bees, they were happier about the garden I installed. I grow them for my bees, but the residents here all enjoy coming to pick the harvest."

Paulina walked past him to the lavender bushes. It was her favourite scent.

From here was a view of rooftops and sunny skyscapes that made the cars below glint and burn her retinas. She closed her eyes. She thought of the mountain Zeinab had pointed to in the coffee cup. She was in the midst of an urban space with a haven for bees and honey on the rooftop of high rise. And then she did what she had always done as a child, something her mother had begged her to stop. She moved away to stand near one of the hives, stripped off her long dress and stood naked, her arms outstretched and closed her eyes. She heard Gustav gasp. For a moment Paulina was concerned about her unruly pubic hair, and the memory of herself trembling with fear at Old MacKenzie's farm ebbed through her... but the compulsion was, as always, too strong. The humming in her beehive heart became louder. She knew he could hear it, and the bees in Gustav's hives heard it, too.

They crawled out from their hexagonal cubbyholes of honeycomb, darting and buzzing around Paulina like a flock of pigeons circling a cathedral spire. The hot sun had made her body break a sweet sweat, and they landed on her naked skin. She could sense their delight at the honey-flavoured nectar, devouring her with their little stick tongues that were velvety against Paulina's dimpled skin. She shivered in delight.

And he watched.

Gustav watched her from the rooftop railing, knowing better than to flinch or make a move as the bees cloaked her skin like a high ruffed collared shirt.

She opened her mouth in ecstasy as they crawled around the arc of her earlobes, the backs of her knees, the dip in her throat. All the places she would kiss him with a flicking tongue like the searching bee. She waited for that moment of delight when they stung. But they did not. It made her hungry. Her eyes met Gustav's.

He was hungry, too.

Paulina squatted slowly, and then jumped! The bees exploded into the air and flew away, Paulina knew, to gather pollens and bring them back to the hive.

Gustav walked towards her and put his hand in hers, his head nuzzled in the curve of her neck and shoulder, and they stood in silence. Paulina felt the soft texture of his lips as she watched the bees fly into the clear empty sky with the promise of pollen and good honey. Some still sat on the railing, rubbing their furry bodies with their front and hind legs, preening like cats. A wanting made the honeyed saliva build under her tongue. She wanted him to kiss her.

He lifted his head to face her. His fingers brushed hers.

They made love that night cloaked under a sky of cold stars. Each thrust was like one of those first pleasurable stings where she wasn't sure where the pleasure ended and the pain began. The buzzing returned. It was so loud it drowned out the sound of the night cars. Over and over: now she was the blooming flower and he was her curious finger that she had poked inside them as a child.

He rose quickly and took her hand to take her into his apartment. "I need to take a shower and you'll have to go soon."

"Oh?"

"I have someone coming soon for a meeting." He gestured to the dining room table scattered with papers and grabbed a towel from the linen cupboard in the hall.

Paulina didn't answer. It had happened so quickly. This sense of busyness so soon after being caressed in his arms. She put her fingers through her hair to untangle it and browsed the bookshelves for familiar tomes and then the papers on the table.

She stopped short at the thesis she saw sitting at the table. The title made her not want to read any further. Then Gustav was there, wiping himself dry. He moved close to her and squeezed her hand.

"I'm a scientist, doing research on genetically modifying wasps so that they make honey too."

Paulina stepped back from him. His words disorientated her and the world spun around. She moved her hand away from his touch. The buzz in her heart was silent for a minute. Caution. Proceed with caution, lest you sting. Bees die when they sting. She straightened her dress.

"I would rather spend my time preserving the honey bee," she said. "I thought that's what you wanted, too."

"It is up for debate. The disappearance of the bees might be inevitable."

For a moment the memory of Mustapha came. A man she loved, and he allegedly loved her, but did not understand her nature. Now she was drawn like a finger in a flower to a man that wanted to genetically modify wasps, yet he kept bees. She wanted to run towards him and run away. She felt itchy inside her skin.

"I need to go now," she said. "Don't want you to be unprepared for your meeting."

"That is best. Can't wait to see you again."

She walked home alone. The afterglow of love was gone, and it left her confused and cold. She pulled her collar tighter around her throat.

There was the gentle sound of a whirring buzz near her ear that didn't come from her own heart. Paulina's face broke into a smile at the sight of a little drone. It crawled onto Paulina's forearm and she watched him preen the day's collected pollen from his fur. He told her why, in an old man's voice, why this man would never be hers to have.

"Even the honey bee drones don't mate with the Queen of their colony," the drone whispered. "And their work is seasonal." Then he fluttered up to her ear and tickled her ear lobe with his furry strands of black and yellow hair. "Do not give your beehive heart to a man that chooses wasps," the little drone said, and flew away.

Paulina was surprised. This was the first time a bee had spoken to her. She wanted to run away and run towards. She thought of the moment Gustav lay next to her, brushing her long hair behind her ears when she looked into his eyes, the fullness of his lips, and back to his eyes. She would run towards. Surely he was more bee than wasp? Zeinab had been right. She wasn't coming back.

She had sought lodgings in a boarding house only a few kilometers from his home; the little drone always visited her, even when Gustav could not. There were many reasons, he said, that he could not. Grant applications. Academic Papers. And the little drone said: "I told you Honey Bee Drones don't mate with the Queen of their colony."

He buzzed secrets in her ears about love and its nature, about the inertia of people, individual greed over communal wealth, and the terrible things that would happen if the wasps became the new honey bee. "Wasps cannot make honey and they don't die after they sting. They don't have the pure heart of the bee. Like you and me. Colony Collapse Disorder", he whispered in a buzzing purr, "means more than the disappearance of just us. It also means the disappearance of you."

For the second month of summer, Gustav and Paulina saw each other more frequently. The little drone less. She had left the window open for him, left honeysuckle on the sill to welcome him in, but he didn't come. Paulina was preoccupied with Gustav, their urgent lovemaking overwhelming her so that even she stopped hearing the buzz in her heart. They argued passionately about the wasps. How their honey could never match that of the honeybee. Of stringy bark or manuka and the rising price of oranges and orange juice.

The visits were frequent but short. It made her frustrated. He would leave soon after lovemaking. That frustrated her as well.

"Why don't you stay a bit longer?"

"I can't. I'm supposed to be working. Wasps don't wait."

She looked away and didn't answer. She didn't understand how someone that kept bees and loved the buzzing in her heart, would dedicate his life to the wasps.

Why? But she knew what he had been thinking. The little drone had told her. Gustav was waiting for the right moment to tell her. She had hoped what the little drone had told her was not all true.

Summer soon turned to autumn and Paulina had stopped asking him to stay. Stopped asking about the wasps. She did not understand the lure of money that made the research into the wasps an attractive option for Science PhD. Graduates. Now they made love with a sense of futility. The absence of words needing to be said created a sense of pointlessness. Of sweet stings and honey nectar, of the fallout between the reality of the situation and her feelings for someone that would betray the bees.

Paulina had a beehive in her heart. By betraying the bees, he would betray her. But she said nothing. For she knew that if she left and walked away – just like the honeybee after he has stung, she would surely die.

She loved him.

So she stayed. Taking jobs waitressing and helping out with other urban bee keeping places. Word soon got out that she could enchant the bees. But she told no one of her beekeeper lover or of the little drone that came to speak to her about truths.

She knew Gustav was leaving before he told her. He had been given a grant to spend a year researching the common wasp and genetically modifying them to make honey wasps. Wasps were common.

He was going with his wife.

His wife. The Queen of his colony. She'd co-wrote the proposals.

It was quarter to midnight and they were sitting in a coffee shop huddled over a small round table in the right back corner.

"I will miss you," he said.

"I will miss you, too." She wanted to kick and scream, beg him not to leave, the bees needed him. She needed him. But Paulina knew the rule of the bee, to sting someone meant a piece of her would die. Honey is pure.

"I'll see you next week before I leave," he said and called the waitress for the bill.

He stood up, and tucked his chair in, leaned forward and kissed her on the lips goodbye. Then he departed. Quickly. He didn't look back. She looked out the window and shivered. She was glad she'd packed a cardigan. The weather was getting cooler. More bitter at night. Her eyes welled with the sticky goo of honeyed tears.

"Hey honey," the waitress crooned as she picked up the dirty cups from the table. "You look like you're getting a mean case of conjunctivitis."

She smiled at the waitress, left some change on the table and departed.

Tonight the road seemed quiet, deserted and wider, even. She pulled her cardigan up around her ears and shivered. She felt alone. She couldn't get warm.

And then it happened. It was a pain of a deep burn. She keeled over, the stinging behind her breastbone making it impossible to breathe; she fell down to the pavement, scraping the palm of her hands to endure the fall. Her heart throbbed with stings and soon its rapid rhythm fluttered at the bottom of her throat so she became light-headed and she choked for air. The bees inside her heart finally left their hive and stung her internally. Heart break.

The little drone appeared. He buzzed worriedly around her ear telling her over and over: sorry, sorry, so sorry. He was sorry but couldn't do anything anymore. That soon, he and his colony would be gone from Gustav's rooftop, too.

Paulina pushed herself up off the ground with her forearms. "Don't leave," she said to the little drone.

He rested on her breastbone, where it hurt the most. She wondered how she would make it home. It hurt. Physically hurt. This wasn't a pleasurable sting, but one that burned and then left her empty heart stinging of what felt like needle stings. The same sensation her school friend Nettie had described when being stung by a bee in the playground at netball practice.

That night she lay awake tossing from side to side on her mattress. She couldn't get comfortable; she couldn't keep warm. The sounds outside the window of her small apartment were loud. The wheels of cars on the wet asphalt, the sound of a cat meowing, a child wailing. She heard everything, now that her heart had grown silent. The bees didn't buzz anymore. All the ones that had lived there had died when they stung her. The little drone had gone with his colony, too, flying out the window when she arrived home. Sorry, Paulina, was all he could say. He didn't say goodbye. Paulina knew that he wouldn't be back. And when the sticky tears fell down her cheeks and sweetened her lips with the taste, she wondered…what if…what if…she would never be able to enchant the bees again?

Drawn against her will, she saw him again. He had said he would see her again and he did. Gustav was leaning against the balcony balustrade of the rooftop garden. He chewed on his bottom lip and shook his head. "I find it so strange all my honey bees have departed. But the garden I harvested for them is still in lush abundance! It doesn't make sense."

Paulina said nothing. The time had come. He was departing next week. She had promised that she would look after the bees in his rooftop garden for the year he was away. Promised.

She looked at him and her lips parted. She kissed him. It was long and loving. She poked her tongue in and out of his mouth as if she was a bee searching a flower for nectar. He sucked her tongue hungrily.

So much potential. For him. For her. For the honeybees.

They said goodbye. He was cold. Callous almost. It was over quickly.

She gathered the little jars of honey she had collected from the bees in Gustav's garden over the last nine months of their relationship, all lovingly collected and labelled. *Almond Honey. Lavender Honey. Apple Honey.* Binding them up, she walked the ten blocks to his home, up the flights of stairs until she reached his front door. She knocked and waited.

For a moment she wondered if she should run. What had brought her here?

He had asked her never to come without an invitation. In case he was working. For a moment she turned to walk back but froze when she heard him shuffling through the hallway. It was futile. She knew why. She heard her voice behind the door. The little drone had told her, the honeybee drone doesn't mate with the queen of his colony.

The honeybee drone relies on the worker bee to feed him. The honeybee drone is only present during the summer. His wife was the queen of his colony, and the worker bee he relied on to feed him for this seasonal work had been Paulina. And autumn was coming: the season when the worker bees stop feeding the drones.

She placed the jars of honey behind the door, hoping they would sustain him while he was away. The door creaked open. Paulina bolted behind the corner of the long corridor. Was it him? Had he come to her? He had been her hive, and she was drawn to returning to him. She pressed her sticky palms against the wall and peered around the corner.

She felt as if something had caught in her throat. It was his wife. Paulina had never seen her before.

She stared at the woman, almost twice the height of Paulina. It was her thin lips, large probing eyes and long fingers that caught Paulina's eye. The way she snatched up the honey, eyes darting back and forth and then slammed the door shut. Paulina's heart skipped a beat and it made her catch her breath. She didn't expect his wife to be so waspish in manner.

Paulina jogged down the flights of stairs, her feet treading lightly, when a spasm of emotion contracted in her chest and she gasped at the memory of Gustav's love. It came in sweet whirrs and buzzing and tickled beneath her breastbone. The memory of his tongue on her lips, him moving inside her. She knew what to do. She remembered that day she had showed him how she could summon the bees. She closed her eyes and held her breath. She would call them – the bees that had disappeared from Gustav's colony.

Out on the street it was already midmorning, a time when bees would be busy. She did what she did best as a child, stripped her clothes off until she had nothing but a petticoat slip on. Arms outstretched, head tilted back, eyes closed, Paulina stood frozen like a piece of holy stone and felt the beat of her beehive heart summoning them.

At first, one by one they came, a gentle whirring, a fluttering; then, a swarm hovered like swallows in circular flight. They crawled inside her eyes and up her nostrils, over her lips, anywhere there was an opening to get behind that skin and breastbone. They crawled inside each orifice to make their way to their destination.

And as each bee arrived to the hive of her heart, the buzzing began again. It was loud, but Paulina would never apologize for this, nor try to quell the noise. It was the part of him that could never betray her and a part of who she was.

Annabelle's Sleepover

Jan Stinchcomb

You don't need to be afraid. I have helped many girls like you.

Everyone gets scared, of course. It's a natural reaction to all the lore surrounding me, those crazy stories they whisper at sleepovers and in the hallways at school. I understand how you feel. Aren't you the one who tried to make eye contact with me in middle school? Did you defend me when they called me a slut, a piece of trash or a killer? You were curious about me. You wanted to be closer to my story.

Little did you know that you would land right inside my house, in my bedroom, in fact, scared to death. I'll bet you never saw that coming when you opened the sparkly pink invitation to a popular girl's slumber party. You were happy not to be excluded.

(It's a frightening time of life, isn't it? You would rather die than be humiliated. Die. Just like the girls in the slasher films, running from a glinting blade through the halls of a haunted house. Well, when you come to my sleepover you get to die, a little. But it's nothing to be afraid of, I promise.)

Let me show you:

1. RONNIE

They come to me from different parties, sometimes on Halloween night, sometimes because there's a birthday. Truth or Dare is a great way to enter my house. That's what happened to Ronnie.

Ronnie is my favorite kind of girl. She really needs me. She's had eczema from the time she was in preschool, and it's like she's a prisoner in her own body. Her skin keeps her from getting close to people. She won't make eye contact because she assumes everyone thinks she's ugly. She deflects the hate she can feel coming her way by being super-nice. It's too much. Her incessant accommodation of others and all the pains she takes to erase herself makes it that much easier to hate her.

Ronnie looked terrified, barefoot and in her nightgown, when she stepped across the black and white tiles of my kitchen floor. I had to pull it out of her, what she came for.

"Come on now," I said. "Tell me what they want you to do."

For a long time Ronnie said nothing. My black eyes must have scared her. I could see her taking those little telltale steps backwards.

"Did they tell you to do something? No? Did they want you to ask me something?"

She nodded after the second question. "Okay, so what was it?"

Ronnie's voice was tiny. "I'm supposed to ask you for a cup of sugar."

I smiled. I like the sugar request. It's more discreet than those girls who come in here asking to touch my breasts or see my privates. And it's scary in its own way. I took the sack of sugar and spilled the contents onto the counter, and then I left the sack hanging there in the air, endlessly pouring, until sugar was piled all over the floor. The look on Ronnie's face was worth a thousand dark winters. She knew she wasn't going back to the party she'd come from, or, if she did, she wouldn't be the same girl she was on her way out.

"There's your sugar," I said to her.

She started crying. "All those stories," she began. "The things they say about you at school…"

"The things they say about me?"

"I didn't want to come over here! They made me."

"Ronnie," I told her, "nobody can make you do anything."

I know that I confuse these girls. I'm shorter than most of them, and my voice is that of a much younger child. I'm someone they've seen at school – although now they're not quite so sure – but they suddenly realize that they don't know me at all. They never really gave me a close look. They regret this and want to make up for it, somehow. They swear that when they go back to school on Monday, they'll be nice to everyone.

But they're not going back to school anytime soon.

I broke the truth gently. "We'll start slowly," I told Ronnie.

Her eyes got big, something I must confess always pleases me. It's like each girl is suddenly getting younger, even though she's just about to grow up for good.

"It won't hurt," I went on. "We have to fix you."

She said what all the others say: "Fix me?"

"It's your skin. Anyone can see that. I'll take care of it."

Ronnie froze. The hair stood up all over her body. I wondered, for a second, what my house looked like to her as she approached it in the dark. It delights me to think of my house, with its flat roof and black shutters, a house full of secrets, a haunted house. Why would any child want to go inside?

Because they will be tortured by their peers in the daylight hours if they don't do what they have promised to do. Nobody wants to break the rules of childhood games.

"Take a breath," I told her. "Take a breath and you won't feel a thing. It's just like being at the dentist, as I recall." I laughed for a second, drawing her in. "Can you imagine: it's been forever since I went to my dentist!" And I opened my mouth to give her a good look at the state of my teeth. There it was: the bad breath that has become a playground legend. But it's not because I eat children, no, it's because I have lasted longer than anyone else in this neighborhood.

Then I took the first steps toward Ronnie's transformation, knowing that when I was done, it would all be up to her.

I scratched off a strip of the red, scaly skin on her wrist, and then I began to peel away the years of disappointment and humiliation. All the while her eyes grew and grew.

2. RUBY

It was a rare night for me. It had never happened quite like this before. On this night I had four girls. A whole slumber party. A sweep.

When I was finished with Ronnie and had installed her in the window seat in my bedroom, I heard someone else enter my kitchen. I knew it was a girl. I could tell by her light footfall, her hesitant approach. The light was on, so she must have taken that as a sign to proceed. And what was she doing in my house? Very simply, she was looking for her friend. It was her job. The others had sent her to find out what happened.

She was it.

This one's name was Ruby. She wore the same attire, a nightgown and bare feet, like a lost bride on her wedding night. She was shivering, having dropped her sweater behind the couch at the birthday girl's house. Her feet were damp from the grass. I let her come to me. It is a ritual that each girl unwittingly performs: the search of my house as her eyes get used to the low light, the panic that creeps into her voice as she calls and then shouts frantically for someone to appear, the unwilling but resolute climb up the stairs to what she assumes is my room. I suppose that they have all seen my face floating in the window at least once. Or they imagine that they have seen it, which is even better.

Ruby's feet would have been sticky with sugar, which was still pouring from the sack in the kitchen. What did she make of that? Did she think it was some Halloween trick? Will she ever be able to get rid of the sensation of sugar grains stuck between her slender toes?

What does a child feel when she finally arrives at a real haunted house, one that is better than anything the movies can offer? What is it like to be the heroine, the one climbing the stairs, the one trying not to get killed? Do these girls appreciate the privilege, or do they waste it because they are so overcome with fear?

There isn't much to look at in my house, I'm afraid. It is nearly empty, almost as if nobody really lives here. Even my bedroom, with its black floorboards and blank walls, has only a four-poster bed and a small vanity. I don't sit at the vanity, though, because I already know what I look like. And I don't need to sleep anymore.

Ruby didn't want to go upstairs. She tried to call "hello" a few times, but her voice was so small and scared that it died in her throat. And then she thought that maybe we were hiding upstairs, trying to scare her. Did she swear she'd make us pay later, maybe on Monday at school? But Ruby was a girl who hated conflict, a girl who would never start a fight.

"Come on, you guys," Ruby called, resigned, as she climbed the narrow staircase. She could barely see, since the kitchen light doesn't reach all the way up there, and then she stepped on something odd at the top of the stairs. It felt fleshy and warm against her bare feet. Ruby was afraid to touch it.

I can still feel how fast her heart was beating.

"Ronnie?" she called, one last time. Then she pushed open the door to my bedroom, which was illuminated by candlelight, and at first she wasn't quite sure what she had stumbled upon. Was she interrupting something private?

I had been talking to Ronnie the whole time, you see, testing her, guiding her. It was up to Ronnie to transform, to go from a selfish, silly middle school girl to someone who can show a little compassion. Yes, I was asking for compassion. Is that too much to ask?

What do you think?

3. JASMINE

There were two girls left: the birthday girl, Sophie, and her best friend, Jasmine. They were hysterical. They had been trying to find my name in the school directory but it was like I didn't exist. Surely they took this as a sign of my evil nature.

"Wait – Annabelle goes to our school, right?" Jasmine asked. Sophie shook her head. "She's not homeschooled, is she?"

"She was in the fall picture, wasn't she?" Jasmine stared into space as if she was trying to make out a shape in the distance. "I know I saw her on campus."

"I thought so too. Did she drop out?"

"But she would still be in this year's directory!"

The two girls shivered in their nightgowns, trying to make sense of things, waiting for another idea.

Jasmine thought of the cell phone possibility.

Sophie had to remind her that I didn't even carry a backpack, much less a cell phone. Sophie lamented my loser status, and then wondered aloud how anyone could choose my company over hers, my house over hers. But by then it was much too late in the game for Jasmine to listen to her.

In the end Jasmine was the one sent to my house next. She didn't want to go alone but Sophie was playing up her birthday-girl status. She warned her friend that the police would be called if her mother came downstairs and found everybody gone. That was a good point. None of the girls at Sophie's party wanted any adult involvement, especially not from the police.

Jasmine walked outside like the other two, barefoot, in a nightgown, aware of how crazy she looked. She must have felt very self-conscious as she stepped across the wet grass. That is the purpose of the sleepover, after all: you have to expose yourself, show the others what kind of body you have so that they can read the sexual future that is written on your skin. The march to my house was just another humiliation.

Jasmine was much more vocal than her predecessors, shouting for Ruby and Ronnie as soon as she entered my kitchen. Her energy was frantic and careless, propelling her through doorways and into what little furniture there is. She cursed the sticky sugar and only then did she stop, worrying that perhaps my mother was asleep upstairs.

But then she noticed how quiet the house was. Was it empty? Had everyone left? Was it possible that the other girls were back at Sophie's house, having gone out the front door just as she was entering the kitchen? Was this one giant prank? Jasmine tried to picture herself laughing it off at school on Monday, or getting back at everyone, miraculously, before the party ended. I can understand her panic.

The problem is: she's a coward. She was afraid to climb my stairs. Jasmine, a famous drama queen, is ruled by her anxiety. Life is too much for her. Jasmine's emotions overwhelm her body and she cannot release them fast enough.

Jasmine was a mess. That was why the voice at the top of the stairs was so consoling, like pure honey. Jasmine thought it was my mother, and she was relieved that all this late-night stupidity was finally over. She was willing to apologize and get her friends back. She wasn't even worried about the consequences.

"Jasmine, I knew it would be you," I told her.

Jasmine squinted at the top of the staircase but all she could make out was a small female in a nightgown. "You know who I am?" she asked.

"Of course. I've watched you grow up."

"I'm sorry, ma'am. I don't recognize you." Jasmine tried to sound relaxed but her voice cracked. "Are Ruby and Ronnie up there? They kind of need to come back right now."

"Everybody's up here. We've been waiting for you. I'm so glad you could come to Annabelle's sleepover."

That must have been a terrible moment for Jasmine. She looked both sorry and impatient. "Oh, actually, I'm supposed to be at Sophie's sleepover. It's her birthday. And we all have to go back right now."

It was no use. Jasmine found herself climbing the stairs. She'd have to suffer through a round of social awkwardness for all of this to stop. Some people just don't have a clue, even adults. Her mother had explained this to her: some people don't actually realize how unpopular they are. They have to wait until high school to figure it out.

At the top of the stairs, in the light from the street, Jasmine began to be terribly confused. Was she seeing me, Annabelle? But then whose voice had spoken to her? It sounded like the voice of a much older woman. A mother's voice. But there was a little girl standing right in front of her. It had to be Annabelle. Was I pretending to be my mother? What a freak. Jasmine couldn't wait to tell the kids at school about this.

"I can see you're confused. Don't worry," I told her in the voice of countless reassuring mothers.

"Who are you?" Jasmine asked. "I am Annabelle's mother."

"But…"

"And I am Annabelle. I never really grew up. You can be two people at once, or three, or four. However many you need. I've lived in this neighborhood longer than anyone. I remember when you were conceived."

Jasmine started shaking. A little trickle of pee ran down her leg. She did not know how to respond to my last remark. "Look, just let me see my friends and get out of here."

"I'm afraid not," I had to tell her. "You've come too far. I have to fix you."

"Fix me?"

"For Ronnie, it was her skin that made her unpopular. It was unsightly. We took care of that, as you can see." I pointed to the pile of Ronnie's skin on the floor. "And for Ruby it was those buck teeth of hers. We got rid of them." I opened my left hand and sent two small objects clattering against the floorboards. "What will it be for you, Jasmine? Is it your frizzy hair? The pores on your nose? Your chubby knees?"

Jasmine lost all her words. I can understand that. Her body must have felt like jelly. The house was suddenly so dark that she could not navigate the stairs, much less run away. I took her by the hand and led her to my bedroom, where the others rose, their faces shining with expectation.

4. SOPHIE

'Now it's your turn, Sophie. It is almost light outside. You've been crying so much that you're thirsty. You want to die, or so you say. The worst thing that can happen to a girl on her birthday has happened to you: all your friends have abandoned you, and for what?

You don't know what they'll say about you at school on Monday.

I'm sure it felt good to go outside, where everything was cool and clean. You were dizzy, Sophie, as you walked across the dew. No sleep and too much worrying. You couldn't imagine how you'd get through breakfast. You didn't think that the party could possibly be salvaged. You could hear your own heart pounding as you knocked on the door to my kitchen where the light was still on. You did not even understand why you were so scared, except for the fact that a life without friends is not worth living. And that ugly Annabelle had stolen your friends from you.

My door opened by itself, inviting you inside to confront the girl who had stolen everything from you. Me.

I resisted the impulse to rush downstairs and take you in my arms, to tell you not to worry, that it was almost over. You're just a kid, after all, like I once was, all those years ago. It's so easy, really. Just be nice for a change. Act the way they want you to act when you go to church on Sunday, but act that way all the time.

Or just on this one very important night.

Your friends learned their lesson, Sophie. That's what you have to understand. Ronnie got her skin back. Ruby got her teeth back. Jasmine regained consciousness and did not have to go through a moment's pain. They all wept and apologized. They took me in their arms and kissed me on my lips even as they winced at the smell of death. They told me they loved me.

I can tell from your face that you might not make it through this night. You're too angry, too wounded. You cannot understand a world in which you are not the reigning queen, but that can never be possible in the dark realm of the sleepover, Sophie. This is my kingdom and I will always win. You are standing in my house.

Please don't make such a terrible mistake. Here, I will open my arms so that you can understand what it is you must do.

Don't make me kill you.

Come on now, birthday girl. What are you going to do?

Bones in Boxes

Frances Pauli

She kept death in tidy little boxes. A cat's skull rested in a shoebox under her bed, painted with her mother's nail polish so that the white bone bore a ruby-red heart between its ocular cavities. A squirrel skeleton hid in the bottom of her closet, its ribcage wound through with satin ribbon, a ghastly corset that had taken her three days to finish.

The bird box lay open on her bedroom floor. The newest, a ghost pale blue jay, had just finished its pre-requisite sun bathing. Now, the bones shone white, if a bit scattered, and she did her best to arrange them with dainty, nine-year-old fingers. The wings needed to be open, like fingers reaching, like the bone bird might suddenly take flight and slip free of the cardboard carton.

It needed something else, too. Not paint or ribbons. Something different.

She squatted on the carpet beside the box, chewing her lower lip and examining the skeleton. The bones were so tiny, lightweight, like her brother's balsawood glider. They'd snap if she messed with them too much. She'd learned that the hard way. Some of the other birds gapped with missing segments or boasted pathetic, crushed skulls. Still, the jay deserved something.

The curved beak had frozen half open, just parted enough that it looked as if the blue jay were screaming. She heard it cry when she looked at the beak, heard it as if it still rang in her ears. One finger stroked the fragile lower jaw with only a slight tremble. That was it. Perfect. She jumped up and skipped to her bedside table.

Inside her princess jewelry box, she kept her pretties, the little jewels and sparkles that somehow rained down upon little girls whether they liked them or not. She squinted at the treasures, plucked the largest jewel; a square plastic emerald with some kind of shimmery metal glued to the back, and let the top of the box close.

The gem slid easily between the upper and lower beak, rested in the Jay's mouth with just enough showing to be pretty, to look as if the bird had stolen one final shiny bit before death claimed him. The girl rocked back on her heels, squinted at the dead bird, and let a satisfied smile twist her little lips together. Then she sealed the casket, fit the Nike lid gently on top of the box and slid it under her bed with the rest of them.

Donna leaned her elbows on her desk and frowned at the glossy photographs. She'd seen grisly before. What cop hadn't? She'd seen things that would make most people throw up, cry, and seek professional help. These were nasty. Something about the animal abuse cases always made it worse, harder to sleep afterwards. These would haunt her even after they'd collared the piece of shit responsible.

She shoved them back into a pile and forced the images down with a swig of black coffee. She'd been in the game too long to ask questions. They came anyway. Who was this woman? What possessed a human being to go that bad? What could warp someone so much, allow them to detach enough for this? Or maybe they didn't detach. Maybe they enjoyed it. Donna shook it off. The questions never went anywhere, never made it any better.

Her office door opened – no knock, damn it all – and a pale-faced rookie peeked in, raised one reddish eyebrow, and then cleared his throat.

"Come in, Doug. You already forgot to knock."

"Sorry." He shuffled in, looked sideways at the desk, and the open file. "You seen the pictures?"

"Yeah. Nasty shit."

"I don't know how the pet cops do it." He'd coined the term on his own and was far too proud of it.

"The Humane Society, Doug."

"Yeah."

They'd backed up the HSUS before. In a city their size, animal cruelty cases weren't rare. It made Donna's teeth grind, but the city was full of useless shits who left their pets to rot when they got in a bind. Usually, the Humane Society handled it. Usually, she didn't have to see photos like the ones on her desk today.

"They counted seventeen animals in boxes," Doug said. "Report says more than that loose in the house. Feces, filth, several carcasses."

Donna grunted. This one was tricky. The woman had refused to sur-
render a single cat, had gotten physical with the HSUS gal, and wouldn't
answer the door on the second visit. The images had earned Donna a
warrant, but she didn't just want to seize the animals now. She wanted to
catch a killer, and the woman hadn't been home in three days.

If she let the Humane Society folks in to save the cats, Donna would
lose her perp. Her hand reached for the photos, tapped the file while she
stared at the buttons on Doug's uniform. How many days should she
wait? How many deaths would be worth catching her piece of shit? How
many would she have to lose to save them all?

"Said the gal's back." Doug was talking, hadn't stopped talking, in fact.
Only the last bit actually reached her.

"What?"

"Just got the call. They spotted her slipping in the back on foot."

Donna stood, knocking the desk hard enough to slosh her coffee onto
the papers. She let it soak in, already reaching for her jacket and her piece.
Doug backed out of the office in front of her and Donna stormed over
him, rattling off orders to the rest of the crew on the way to her vehicle.

The rookie scrambled in her wake, quick on his feet, a good man to
have with her if she needed to move fast.

"Get a move on, kid." She plowed through her precinct like a dozer
and snarled at him even though he was keeping up just fine. "We're going
in."

The dead cat had almost lost all of its fur and muscle. Some neighborhood animal had been at it, picking, and she'd had to chase down some
of the bits that had pulled free, drag the carcass back to the rock and the
sun. She hadn't figured out how to keep them from chewing on death,
how to keep the bones safe. Maybe up in a tree would work, but she'd
never been good at climbing, wasn't athletic according to her parents.

They'd found the first few boxes before she'd learned about rot and
smell, before she'd learned to be patient, to let the sun and the animals
clean the bones for her. The stink had brought her mother snooping, and
the discovery of a box of dead birds under her daughter's bed dragged a
child psychologist into the mix.

For two months she'd sat in a well-appointed office and smiled for the
doctor, told her that she'd only thought the birds were pretty, that she
didn't understand about death. The cat would need another week to be
clean enough. Then the smell wouldn't be a problem.

She lifted the chin. Exposed bone showed between the dried skin
there. If she painted this one, it wouldn't be hearts. This time, she'd do
flowers. Flowers would be nice.

The bushes rattled beyond the rock. Boys' voices whispered. Their
steps crunched. She dropped the cat's chin and backed away from it,

scooted farther into the brush, and held her breath. If they found it, found her with it, they'd crush the bones. They'd take it away, destroy it.

"It was just over this way."

She couldn't save it if they took it away. "Come on, Stew, it's just a dead cat."

Her fingers reached for the carcass, but it was too fresh. She couldn't take it home yet, and there was no time to hide it. She'd learned the hard way not to confront them, too. She'd learned. Maybe they'd just play with it and leave it here. Maybe.

She turned and wriggled into the brush and away, sprinting for home with her thoughts racing. Maybe they wouldn't find it. Maybe she could still save it.

"Have Wills park in the alley." Donna let the rookie drive so she could focus. She knew the neighborhood better, but the kid had to learn it eventually. "Get us close to the curb and across the driveway in case her car is there."

"Sure thing." Doug punched the gas and the cruiser lurched forward.

"Don't kill us on the way there," Donna said.

"Right."

"But don't dawdle either." She bit off further comment, wanted to hurry and also wanted to think. The animal cases got to her. That was the problem. They got in her head, under her skin. She could still see the pictures.

What kind of person?

You weren't supposed to ask those questions. The answers didn't matter, really. You caught the bad guy. You locked them up. You let the justice system handle it, the psych freaks worry about why they did it, how they could live with themselves afterwards.

All the animal hoarders had some excuse, some ghost of abuse or trauma that left them incapable of resisting. She'd heard the HSUS officers talking about it. Pathological rescuers. They meant to save, but they over-extended, took in more than they could care for and then, then it all went to hell fast.

Donna didn't believe in excuses. She couldn't be a cop and think soft thoughts. She'd spent her life cleaning up the mess, waist deep in the repercussions. She'd seen way too many grisly photos. Motivation was for lawyers to worry about. As far as she was concerned, there was no polishing a turd.

And this turd was the mother of them all.

"One more block and take a right." She barked her directions to Doug and pressed her lips into a pale line. "Tell Wilks to secure the alley."

The first time she'd caught the boys killing something, she tried to stop them. They had the squirrel tied to a branch, and they were taking turns at it with sticks, poking it, making it squeal. She'd ran straight into them, slapped, and kicked, and screamed until they dropped it.

They'd held her down then, made her watch while one of them stepped on its head.

She came home with a black eye, mud stains, and tears. Her mother fed her a cookie and pressed cold meat against her skin. Her father had told her that, "boys are just boys," and shrugged the whole thing off after reminding her not to get into tussles.

Neither of them worried about the squirrel at all, but then, neither of them had heard it screaming.

She'd heard it for weeks afterwards. She heard it when she slept, and she heard it again when she crept back to the spot and found its decimated carcass. The skull was past saving, but she'd gathered it all up, just the same. She'd wrapped it in one of her shirts and left it in a drawer.

But she hadn't understood about the rot then. She hadn't known about the smell.

The house reeked of death and excrement. The carpets had been torn free, but badly, so that bits of urine-soaked shag still clung at the living room's edges, still peeked from underneath the stacks of wire crates and plastic kennels. The cats inside yowled and paced if they could still walk. Others lay like dark shadows against the wires, maybe breathing, maybe not.

Donna kept one hand on her piece and the other on one of the peeling walls. Urine stains reached nearly waist high on these, visible even in the low light. Golden eyes flashed from the spaces between the towers. The overflow cats slunk and hissed and cried out at the injustice of their situation.

No food in the filthy dishes. No water. No excuse.

The entry darkened as Doug closed the front door. Wilks from the Humane Society had the back of the house covered. He hadn't seen any movement since the first report. It might have been the cats moving the curtains. It might have been nothing.

Donna was glad either way. Sure, she wanted her turd caught, but these cats couldn't wait any longer. It was time to get them out, to save the ones the HSUS people could save. Some of them were too far gone. Some were long gone.

She waved Doug into the kitchen and then inched between the kennels and into the living space. A hallway opened off the back of the room, but even there in the main space, there was only just enough area to maneuver between the kennels, to slide between them while the occupants wailed and batted at her as she passed. If her perp was there, she'd be down the hall, hiding in a room or under a bed.

Donna made it across the living room, paused in the hallway and stared into the nearest corner. She'd seen this in the photos. It shouldn't have stalled her, shouldn't have distracted her from securing the building. She stopped anyway. She bent down and plucked a skull from a pile of bones.

Down the hall, a kitten mewed. A chorus of cat fury echoed through the house. *Who would do this? Who would let it come to this?* Donna turned the cat skull over in her hands. She felt the bone, light as a feather in her palm. She stared into the empty eye sockets while the cats around her screamed.

She'd never interfered with the boys after that first time, but she hadn't forgotten them either. She'd follow them at a distance, wait, watch where they went. Then she'd slip in after they'd gone, gather up the mess they'd made, and find somewhere to hide it, to let the sun purify the bones so that she could carry them home without fear of discovery.

She'd save them, decorate them, tuck them away all the while whispering, "I'm sorry. I'm so, so very sorry."

She couldn't really save them. She was only one little girl.

They were bound to catch her at it eventually. When she went to fetch the cat, the boys were waiting for her, hiding in the brush. They'd sorted out where their toys were going. They'd been following her, too. They pushed her down and crushed the whole thing, ground the bones beneath their sneakers and laughed at her for crying over it.

She knew better than to kick them this time. Instead, she held her arms around herself and sobbed until they'd turned the cat to dust. No painting this one. No flowers at all.

"What's the matter, weirdo?"

"Shut up, Stew." One of them pushed at her with his toe. "She'll tell her mommy again."

"Don't tell me to shut up," Stew snarled.

"Shut up." The rest of them sang it. "Shut up, shut up."

"You shut up!" Stew was the biggest, a square boy with white hair and a lot of freckles. He leaned over her and hissed through a gap in his teeth. "She ain't gonna tell again. Is she? Her parents'll send her back to the shrink if she does."

That sent a snicker through them all, a wave of mirth that shifted the power back to Stew. "She ain't gonna tell," he said. "Or we'll tell on *her*. And she ain't gonna take our things anymore neither."

No more saving them, they meant. No more bones in boxes.

Hot tears fell in her lap. They soaked dark stains on the cotton fabric. She wasn't going to tell. It hadn't done any good the first time. She hadn't *really* saved any of them.

"Say you're not gonna do it anymore," Stew said. "Say it!"

"I'm not gonna." She sucked in a ragged breath and shook her head. "I'm not gonna do it anymore."

"That's right." Stew stood up, satisfied. He nudged her with his toe again, but knew better than to really hurt her. She'd heard it at school afterwards. Her mother had called their parents, and they'd gotten it for hitting her, at least. Not for the squirrel, but for hitting her, they'd been switched.

He grinned down at her now, but she could see the shadow of fear there too. He wasn't really sure she'd stay quiet.

"Now get up and go home," he said. "Not gonna tell nobody. Not gonna, Donna."

The boys all laughed when she ran away. They laughed at Stew and at her, and they chanted the new song. "Not gonna, not gonna, not gonna Donna."

The cat skull stared back at her. Plain white, but she could imagine little flowers around the eyes, and she painted them in her mind. Blue flowers, and a heart between them.

Wood creaked down the hallway. The screech of a window dragging in its track brought her back to the present. Her turd was running. Donna dropped the skull and drew her weapon. She listened to the window sliding, and she stepped with each squeal, hiding her progress until she heard the thump, the shuffle of a body moving, squeezing to freedom.

Then she ran, shouting for Doug and leading with the muzzle of her gun. She slid into the end of the hallway, pushed off and burst into the master bedroom in time to see the woman's legs fall out of sight.

"Doug, get out back. Get Wilks. Move!"

She spun around and hauled ass. The back door was off the kitchen. Doug would be out in a flash. Donna crashed through the front door and hooked around the driveway side of the house, ducked an overgrown rhododendron, ready for anything. The HSUS van was in the alley. Doug and Wilks both stood in the center of the back yard. Where the hell had her perp gone?

The rhodie rustled beside her. Donna spun, trained her piece on the bush, and peered between the scraggly branches. The woman crouched against the house, only half hidden by the bush and staring wide-eyed at Donna's gun, at the furious police woman towering over her.

She wore a nightgown, shoved up to her thighs in her haste to get out the window. Her skin was blotchy and laced with sores, her eyes as wide and terrified as the cats' had been. Like an animal's. Donna clenched her teeth tighter. What kind of person?

Not gonna, not gonna, not gonna Donna.

"You got her?" Doug slid around the house, then turned to follow the line of her aim and laughed. "You got her."

"Yeah." Donna stared down into the bush and nodded. She closed her eyes. "Get her in the car, Doug. Read her in and get her locked in a cell."

She'd help Wilks get the cats out, save what they could. Not all of them, of course. Not ever. Justice was in someone else's hands, someone who might care about excuses. Donna was just one cop. She did what she could. She put them away, now.

Now, she kept killers in tidy little boxes.

Marco Polo

Calypso Kane

Lotte Piper woke up on the first morning of summer break with the vestiges of an old dream still clinging to her. It was a familiar thing, featuring the phantasmagoria of older visits. Upon entering it there'd been an intense brackish odor. After that had come the lapping or tempest roar of the ocean. No seabird cries, though. No din of boats. Light from a swollen red moon lit a barren shore. As the dream continued the latter had grown distant until it stopped showing up entirely. It was all very slow, very tranquil.

Yet there was a quiet wrongness to the visits. In them she swam in the black glass of the sea, superficially alone, but undeniably examined. The moon trained on her like a dying eye while nameless things scrutinized from below. Her waking life had no similar experience to steal from, and the fear in her sleep was alien and raw. That summer morning her internal clock rescued her from the first dreamt visit to dissolve into a legitimate nightmare.

Lotte had been swimming. She had been whirling in place, trying to find a direction, a shore, an island. Then something grazed her leg. Smooth, boneless muscle snared her calf. Lotte was pulled under. The bloody speck of the moon shrank until it was a pinprick and then nothing at all. Wet darkness hugged from all sides, squeezing, crushing, strangling. Lotte opened her mouth.

When Lotte woke up she went into a brief spasm on the bed, certain she had to keep swimming. Then her room was there. Dry and safe. Lotte returned to her back and sighed. She didn't understand where such a gruesome thing came from.

Swimming had infected her legs before walking could. She had learned in the pool of their first apartment building, a squealing infant bobbing along in water wings and mother's skinny white hands. Springs and summers had been passed in that chlorinated pond and in the warm Atlantic surf. At least until Mrs. Piper left them. After that Mr. Piper had moved them to an apartment further inland. When he could, he would take Lotte to the Blue Surf Water Park to scream her way down the tubes and around the whirlpools. That was to say, once, maybe twice a summer.

But that had been before the promotion, before the second move. Now the Pipers were flush enough to visit Blue Surf three times in that year's spring break and at least one weekend out of each warm month. But for all the joys of water slides, Lotte had found herself more enamored with the gift attached to the new house: Gray Lake. So far she'd found the temperature never dropped low enough to shoo her back to their tiny pier. That might change come winter, but until then Lotte was giddy over access to water that she didn't have to fight for space in, and that her father didn't have to pay for admission to. The thought of it tugged her to the window. She pulled up the blinds and found a surprise.

The other night there had been a small storm. Some purring thunder and several balmy showers. Now the morning was packed with fog. When she worked the window open, a humid gust rolled in. Lotte smelled sodden earth. *The point is, it's warm. It'll be fine.*

Except it wasn't. Gray Lake was nearly gone. No matter how she squinted, she couldn't see the other side of the water. It was like being in the middle of a raincloud. *A warm raincloud. It isn't like you're going in the lake to stay dry. Dad won't care.*

With this in mind Lotte shucked her pajamas and dug out a bathing suit. She took sandals and a beach towel from her little side bathroom and went into the hall. Once at the top of the stairs she could hear a murmur of infomercials. Mr. Piper often stayed up late watching TV, always making sure to crawl up to bed before a workday. On weekends it was a fifty-fifty chance. Lotte had occasionally found the man snoring in front of commercials to do with laser lady razors, diet pills, and technologically advanced mops. As she descended the stairs she could hear the trademark drone.

"You sound like a beehive," she'd told him once. Afterwards, whenever she woke him asking if he wanted her to make breakfast – frozen waffles, toast, and microwave oatmeal were specialties – he might wake up just enough to tickle her to breathlessness while declaring she shouldn't have woken the Bee Lord.

When she passed by the living room now, Lotte saw her father stretched across the sofa, his cheek nestled in a drool stain. The current infomercial was telling viewers how beneficial a piece of equipment made from strange bars and bends would be to their quest for stiff abs and rumps.

She went to turn the TV off and stopped. *Dad might hear you going out.* Lotte mouthed a mute, 'So?' *So, he might tell you to plant it until you can see the rest of the lake.* On the surface this sounded fair. The June sun would burn the fog eventually. *In which time you'll be too hungry to skip breakfast, then Dad will make you wait some more, and by then it'll be too late.* Lotte looked out through the glass backdoor and felt a pang of want. The world looked mystic out there, as if a mermaid might raise her head out of the water and take a rest on their pier. She could imagine other things out in that fog: good sea creatures to counter the eerie denizens of the nightmare ocean.

Mom could be out there. Reflexive shame ordered her to dig her nails into her leg until it stung. It was a stupid thought, a blasphemous thought. The sort of thing a toddler who didn't know better would tell her grieving Daddy who did know better.

It hadn't even occurred to her at that age why they had stopped visiting the beach. Not even once during the summer. No more fresh fish, no more dribbling ice creams, no more sandcastles. Lotte's first thought was that the traffic-clogged drives to and from the water were simply more trouble than they were worth. Then Dad had moved them inland to their new little apartment. And still Lotte had not understood.

Not until the cooking August day that Lotte had asked, "Why haven't we gone back to the beach yet? Mommy's probably waiting." Dad had explained. Explained and explained until they were both crying. *But we did bury an empty box. Mom could still be out there. She was a big swimmer too— maybe she went all the way across the Atlantic and when she swam back we were already gone. She made a new life for herself at the shore. Teaching swimming lessons or catching lobsters. Or maybe she became a mermaid. She could be racing dolphins somewhere.*

It was a nice daydream. Infantile, but nice. Whether her mother was in Gray Lake or not, the fog added a touch of newness to the water. And it really would burn up soon, wouldn't it? There was no harm.

Lotte stole a sticky note from the kitchen's pad, scribbled a note – GONE SWIMMIN' – and stuck it to the backdoor. She slipped silently out. The humidity was comfortable and she idled her way to the lake, enjoying the spongy tread of her sandals through the grass. She moved no quicker on the pier. In the morning's hush there was no one clamoring around barbeque pits or churning the lake with their boats. Even the birdsong was on pause.

You're somewhere else now. A private pool no one else knows. You found it by taking a forest trail no one else knew or will ever know. It was waiting for you beyond wild green shadows and water-polished boulders. This pier isn't wood, but an ancient stone platform carved with dead—

How dead?

—men's languages. Their arcane—

profane

—languages and images of their forgotten idols. It's magic and secret

and when you dive

in it will be yours. Your water, your mist.

Yours and who else's?

Lotte paused at the pier's end. The daydream had gotten away. Her brain sloshed weirdly in her skull. Had she been older she'd compare it to inebriation. But the strange rush trickled away.

Once it was gone, Lotte kicked off her sandals and covered them with the towel. She gave the house a parting glance. No movement at the backdoor. Lotte took in a long breath and dove in. This she did with her eyes open. It was an old talent she'd managed in chlorinated pools and seawater, but always with a squint. In the lake she could keep them open wide. Slick rocks and water plants stared up at her. Faraway motes of fish flickered in the murk. At a brighter hour she'd have been able to tell the species.

What she saw now was confusing. They were heavy specimens, waving the ribbons of over-long fins. Perhaps someone had dumped unwanted pets in the lake. Lotte resurfaced and floated onto her back. With a corner of her eye on the pier, she began to stroke away from shore. She pretended to be a corpse for a time. When death grew old, she turned onto her belly to be a mermaid. The urge to be a cannonball struck her and she looked back at the pier. Her distance had made it a wooden tongue sticking out of the mist. Lotte swam to it, envisioning a running leap from its edge.

"Marco!"

"Polo!"

Lotte spun around. *Other girls,* she thought. *Where are they?* Splashing sounded from all directions.

From the predator, "Marco!"

From the prey, "Polo!"

Their voices had a queer echo to them, reverberating off walls that weren't there. Lotte waited for them to pass. Instead, their shapes grew dark in the mist. Three small bodies bobbed through the haze toward her. Two of the girls had their backs to her, both snickering lightly. The third had her eyes screwed shut and her arms outstretched.

"Marco!"

"Polo!"

Lotte observed their progress and swam back as the Polo girls drew too close. They turned to see her. Both girls were of her age and of the same sun-bleached blonde. By contrast their eyes were massive and dark. Upon acknowledging Lotte they regained their wide smiles and held fingers to their lips: *shush*. Lotte signed back an okay, meaning to wade out of the game's path. The closer of the girls shook her head and gestured for her to linger.

"Marco!" their hunter cried. She was startlingly close now, her own pallid hair dragging behind her in flaxen tendrils. To Lotte they made her head look like a pursuant octopus.

She and the others cried back, "Polo!"

The Marco girl paused long enough to ask, "Oh, did we pick someone else up?"

"Keep Marcoing," the furthest girl ordered. As a result the Marco girl shot forward and latched a hand onto the speaker's shoulder. There were twin shrieks of delight before the Marco girl spun towards Lotte and the other survivor.

"Marcooo."

"Polooo." It was a quick affair after that. The girl beside Lotte went first, then Lotte herself. She bristled when the hand found her arm. Aside from being too strong for its size, there was an unpleasant smoothness to the grip. *That's how bodies feel when they've been underwater too long.*

Don't be stupid. How do you know what corpses feel like?

The fact was she didn't know. She uprooted the thought and threw it away. Around her the visiting trio smiled and Lotte was pushed to smile back. "Hey. What side of the lake did you come from?" *When are you going back?*

The girls all looked to each other, black pearl eyes pitching invisible messages. They were sisters, Lotte decided. Too many features were mirrored in them otherwise. They even smiled the same and giggled the same bubbly titter. The eyes slid back to her.

"Way on the other side."

"All the way on the other side."

"The other sides of lots of sides."

Lotte considered them all warily. Her own smile was pinned in place by sheer force of politeness. "Oh. I've, uh, I've never seen you guys out before."

All three nodded. The centermost girl offered, "We've never been here before." Then she sank under the surface without taking a breath.

"Did you just move?" Lotte tried.

"We're visiting," the right hand girl said before submerging as well. Lotte turned to the last girl who now floated prostrate on the water. Cold shock slapped into her when she saw what the girl wore. Covering her torso was a thin suit of scales that molded to the early buds of breasts and the cleft of her sex. She may as well have been wearing paint. Lotte turned away, but was hooked by the floating girl's stare. Her head was tilted back so that she could mirror Lotte's eyes, her neck plastered with coils of hair.

A lump danced in her throat before Lotte asked, "You're here for the summer?"

"As long as we need to be." With that the girl turned over onto her front and dove after the others. Lotte considered herself excused. She'd managed one stroke back to the pier when sleek little fingers caught her leg. Lotte gave the desired flinch and three bleached heads bobbed up to laugh. It wasn't a mean sound, but one that expected Lotte to answer their laughter again. As if they were playing an old game and she was missing her cue. Lotte giggled obligingly.

Breakfast is sounding really good right now. Maybe waffles. Time to go. "Okay, so, in case you come by again, my name's Lotte." On reflex she offered her hand. It was seized with a wet snap of the left hand girl's fingers.

"Kendra," she said.

"Mary," said the one beside her.

"Nixie," said the last. Lotte tried to collect some differences between the lot as reference should she have to address them another day. They all seemed to wear the same scaly suit, the same face and length of limb. She examined their hair. Kendra's was the darkest of the platinum blondes. Mary's held a bit of natural curl. Nixie's was the longest.

"Well, it was cool to meet you guys, but I've got to head in for breakfast. Maybe I'll see you later?" The question sounded polite enough. In truth she'd be fine without running into them again for the rest of their visit. The girls struck her as off. They made Lotte think of friendly sharks – animals that could rip a body into gory chunks if the urge struck them, but were currently full and amiable. Lotte believed that if she'd met them on land she'd find them better company.

But they were in the water and Lotte had lost her private time in the fog. If she woke early enough the next morning she could try again. But then there was a chance her father would snap over her swimming without a chaperone. *Shouldn't have left the note*, she groused. Lotte kept her smile in place and aimed for the backyard again.

"We can all go to breakfast." That was Kendra.

"Just on the other side," Mary added with a gesture at the mist.

"Way better than waffles," Nixie concluded.

What? "Oh. Nah, I wouldn't want to bug your parents."

"You won't," they chorused. Kendra: "It's a buffet."

Mary: "Grab what you want, eat what you want."

Nixie: "And we can play Marco Polo on the way back!" The girls shared identical glee at the idea.

"Come on, it'll be fun! You can be Polo with Mary and me." Kendra faked a grumble.

"Please?"

"Please?"

"Pleeease?"

Lotte's temptation to go in for defrosted waffles and gummy vitamins didn't diminish. But the trio was trained on her again. They beamed unblinkingly. A pressure seemed to build inside, pushing from within her head and chest. *Don't be rude*, the pressure insisted. *You can have waffles anytime. You don't have any friends around the lake anyway.* She might still have steered for home if not for the last point: *Do you really want to waste this fog?* Lotte knew she didn't.

"Okay. But I need to call and leave a message for my dad when we get to your side." The girls hummed agreement. Kendra shut her eyes and waited as Nixie, Mary, and Lotte waded out of arm's reach.

"Marco," came the cry.

"Polo," came the response.

Kendra swam after them. "Marco!"

Nixie led Mary and Lotte into the mist. "Polo!" The name was parroted again and again until they were swallowed by walls of vapor. Worry fluttered in Lotte's ribs at the white blindness. Several late thoughts barged into her as she clung to the sight of the sisters.

What if they got turned around in the fog and ended up at a stranger's yard? What if they came to the mouth of the stream that played umbilical between the lake and wilder waters? What if some other early bird got up and took their boat out for a little whirl and struck a gaggle of swimmers who couldn't get out of the way? What if the girls' parents got upset because she hadn't asked Dad's permission and called him to pick her up? What if she didn't even like the stuff they had for breakfast?

Lotte may have gone on accumulating such scenarios if a more pressing threat hadn't lapped against her: the water had gone inexplicably warmer. Disgust shot into her belly. As she tried to determine which girl had used the lake for a toilet she saw that the fog was getting thinner. Sunshine filtered in through the haze. Warm air rippled the low cloud and made it fracture. The lake began to feel like fresh bathwater. She allowed herself some optimistic relief – maybe neither Nixie nor Mary had relieved themselves – before she followed them out of the mist and lost all manner of rational thought.

Further ahead of her Nixie and Mary went on calling Polo, Mary whispering that Lotte should hurry, Kendra was coming. Lotte stayed where she was until Kendra came. Her searching hand found Lotte's shoulder, "Got you! You're out!" Then she was swimming blindly after her sisters. Lotte continued to gape, then to slosh cautiously forward. If she moved too fast the vision might shift on her. She couldn't tell whether the latter would be a better or worse turn of events.

The houses were gone. As were the piers, the backyards, the one ugly yellow speedboat that buzzed around on weekends. Gray Lake itself had gone missing. What Lotte floated in now was an expanse of water so clear she could see the white sand at its bottom. A tiny school of primary-colored fish swam past her. Up ahead was a clean strip of a beach. Its sand reached back into a tropic wilderness whose green burned in her eyes. The shore's morning sun blazed in a cloudless sky. Seabirds threw their flapping shadows across her as they passed.

"Marco!"

"Polo!"

Lotte followed the shouts with eyes that seemed to creak in her head. The other girls were nearly to the shore. Kendra was gaining speed and her quarry's giggles were giving them away. Mary was caught. Then Nixie. Everyone laughed. They turned to Lotte when she missed her cue again. Lotte's mouth squirmed until the corners bent up. The sisters were satisfied and beckoned her to the sand. Lotte swam to them with rubbery legs. When she closed the distance, the four of them sloughed through the crystalline shallows. Warm sand glued to their feet. Lotte stood frozen in place as the others idly wrung out their hair and stretched their skinny limbs.

"Hey," she ventured. The sisters smiled at her. "What…what is this?"

"What's what?"

Lotte gestured around them, at the palm trees, the beach, the water, the mist that squatted on the meager waves like a patient dog. "This."

"Oh." The trio made a show of scrutinizing their surroundings. A seashell was examined. A damp trench was made in the sand. A tiny crab was tweezed between thumb and forefinger and flicked back into the ocean.

"It looks like we're on an island."

"Somewhere in the Atlantic Ocean."

"Somewhere with breakfast." Without prompting Mary marched back into the water, not diving, just walking until her head disappeared under the surface. Lotte could see her wave as she left, silvery bubbles trailing behind her. The remaining sisters waved after her.

Lotte waved too and swallowed dryly. "Okay. Alright. Why are we on an island in the Atlantic?"

"Because we swam here."

"The lake was alright, but there was no good food."

"Want to make a sandcastle?"

Lotte Piper gaped at them. In her head there was a rising choir of uncomprehending screams. *What is this where am I can I get back have to get back have to go have to get away from them have to—*

"Sure." Lotte joined Nixie in heaping up the wet sand while Kendra gathered ornamental shells and pebbles. The screaming did not leave. It had simply been muffled by an acceptance that seemed crucial to keeping her head from splitting apart. When whatever this was ended – *Dream?*

Am I crazy? Dad thought Mom was crazy. Could've been passed on. – she would dissect the pleasant madness to her heart's content.

And it was hardly an awful thing, was it? If she was insane, her mind had conjured somewhere quite pleasant to drop her in. Or, she supposed as she squeezed a grainy spire into shape, *this is real.* A combination of accepting youth and the overly-realistic threat of sunburn resting on her back made the idea plausible. The idea sharpened into something more precise: a daydream fixation given life. *Mermaids. They must be mermaids.*

Panic leaked cautiously away. She was among little mermaids taking a break from their tailfins. They'd come from their pretty island, decided to slum it with the humans, and took a fellow swimmer on a trip. Maybe it was the magical equivalent of leaving a waitress a hundred dollar tip. *Maybe. Maybe it's something else.* Lotte frowned over a spiraling shell as she wondered what that 'else' might be.

"Um," Nixie and Kendra looked to her, "what are you guys? If it's okay to ask." Lotte raised her head from the castle, which had turned into a city. The structures were all spires and swirls and warped geometry. Nixie was busy sketching some nonsense squiggles around the sandy metropolis while Kendra doodled an animal at its heart. A cephalopod.

"It's okay to ask." Their eyes met Lotte's, then their own. "We're mermaids," they decided.

"What's that like?"

Twin smiles rose. "Wet."

"Do you like saltwater or freshwater better?"

Nixie: "Saltwater."

Kendra: "Freshwater."

"Where are your tails?"

They looked at their legs – smooth, with toes that wore subtle webbing – and shrugged. "We put them away."

"So you're amphibious."

"When we need to be."

Kendra perked up. "Want to see the gills?" Lotte watched as Kendra bent her neck back. Four thin lines showed along either side of her throat. Kendra took in deep breaths and the lines flexed open into organic darkness. "Aren't they neat?"

Unreality and delight crashed against each other in Lotte's head. "Yeah. They're, ah, they're cool. What's it like breathing through them?"

"Easier than breathing through this," Nixie chimed in as she tapped her nose. "There's less to breathe, fewer smells." Her brow puckered and her own gills flapped. "Mary's back." Nixie and Kendra turned to the water and Lotte followed. Mary's head was rising out of the surf. Her hands were full of squirming marine life. More jittered between broken jaws. Only they weren't exactly broken. The teeth and gums jutted out beyond her lips. Behind the squared off human teeth were rows of serrated points. Lotte remembered something similar from an animal documentary.

That's how shark mouths work. They stretch out to take bites. Their teeth come in rows because they lose so many. "Wow," was all she could say. Mary saw her looking and her stuffed maw somehow managed to smile. Lotte smiled back. When Mary reached the shore, Lotte found herself helping the other sisters take careful hold of the catch and arranging them on dryer sand. There were fish bright as rainbows, fish that were silvery and bloated, two lobsters, and four snip-snapping crabs. When the crustaceans tried to scuttle for the sea they were grabbed up, their claws and legs broken by six sleek hands. Lotte jumped at the first crack and grimaced at the rest. The sisters grinned. Lotte's smile jerked back into place.

"We know."

"We should have brought butter."

"Just pretend it's sushi."

Lotte had tried sushi a handful of times in her life. Those were in the small years before Mom had been swallowed by the ocean. Mrs. Piper had been the one who'd introduced the family to a restaurant whose sign bore cheery cartoon fish, crab and octopi caught in the net of a likewise giddy dragon. She recalled the blissfully suicidal sea life and the place's name, a backlit declaration of, Dragon Dining Sushi Bar, with the dragon's R eternally fizzled out. In its walls Lotte had been introduced to rolls of makizushi, boxy nigirizushi, and the colorful displays of chirashizushi. Her toddler tongue had done back flips. Mr. Piper had been happy to stick with fried lumps of inarizushi, no more than pockets of rice. After the move inland, the remaining Pipers had frequented the odd Red Lobster, maybe gnawed some calamari, but never tried another sushi bar. She missed it.

She missed it a great deal less when the sisters dug into their still-sentient meals. A fish gawked desperately at her as Nixie ate through its belly, not even bothering to pry out organs or bones. Crippled lobsters fidgeted as their snapped limbs were wrenched off and sucked empty. Lotte ogled her own options, trying to spot an animal that had stopped moving. There were none. Her stomach bubbled with impatience. *It's just sushi.* She wrapped both hands around the smallest fish of the catch. It jittered slickly in the hold. Her fingernails dug into the scales. *Interactive sushi.*

Lotte met the fish's frantic doll eyes. Her face shined in them. "What do I do?" The sisters looked up, their jaws all wide and heavy with meat.

Around their mouthfuls they instructed, "Eat."

"I don't want to eat it while it's…" Lotte shrank under the girls' uncomprehending stares and held up the writhing fish as explanation.

Mary finally swallowed. "How do you think other animals in there feed themselves?" She pointed to the water. "It's really simple."

Nixie gulped. "Quicker than letting them drown on the sand."

Kendra picked her serrated teeth. "Want me to open up its guts for you?"

"Aw, she can do it." Nixie nodded at Lotte. "You can do it, right?"

Lotte looked again at the fish. Its spasms were slowing, the life seeming to wriggle out of its skin and up into the sunny air. She could almost see it. *It's hurting. Either chuck it back in the water or—*

Without thinking she brought the creature's belly to her mouth. Her teeth snapped down and ripped open a jagged hole. She chewed and swallowed so fast she nearly didn't taste it. What little she did taste was... not bad. *Definitely fresh.* A more frantic voice yelled from its corner of the mind about how sick this might make her, about how she should at least get the organs out, watch out for fish bones, there could still be feces in it, and on and on and Lotte was taking another bite.

Another, another, another.

She kept taking bites until only head and tailfin remained. Then she twisted the slow- snapping claw off a crab. Nixie shared the meat from another one's carapace. Mary handed her another fish. Kendra split a lobster tail. By the end Lotte's face was greased with the slime of fish innards and she was joining the other girls in a battle of crustacean shell puppets. Kendra frowned over the pieces and looked to Nixie.

"Which one is Grandpa?"

Mary snorted and snapped at her with a lobster claw. "These are way too little to be Grandpa. They're just, you know, citizens and stuff."

Nixie nodded with authority. "Or the people who fluff his giant pillow."

"He does not have a giant pillow!"

"Bet he wants a giant pillow."

"If Grandpa wanted a giant pillow he'd send somebody out for a giant pillow."

"He's never said anything about it."

"Only because he's always asleep. He's resigned to uncomfortable sleeping conditions."

Lotte looked up from her craft of linking crab legs into each other in an odorous, fragile necklace. "Is your Grandpa okay?" The girls grinned at her. There was genuine joy in the smiles but also a touch of proud malice. On school grounds they might've looked at home on a boy informing his friend that his father could beat up theirs.

"Oh, Grandpa's great," Nixie assured.

"He's really old and he sleeps a lot," Mary amended.

"But he takes care of everyone at home," Kendra finished.

Lotte nodded and gave up the necklace, opting for bracelets instead. "Do you guys have a big family?"

"Very big." They explained that they had more aunts and uncles than they could count and several more siblings and cousins besides.

"Where do you come from?"

Nixie beamed and began to scoop out a hollow in the sand city's middle. She exchanged a glance with Mary and Kendra who smiled in turn. Lotte watched the latter pair wander off in opposite directions down the beach. "Looking for tide pools."

"Why?"

Nixie shrugged and shooed the question away. "Grandpa and most of his progeny live in the old city in the sea."

Intuition sparked. "Atlantis?"

"No."

"Oh. So there's no Atlantis?"

"Atlantis is real and there are still people there, but they're more like neighbors. Our home is older and made of black shapes that present man cannot reconcile."

"What?"

"Are you making bracelets?"

"Oh, ah, trying to. What'd you mean about shapes?"

"The city's shaped funny. That's all." Before Lotte could press on, her crafts were snatched out of reach, examined and pulled apart. "We don't need these. There's better jewelry where we're going. Better bones and better beauty." So saying Nixie began planting the hollowed legs around the chasm in the city. The remaining claws and fish bones went to the same decoration. Minutes later Mary and Kendra returned with new catches. Mary carried a wriggling glob of a young octopus. It curled and uncurled its little tentacles like royalty waving to subjects. Kendra had acquired a dead fledgling seagull. The feathery carcass was sodden with seawater.

Lotte met Kendra's eyes. "It drowned." Lotte tried to accept this without noticing the limpness to the bird's neck. Her breakfast flipped over in her stomach. The flipping turned into a nauseous roiling when Kendra retook her seat and tore the little gull's wings off. Then she plucked the feathers away until there were only fleshy nubs. Lotte was half-hypnotized by the process when she felt a prickling at the front of her mind. She turned to Nixie. Mary was holding the octopus out to be petted and to, 'shake hands,' which Nixie did dutifully. But she was looking at Lotte. Smiling.

An impulse tugged at brain and body and it occurred to Lotte that the only living animal among them must need more water. She got up and went into the surf. As she knelt she cupped a pool into her hands. When she walked back it was with cautious steps, never spilling a drop. On returning to the sand city she saw that the central hole had been layered with little stones. Lotte poured the water in and went back for more. She did this until the cavity was filled. Then Mary set the octopus in his watery throne. Kendra gifted the creature with the gull wings.

Nixie wrinkled her nose. "We should've gotten a bat or something. Baby bird wings are too chubby."

Mary shrugged and snickered. "We don't know. Maybe he was a chubby baby."

Kendra snorted. "He was never a baby! Grandpa was always old!"

Nixie: "No, everyone's young first. Even the really, really old ones like Grandpa."

Mary: "That's right. And Grandpa was definitely a chubby baby."

Kendra: "He's so squishy now I bet he was only a blob when he was little. If he was ever little."

Lotte: "Your Grandpa is an octopus?" The trio turned to her as one and broke into giggles. When they calmed down they explained:

"No."

"Kind of."

"He's too big to be an octopus."

Lotte smiled and nodded and tried to keep her guts from crawling up her throat. Despite the thrill of unreality to this visit, she felt a distinct tilt into something grimmer than fairytale magic. *That's the wrong word. Grim is wrong. Grim is the bloody ending to Little Red Riding Hood, and Cinderella's stepsisters mangling their feet for the sake of the glass slipper, and the Little Mermaid dancing on knives for love. Grim is ugly but with a happy ending or a moral at the end. This, whatever this is, feels odd. Odd and mean. Uselessly, creepily mean. It's... the word is...*

Eldritch.

She couldn't remember hearing or reading the word, yet it clung to the folds of her mind, a mental scrap that wouldn't float away. Thinking it brought bad images to mind.

Fat moons with faces full of apathy. Stars that burn in terrible constellations. Deep, blind earth and waters riddled with deep, blind creatures. Subterranean ghouls and worms that eat, eat, eat. Submarine things that do worse. All boneless and heavy with happily hating minds.

"Mary's Marco this time!" Lotte fell back into herself and saw the sisters getting to their feet. Kendra offered her hand. Lotte took it and only frowned a little when that hand towed her out into the water. Nixie was already wading towards the lingering fog.

"Are we heading back to Gray Lake?"

Nixie and Kendra beamed at her. "We'll get you home."

Nixie: "Just taking a detour."

Kendra: "Promise."

Behind them Mary's eyes were shut and she was giving the call, "Marco!"

"Polo!" came the return. Marco Polo was called all the way into the fog. Lotte stayed close to Kendra. Between Polos they whispered.

"I'm sorry, but I need to get back soon. My dad will freak out if I'm not there."

"Don't worry," Kendra whispered back, "We'll get you home. Everyone goes home after we play. Do you like pearls?"

"Marco!"

"Polo!"

"What?"

"Pearls. We have those. Oh, and metal prettier than gold. Better than crab leg bracelets."

"Marco!"

"Polo!"

"Cool. Do you wear pirate treasure too?"

"We do. Nixie and Mary helped collect a lot of ships before I came."

"Marco!"

"Polo!"

"You…are you the little sister?"

Kendra masked a giggle and nodded. "Younger, yes. That's why I haven't gone all the way white yet. See?" She showed Lotte a lock of hair a couple shades dimmer than her sisters' stark white. "A lot of us are born darker, but we go lighter with time and depth."

"Marco!"

"Polo!"

The fog was thick around them now. It moved in opaque coils. The longer Lotte watched it, the more she felt like she was cloud-watching. Figures grew and faded in passing. Eyes, faces, bodies. Some were human. Most were not. She was transfixed by one swift image of a woman – Mom? – staring back at her before her image stretched open in a hideous yawn. Lotte's heart tightened. Then the fog was thinning. The light that came through was not as dazzling as the beach's dawn. Here the light was cut up into beams. When they left the mist entirely she saw why.

They were in the middle of a lagoon fed by skinny waterfalls. The light was severed by the boughs of a forest that ringed the water. It smelled of healthy foliage and damp soil. No birds twittered, no creatures blundered through the green shadows. There was only the burble of water meeting water. A darker, sullen beauty compared to the tropics.

Something gray caught her eye. Nixie and Kendra swam toward it, shouting their Polos and laughing. It was a pier made of gray, carven stone. Countless years had washed away its roughness and much of its illustrations, but she knew it for what it was.

A stone platform made in an older time. Carved with dead men's languages. Forgotten idols crawl over the rock to spew their forgotten messages. It's magic and secret, and when you dive in it will be yours.

"Marco!" The cry came from directly behind her. Mary's slick arms latched around her in a hug. "I got Lotte!"

Nixie and Kendra hugged the legs of the pier, calling back, "Have to get us too."

"Fine. Marco, Marco, Marco!"

"Polo, Polo, Polo!"

The chase resumed. Lotte waded after Mary until all the Polos were gotten. Then the four of them scaled the little pier and took running leaps off. There were dives, cannonballs, belly flops, and even a cartwheel over the edge. After her fourth plunge Lotte was snared and towed deeper. Mary had her by the arm. She beckoned with her free hand to follow her to the bottom. Lotte couldn't wrench her arm free, and so dove. She observed the flex of the girl's gills and the jagged saw teeth of her smile. It was more excited than cruel. Not that that isn't there too. Air strained hotly in her chest as they reached the bottom and Mary began to claw at the silt.

Glassy bubbles snuck from the corners of Lotte's mouth. Mary went on digging, finding chunks of debris – pebbles, a small animal skull, more pebbles, a pocket watch crusted to uselessness – keeping her iron grip on Lotte's arm. She did so leisurely. Black flowers grew in Lotte's eyes. When she tried to pry up the other girl's fingers they wouldn't bend. Lotte yanked and spurted her used air through her teeth. Mary dug. Pain throbbed in Lotte's lungs and throat and panic floundered in her head. Just when she thought she might suck the lagoon in, another hand found her.

She was pulled taut for a moment, her arms stuck in an awful T. Then Kendra was bringing her to the surface. Lotte caught a brief glimpse of Mary shrinking beneath her. Perhaps it was a trick of the light, but her eyes seemed to have gone entirely black. Lotte turned her head up to the air. She broke through the water with long, coughing breaths. Kendra brought her to the pier as she wheezed and spat. "Sorry about that," Kendra murmured, for once unsmiling, "sometimes we forget when we're with others."

"It's…" *Not okay, not okay at all, I'm all done, time to go, I want to go home.* "It's fine. I'm good, I'm fine." She waited until Kendra looked away to snort and squeeze water from her nose.

Nixie was kicking her feet as she sat on the pier's edge. When they grew close enough she reached an idle hand down and helped Lotte onto the stone. She smiled blandly as Lotte stalked over to the trees for a dry root to sit on. Kendra exchanged a wave with her before the girl dropped back into the water. Nixie followed after. Fear leaped onto Lotte's tongue. They were leaving her here. She would be abandoned to this nameless pool with no way home. But two blonde heads bobbed up at the water's center. Lotte relaxed against her chosen tree and watched the sisters stroke toward the waterfalls.

Neither girl smiled or spoke. At least, not aloud. Their dark eyes conversed. Once, they darted in her direction. The smiles returned for an instant. They dropped again when their mute conversation resumed. Lotte turned away from the water and tried to see through the forest. Despite the heaviness of the flora, all the overgrowth and snarls, there were signs of visitors. A ghostly trail snaked between thick bunches of greenery – *Not all green, though. Strange colors in the flowers. Stranger shapes in the petals, the leaves, the zigzags of the bark. More faces. More words I shouldn't know* – and there was graffiti.

Odd little notes left by strangers' pocketknives. Lotte read:

SWIM AT YOUR RISK

GONE RISKIN'

LOVE YOURSELF AND LOVE THE DEEP

SQUAMOUS IS SEXY!

MARSH WAS HERE

AND THIS MARSH

AND THIS ONE

MISKATONIC UNIVERSITY RULES

DAGON RULES MORE

CTHULHU > DAGON

On and on they went, gibberish exclamations linking to alien names and places she couldn't guess at. Lotte felt unpleasant as she read them. The last note she spied was at once the sanest and the most disquieting. A large heart was carved high up on the trunk she sat against, the expected head and tail ends of an arrow piercing through. In its center was:

DAYTON

+

GLORIA

Lotte knew a Dayton and Gloria. A Mr. Dayton Piper and a Mrs. Gloria Piper. When Mary finally breached the surface and showed her the prize she'd unearthed, Lotte recalled Mrs. Gloria Piper's wedding ring. It'd been set with a pearl rather than a diamond. Mary's offering – "Sorry about before. Sometimes I forget."– was a massive oyster. The shell was painted in surreal colors not unlike those of the flowers'. Mary popped it open to show a pearl the size of an eye.

"It's beautiful." It was. Save for a queer oily sheen. It brought the dancing prisms of soap bubbles to mind. "But I thought oysters only lived in saltwater."

Mary shook her head. "Not these. They're a special breed that were brought up from home. They'll live just about anywhere. Only they filter feed a lot more than plankton. Prying them open might get your skin sucked off. That's how I lost my first fingertips."

"Well, thank you. It really is gorgeous." Lotte looked up through the canopy and frowned at the sun's creeping height. "Listen, I don't mean to be rude, but I really need to get home now. Dad's going to kill me."

"No he won't." The cry came from Nixie, now floating on her back. Kendra bobbed beside her.

"We're heading back right now," Mary assured. She reached for Lotte's arm. Lotte sped to the pier.

Lotte looked to Kendra. Kendra only nodded and waded toward the mist. Mary sprinted past and dove after her. Nixie did the same. She turned in time to announce, "You're doing Marco this time." A second later the fog had eaten them. Dread jerked Lotte into the water.

She tossed the pearl aside and fired into the fog like a shot. "Marco!" The fog rolled over her. "Marco, Marco!"

"Polo!" Their sound was too far.

It's the fog, that's all. Makes things sound different. You're going home. Keep swimming. "Marco!"

"Polo!" Even further away now. Had they grown their tails back? "M-Marco!" *Wait!*

"Polo!" Tiny voices, puny and airy and nearly gone. *Wait, wait, please, you need to wait!* "Marco!"

"Polo..." The sisters petered to nothing.

"Marco!" Nothing. "Marco, Marco!" There was just her breath and the lap of water. She tasted salt. Lotte paused and listened for a splash or a giggle. "Hello? Hey, are you there? Kendra? Hello!" No one answered. Lotte swam straight ahead. The fog would end eventually and the sisters had—*What? Steered it? Steered through it?*—fixed it so she would go home, right? They'd said they were going back. *Right, good. Keep swimming.* Lotte did. The fog came to an end.

She came very near to soiling herself.

Gray Lake was not there. Nor was the sun. There were only stars and blackness and the rotten rock of the moon. "No." *No, no, no, no, no—* Lotte turned and found the mist was gone.

All she had was an ocean like an inkwell. Midnight air stung her face. "You can't. That's not fair, you can't." Tears scalded.

"Polo." It was a whisper. Small, far, and not one of the sisters. "Marco?"

"Polo." She knew she knew the voice. It was husky with age and brackish water. And kindness. It was the sound of someone there to help. Lotte spun in search of them.

"Hello? Where are you? I-I'm lost. Can you help me?"

"You're supposed to say Marco, baby." The voice was a sigh. Yet there was no one there to make it.

Lotte raised a hand to her head. Hair squelched under her palm. "Marco?"

"Polo." The voice echoed inside.

"Ma—," *Mom?* Hands locked around her leg and pulled her soundlessly down. Air fled her in a burbling scream. Inside her a thread of endless horrified denial unspooled. She pawed frantically at the water, scrabbling as if she could somehow climb back to the air. But the plunge continued. The hands on her scaled up to clutch her in a pantomime of a hug. *Help,* she thought at the fleeing air and whatever gods might listen. *Help me, please, I'm sorry. I'm sorry, Dad, help me. I'm sorry, God, help me. I'm sorry, Mom. Mom, Mommy, is this where you went, Mommy?* "Ma…" The sound escaped her and floated up to the surface to burst.

"I'm here, baby." *I've got you, Lotte. Your sisters and brothers, aunties and uncles, and Grandpa—we're all here. We've got you. We're going home. Just breathe deep.*

Lotte did as her mother told her. Cold wet pain filled her for an instant. The instant passed.

She went home.

Teeth Bite Harder in the Dark

Sierra July

"Put her in. Make sure it's sealed tight."

Down Rin went, lowered into a box a head shallower than a grave. Hammers and nails applied the lid that submerged her into darkness. There she would stay, one more month, one more till she was born.

Rin lie curled up, tight fists pressed against her chest. Normal appearance of any human fetus, but for her bud heart gripped in her little hands. In time it would grow so she wouldn't be able to hold it. For now it was her anchor, linking her to the dark because, although she looked human, she was born underground, deep, deep underground.

Voices spoke to Rin and she spoke back.

"What are you doing in here?"

"Growing strong."

"You don't belong in the dark. A flower bud is linked to your chest. You need sun."

"I need quiet."

"What good is dark to a plant? You'll wilt. You'll wither. We belong, you don't."

"I've been here longer than you."

With that the voices went. They didn't know why, but they believed Rin's words. Her voice was old, ancient, cracked like the walls of painted caves. They stayed in the dark, but they cowered there. They shuddered at the thought of what Rin would grow into.

"She's ready. Bring her up."

It takes a full day to get the nails from the box. Perhaps too much caution had been taken in sealing it, but none of the hands doing the work believe it so. Had it been their way the box would have been burned, not set under shaded pedestal in the center of the garden where it could watch the rain. None says a word, but sweat beads their foreheads and their throats feel clogged.

The box is heavier than before, much heavier.

"Stand back. Give her some air."

Rin stands before them all, unclothed, pale and bone-thin. Her hands rest unused at her sides, relieved of having to lug her heart sac. Other than knife bones and paper skin, she carries human attributes. Her eyes are onyx black, glassy. Had the group been standing to observe her on bazaars or even in a forest crowded with bugs and birds, they wouldn't have noticed, but as it is silent, they hear her breath come out in a long, steady stream, the hiss of a gas leak.

"Do you know who I am, my dear?"

Servants' feet rustle as they shift their uncomfortable weight. They look from the girl they'd unleashed to their mistress and see polar opposites, a tired and weary child with dead eyes and a woman flourished in silks red and yellow, fingers laced together, tears wetting her cheeks. One thing they share: raven black hair.

"Mother," the girl whispers.

It's all anyone can do not to shrink away, the girl's voice grates so; all except the mistress, too keen on the word spoken.

"Yes, love, yes. Mother." The mistress stretches out a hand. "Come inside and let me lavish you up. Some clothes, a warm meal, fit you right at home. Oh, and I suppose you have a name?"

"Rin."

"Beautiful. Perfect. Come right this way, Rin."

With no fuss, Rin takes the mistress's hand, follows her in.

Rin stabs her food, sending a spray of red onto the tabletop.

"Be careful with the tomatoes, dear," the mistress scolds. "They have the tenacity to fight back."

No answer from Rin; she continues stabbing.

Once her food is pulverized and eaten, Rin leaves the table and retires to her bedroom. She's been shown the way. Up the carpeted staircase, turn left, door to the right. A black cat streaks past her on nimble pads. Rin pays it no mind, but the cat spares the girl a second glance through squinted eyes before continuing on its way.

As she opens the bedroom, cutesiness assaults Rin's eyes: pink walls, frilly drapes and bed skirt, pillowcases satin silk, floor covered in teddy-hide-fluff carpet, too plush for Rin's feet to find proper purchase. She pussyfoots over the surface before she can sink and prepares to dress in the outfit assembled for her, flower-print shirt and tutu skirt. She frowns and removes the midnight blue gown that had been thrown on her upon entry. At least her formal wear hadn't been something spat up by a cupid. She shutters as she is about to slip the shirt around her neck.

"Do you want help dressing, darling?"

The woman. Rin turns her head and watches the woman's eyes stretch, gawking at her back where her spine forms a white ridge, her bones pressing, pleading to poke through and away from her skin. So much more desperate than when she first ascended. Yes, they couldn't tolerate being near her either. Her fingers and toes have hurt all day from all the tiny bones needle-pricking her. She whips her shirt down and faces the woman, her lips wrenching into a grin.

"Did you want something, Mother?"

"O-only to help you out, dearie, but it's seems you've got it." Her eyes cloud with denial. "So nice to have a ready-made child, trained to handle herself so, just marvelous."

"May I sleep now, Mother?"

"Of course, dear, of course, just call if you need Mother. There's a bell by your bed that I'd hear through the deepest of sleeps."

Rin doubts that. No sound traveled the deepest of sleep, no sound, no light, no— "Ok, goodnight."

'Mother' leaves, switching the lights off on her way out the door. Had she lingered a moment, had she cast a second glance, she'd have seen more than blunt darkness. She'd have seen Rin shrouded in her bubble of nothing, might have confused it for a soft silhouette of light, would have been wrong. Light died on Rin, but none could see it because its death was so bright. The dark shows everything as it runs screaming. About her is her barrier of white nothing, her barrier light can't enter; dark can't retreat.

"What did I tell you about scarfing your food, dear?"

Rin doesn't regard 'Mother.' She eats.

"You are my daughter, and if you bear my genes, you must have impeccable table etiquette."

Rin stops, a hiss rising in her as she drops her sullied knife and fork. They drip from tip to handle in tomato guts.

"Sorry, Mother. It was good." Her stomach clenches in a pout as she speaks.

"Perhaps if you didn't request red food we wouldn't have the mess to clean. Well, no matter, anything for my growing girl. You run and play now but mind you stay in the garden."

The garden is same as always, quiet and crowded. Rin stands in its center where her box was yesterday. They've moved it, the servants. Her hands bunch into fists at her sides. Its smell lingers. She sniffs, sniffs . . . It is back underground. She gets on her hands and knees, starts to shovel churned dirt out of her way.

"Rin, stop this instant! What a mess." She is being handled by one arm, yanked to her feet, her white clothes, now brown, batted and fussed over. "What were you doing, digging like that?"

"Going home."

'Mother' freezes then recovers. "You are home, my child. I know you miss your – your shelter, but a child can't return to the womb. You've grown up and are now meant to live in light, breathe in air. You understand?"

Rin doesn't. She pulls her hand out of the woman's grasp, stands over her box, stomps her feet to hear its voice call and echo to her.

"Come now. Let's just stay inside for today."

Huddled before the servant's quarters, Rin listens to voices that should be too far away and muddled to hear.

"Sin to uproot that child."

"Her child, her business."

"She's his child too."

"Don't mention him. What if the mistress hears? Just hearing his name sends her into fits."

"Sends anyone into fits to mention the dead. Had he not passed, I don't think she'd have lost the child. It's a might shame, but to go through all the ceremony. Bury the wee thing and yank her back up. It ain't right, I'm telling you."

"It ain't right, but it's done. The child exists, back and breathing. Can't do any good to stick our heads in the sand."

"I have a mind never to stick *anything* in the sand, not after this." Silence. Rin gets up and strolls to her bedroom.

Night hurts her stomach. Rin doubles over and heaves. Everything ejects from her looking like it did when it entered, tomatoes, mushy red blobs. This was the only way for anything to come out. Mother and the other mouths in this house hadn't noticed Rin had an aversion to the bathroom, didn't need to go and didn't want to. Mirrors watched her in there. Her other selves, they wanted her dead because she wanted things dead. Her desire bounced from the shiny and it might hit her, might make her dead too. She smiles knowing she never needs to go in there.

Tomatoes aren't red enough. They're a fake red. They make her sick like pink, watered- down red fakers, liars. She wants the real stuff.

She pops from bed, tiptoes about the sick she's made and steps into the hall. It's dark but her nothingness is showing. She'll have to keep quiet; she'll have to stop breathing for a little bit, not hard. Mother's room is right of the staircase, she feels it now, can hear Mother's heartbeat, relaxed in slumber. It's so slow, it's soupy, a *slosh-slosh* like waves. When did she hear waves? No, it was the sound her heart had made nestled in her hands, purring. It made waves like seashells.

She wants to be there for the panic, when high tide comes roaring in (out), drowning her.

It would taste so red.

A black bundle forms before Rin. That wasn't right, no. It had rushed past her in a blur and what stood before her was the cat. It hisses at her, spittle flying from its fangs. Rin hisses back, but the cat holds its ground. She takes a step back, ready to withdraw, try another day, and then a thought strikes her. It was running through the beast too, the red. It ran through everything, everything fleshy and red on the inside.

Rin gets down on all fours, spitting fury. She leaps in a feral cry, but the cat dodges. It doubles back and attaches itself to her back. She shrieks and tries to roll over it but it moves to her stomach, burrowing its claws in her. She keeps rolling and rolling. It hurts, hurts! She wants it over.

She comes to the stairs, doesn't heed them. The cat leaps from her as she clamors down, coming to a dead stop at the bottom.

"Gracia! Jones! What's all the noise?"

The woman's servants don't answer, stay put on the ground floor, and when the mistress reaches them she finds nothing need be explained.

The woman crumbles in a heap, requiring escort to the couch in her sitting area where she faints. The servants go about removing Rin's body before the woman wakes, knowing the past hour or so of their mistress's memory would be moot. They could say the child ran away, was kidnapped, anything but the truth.

"These scratches . . . you think the cat killed her?"

"They're plentiful but not deep. I'd say it was the fall. Though mistress has taken a tumble herself and walked unscathed. Guess the child wasn't as lucky."

"Short flight . . . I don't know. Wait, look at this. Her bones press clear out her back and . . ."

"What's the matter?"

"The back of her head . . . Know that soft spot on babies."

"Yeah, closes as the child ages."

"Not this child. Spot is softer than any babies like her skeleton was splitting apart. Skull's wide open."

"What'll we do with her?"

"Same you do with any dead."

"We can't. She might come back, come back powerful."

"I doubt anything can come back from this. It's a mercy to let the child sleep true now."

To the garden, the servants carry Rin. The girl and her box are reunited and, before the mistress wakes, both are back in the dark.

Rin exhales in a sigh, bundles herself into a ball, relaxes as she reacquaints with her heartbeat and the boom of her box's copy. The voices don't bother her again as they know what she's known all along. She belongs here. She is home.

Sisters in the Art of Dying

Megan Neumann

As a Sister of Mercy, I have trained to endure much suffering. Even as a child, I worked alongside my elder sisters, learning the ways of mercy and the art of leading someone to their passing. All sisters train to endure, but despite this, there are tales of betrayal and weakness. I hear rumors of sisters going in the night, leaving their beds to perform their own passing. This is a sin of the highest sort – to die without the aid of your sisters and before your time of service is complete.

On the night it is our turn to prepare dinner, my assigned elder, Sister Foster, tells me a young sister has thrown herself from the High Tower.

"She was just a babe!" Sister Foster says in hushed, but exaggerated tones. "Not even eleven! She had only been with us two years. Can you imagine?" She folds her arms over her ample chest. She is larger than me, her bosom heavy and her hips wide. At the age of twenty- three, she is matronly. I seem like a twig beside her, easily snapped in half. Her skin is white and laced with blue veins over her hips and arms. My skin is light brown with dark freckles over my nose and forehead.

I shake my head and dust flour from my hands. The bread for the night has gone into the oven, and a sense of pride falls over me. I have always enjoyed cooking for my sisters. This act has been one of my favorites in my time of service. Only the act of mercy fills me with more contentment.

"It's happening more and more," Sister Foster says, warming her hands before the brick oven. Heat radiates around her. I can almost see it moving through the air, rippling the world surrounding.

"Has it?" I ask, removing my apron. I avoid eye contact with her. Gossip holds little interest with me, but I must indulge my elder in conversation.

"Yes!" she says. I glance up, and her eyes widen. She pulls me close, and her palms are warm against my skin. She whispers in my ear, her breath tickling my neck as she says, "They say the world outside this place changes by the day. Fewer come seeking mercy. Fewer and fewer need our services. What will become of us? Some of the younger girls wonder this. They remember their families too well and still long for that life."

I pull myself from her and mutter apologies. "I'm sorry, Sister Foster, but I must not speak with you about such things. You are my elder and should know better. Forgive me." My face grows hot, and I know it is not because of the oven. To speak of a life without our service is a sin.

I turn my back on her and busy myself with cleaning. Cleaning is a service, and though not the service I gave my life for, it must be done.

Sister Foster does not speak to me for weeks after our night to make dinner. This does not bother me much. My time is better spent in the act of aiding those to their passing.

When a man comes to me for mercy, I kneel beside his bed as he drinks the tonic I have mixed for him. For the tonic I use pieces of his hair and my blood – this is part of the sacred formula, though it has no practical value. There are other ingredients that will take his life.

The man, he has lived long and could live much longer. In our world, you must choose to die. Such a sacrifice is honorable, just as a life devoted to mercy. As I came to the service voluntarily, so has the man who comes to me.

When a man comes to me for mercy, he comes because age is too much. Although his health will not fail him, as it would have in a time long ago, age brings with it exhaustion. Life is tiring. Even I know this, despite my youth.

I hold hands with those who wait for death. Some cry. Some speak of their lives at great length until, at last, they can speak no more. Those who have suffered long hold my hands in silence, smiles on their faces, feeling relief come at last.

Once I held a man who, in his last moments, refused to go. He screamed and six sisters were called to restrain him. It was too late to reverse the effects of the tonic. This was a terrible passing, as I recall, but I have trained to endure his suffering.

When Sister Fosters finally speaks to me, it is once more to gossip. Again we are paired to make dinner. The kitchen is noisy with the sounds of pots boiling and the chopping of vegetables on cutting boards. Younger sisters scurry around us, helping prepare the meal that will feed the hundreds of my sisters.

"It has happened again, you know," Sister Foster says. "You denied my words before and accused me of blasphemy, but I only speak the truth and wish to share it with you."

I roll my eyes and say, "Then speak the truth, dear sister. But please spare me any denials of your blasphemy. I am not the one to hear those words. I will not be able to do anything with them." We pray to the God of Mercy. Only Mercy can forgive our sins.

Sister Foster scoffs, and she too rolls her eyes. "You have always been the most faithful. How you take pride in your devotion."

I do not know how to respond, so I fold my hands and wait for Sister Foster to finish. Although she is my elder, we have never been close. I became her duty when she was fourteen and I was eleven. She was still a child herself. The differences between us grew more apparent as I grew older. Sister Foster came to the service because she was orphaned and had no other options. I came, as I have said, as a choice.

"You need to hear this," Foster says. "I worry something sinister lies outside these walls. Something we do not see yet. A drastic change is coming from the outside. Two sisters have died since we last spoke. They died by drinking the tonic. Their ages only nine and thirteen."

"Why have I not heard of this from others? I have not noticed any missing sisters."

"There are hundreds of sisters living in this commune. Do you know them all?" Sister Foster does not wait for my answer. "No! You are too absorbed in your art and work to notice the sisters you once walked the halls with vanish in the night."

What she says is true. I do not pay attention to the others. My days are devoted to the art of aiding men to their final rest.

"Why are you warning of this, Sister?" I ask. "Do you fear I may pass before my service is complete?"

Sister Foster laughs. She slaps my shoulder jovially, and I instinctively pull away. The Sisters of Mercy do not touch one another in companionship. "I never doubt your faith, my dear. I merely tell you so that you might keep an eye out. You are nearly an elder sister. You must watch out for the younger ones."

That night I sleep poorly, the words of my elder turning over in my mind. Was it my duty to protect the other sisters? Sisters of Mercy grow into their roles at the commune by learning from their assigned elder to cook and clean and mend things. We must learn these duties as they are necessities for living. And we, of course, learn the art of mercy. Caring for one another is not taught. It is not something I think about day to day, but it's something that makes sense to me, something I feel I must do. Surely it is a sin to allow a sister to fail in her duties, to give up the art.

I awake not from a dark dream but from a disturbance in the room. My eyes adjust, and I see a naked figure walking across our dormitory.

The other sisters sleep, not noticing what I see before me – a young sister walking to her own passing far before her time of service is complete. I rise without thinking and follow her.

She exits the dormitory and climbs the twisted staircase to our highest level. I know what she seeks.

We climb together, both of us silent in our ascent. I should call out to her, grab her, and carry her to bed. But I say nothing. Instead, I wait for the cold air of the outside world to hit my face as she opens the wooden door to the roof. The wind howls in the darkness. Her body is white and seems to glow in the moonlight. I see her walk trancelike to the edge. As I move silently across the rooftop, I can see her face in profile. Heavy tears stream down her cheek and over her chin. The tears shine and sparkle as though her face were covered in rounded diamonds.

"Dear Sister," I say, feeling some guilt for not stopping her earlier. "What are you doing?"

She jumps at my words, every muscle in her body twitching. I have startled her, clearly. "Go back to bed, elder," she says. "This is no place for you."

"This is no place for you," I say. The girl cannot have reached her thirteenth year. At such a young age, she will have participated in aiding a person to their death only few times. She has not yet lived long enough to do much service to the world.

"Step away, Sister!" she shouts, "Or I'll pull you with me and your service will end as abruptly as mine."

I step back, suddenly afraid. The sister is several feet from me, but still I fear my own death. I fear her threats because I have never been threatened. I reach my hand for the door and hold onto to the knob as though it will protect me from this mad girl.

"What brings on this madness?" I ask.

A mischievous smile appears amid tears still streaming over her cheeks. "I volunteered for this life!" she says.

"So did I," I say, unsure of her meaning. "Many sisters have."

She shakes her head. "Haven't you heard what they're saying out there?" She motions to the world beneath us. "How can you keep going knowing the truth?"

"Sister, you are speaking madness," I say. I summon my courage and edge toward my sister.

She speaks again in low tones, but, though the wind is strong and the noise of the world outside the commune loud with life, I hear her clearly. "I heard it from other sisters who heard it from the outside. They are going to start killing us anyway. At least those who volunteered for this. We are too many now, you know. There are too many women wanting to commit the act."

I pause, but then dismiss her words and keep moving across the roof; each step is slow and silent.

"Do you know why we volunteer?" she says. She giggles, and then the giggle grows into sobs. "It's because we're mad!"

I stop in the middle of the roof. "What?"

"We enjoy killing," she says, smiling at me. "We're killers."

"Our art is a sacred and honorable act."

"Murderers," she says.

"We are angels, bearers of peace," I say.

"Killers who find comfort in the death of those who live forever."

My brow furrows, and I start to panic. "We are angels," I repeat, remembering the day before when a man came to me ready to pass on. I held his hand and in his last moments, he begged me to undo it. I clenched his hand tighter and spoke gentle words to him. He begged me to stop, to please undo it, but I held his throat and poured more tonic down. This was a sacred act. A mercy.

"No," I say to my sister. "You lie."

"It doesn't matter now. They've found an elixir to cure the tiredness of age. Our whole convent will die out. There'll be no more of us soon. Those who can live forever have no use for women who make poisons."

"There'll be too many if we do not perform our art!" I say. "The world is already overpopulated." This is why our commune is so highly honored. After serving thirty years, we women of the commune volunteer for death. Such a sacrifice is highly honored.

"It'll never be overpopulated now because people are leaving the planet. Going off to space!" These words send my sister into fits of laughter again.

She mounts the ledge, throwing one leg over, looking down at the vast city below. I can see it from where I stand, full of lights and movement. She throws her other leg over and sits with her hands clasped to the side of the roof. Her body slips forward, and she lets out a scream. I rush toward her and grasp her wrist as her hand still holds onto the ledge. She breathes heavily and flails her legs, making her harder to hold.

"I changed my mind," she says, "I'm scared to die."

I look at her hanging beneath and realize the truth in her words, all of them. "Everyone is scared in the end," I say and let go. I watch her fall until the darkness engulfs her and I can see her white body no more. I feel some guilt for letting a sister go before her time of service is complete, but there's also some satisfaction from performing an act of mercy. She was frightened, after all.

If her words are true, I will need to leave the commune. I doubt our service is no longer needed, but perhaps others think it is. Either way, I will find a way to continue my art until my time of service is complete.

The Empty Birdcage

L. Lark

Beatrice keeps an empty birdcage in their room. It is bronze, dappled in mint-green rust, and supported by curved legs that end in leopard's paws. Sometimes, Beatrice drapes a cloth over its top, seemingly unaware there is nothing inside for which to feign night.

Ana decides not to mention it. She spends their first two weeks as roommates examining Beatrice's behavior. Beatrice's eyes sometimes dart from her typewriter to the cage, like a rattle has drawn her attention. Once, Beatrice drops a finger between the cage's bars and recoils, nursing the appendage between her teeth.

Ana's request for a new room is denied. The orphanage is structurally unsound. There are few places one can walk without fear of the floor-boards snapping. The remaining dorms have been colonized by house-cats, vicious things with eight toes to the paw, waiting beneath bedframes for an ankle to stroll past. Taxidermy parrots decay beneath jars on the sagging shelves. Climbing vines search for weak spots on the exterior walls.

The dichotomy of St. Sofia's is obvious to Ana from the start; a wild place, struggling to be tamed. Beatrice fits seamlessly into this theory, with her hungry eyes and the tufts of hair in her armpits. A knot of flesh binds Beatrice's toes together. There is a third nipple beneath her left breast.

Ana remains in the room. She watches Beatrice stand fixed before the birdcage, as if testing her self-control. A gnat settles atop the scar of an old piercing on Beatrice's left ear.

The birdcage does nothing. The gnat resumes flight and disappears between the bars. Ana searches for its silhouette bouncing in the draft, but cannot catch sight of it again.

"Did you see that?" Beatrice says, mystified. Ana does not know what she is talking about.

Ana looks like she's been pieced together from parts of other children. Her freckles follow no particular pattern, scattered diagonally across her face. Ana's hair is flat and brown, and her teeth resemble a row of crooked headstones. On her fourteenth birthday, her limbs had surged forth in an unexpected growth spurt, and now jut from her torso at uneven lengths.

All orphans have the same backstory, really. Each of them is the child of a car crash, a cancer, a sailboat tipped by the waves of Cape Horn. Except for Beatrice. The stories surrounding her origins vary in their degrees of outlandishness and probability. Lupe, the oldest girl at the orphanage, claims Beatrice was found wandering naked in the woods, chattering in an unknown language. Daphne subscribes to the theory that Beatrice washed ashore on Tulla beach, accompanied by four crates of blood oranges. When questioned, Beatrice only points towards the sky.

Beatrice is afraid of songbirds, and had once ran screaming from a finch on the windowsill. Beatrice has dark hair and purple skin beneath each fingernail. Her shins are bruised in Rorschach patterns. Ana catches Beatrice pinching the skin on her forearms, or staring down at her feet as if surprised to find human toes wiggling at the end of each leg.

Ana documents her findings in the margins of her textbooks. She prefers the weight of a pen, enjoys the bump of a writing callus on her index finger. The sound of Beatrice's typewriter makes Ana's temple throb.

Day one, Ana writes, *Beatrice watches the birdcage.*

Day two, Beatrice watches the birdcage.

Day three, Beatrice watches the birdcage.

Day four, a moth disappears in the birdcage.

Ana is taping the spine of her favorite paperback together when the moth skids to a halt on the windowsill. It regards the room with a tufted antenna, and then settles on the tattered lampshade. Its wings become pink and translucent.

"Don't," Ana says, unsure of why. The moth swoops in for a landing on the cage's bars. It is gone a moment later, shattering into multi-colored scales. Ana's tape hits the floor, rolls, and settles beneath the desk.

"What—" Ana gasps, inhaling a cloud of pulverized insect.

"You are all strange," Francisco tells them, "Therefore, knowledge of the outside world will be useless to you. You must learn how to occupy your own place."

He teaches them about the plants in the garden instead, whittling into a gnarled length of blackwood with a pocketknife. The wood excretes yellow pus that causes waking nightmares. A blindingbush grows along St. Sofia's western edge. A puff of its pollen in one eye reveals the plant's namesake. There is stinging nettle, which launches barbs at one's bare skin. There is witch-hage for coughing, moonwort for cramps, and diavlo weed for enemies.

Lupe complains about the heat, Beatrice stares at a millipede wrapped around her index finger, and Ana watches Francisco snipping pods from the dying poppies. The other girls sleep on the layer of cool soil exposed by an earlier tilling. Chickens wail in the coop downhill. The dirt is speckled with the shells of snails, withered by the sunlight.

"I've just outlined six ways I could murder the lot of you while you drank your afternoon tea. Why aren't you paying attention?" Francisco says.

The day ticks on. Sensing their indifference, Francisco diverts the lesson to the estate's basement, where they spend the afternoon sweeping out ghosts with straw brooms. It is a pastime Ana enjoys, composed of simple, repetitive moments.

"You haven't heard anything, have you?" Beatrice whispers, disentangling a spirit from the handle of her dustpan. It yelps as Beatrice pinches its tail and drops it into the wastebasket with the others. "In the room, I mean."

"I don't know what you're talking about," Ana says. Her heart gives a double-tap against her chest, but her pile of ghosts remain pale and sedate, tangled like a clutch of cobwebs. At the other end of the basement, Lupe sings the old hymn of St. Hieronymus, patron of the abandoned.

"I can't let you go," Beatrice says in the night.

Ana keeps her face pressed into the pillow, feeling her oxygen run low. In the aftermath of dreams, everything seems heavy with symbolism. The cage looks a basket of rib bones. Monkeys scream in the distance. At night, St. Sofia's reverts to its more primitive form. The cats stray from their territories, and termites swarm the cooling firewood. Predatory flowers tap at the windowpanes.

Somewhere on the floors below, Ana can hear their caretakers joined in a low frequency chant. Francisco and Gabriel are tall men with identical faces, who smell always of dog. Earlier, Ana had seen candles arranged evenly around the seven-pointed star drawn on the floor of Francisco's office. The ghosts on the first floor have been restless, knocking vases off the countertops and unraveling the curtains. Ana wonders if she shouldn't have snapped at them for reading over her shoulder.

"I'm sorry," Beatrice says, pressing an index finger against the cage's top. Her skin hisses as it connects with cold metal.

"Go back to sleep," Beatrice says, but Ana does not know who is she addressing.

Beatrice isolates herself from the other orphans. She speaks to Ana only as a function of necessity, and spends the majority of her time folded beneath the rhododendron bush in the garden. Wasps land on Beatrice's outstretched arms. Mosquitos flatten themselves against their windows at night. At times, it seems as if the entirety of the orphanage exists to infiltrate Beatrice's well-guarded interior, but her walls are too high to be breached.

On their hundredth day as roommates, Ana finally approaches the cage.

Beatrice is somewhere on the first floor. Ana can hear the static of the phonograph playing war-era records. Ana sometimes has the feeling that they are lagging behind time, torn away by a rip current in the fabric of the universe. A spring downpour has turned the orphanage grey and flickering.

Since coming to St. Sofia's, Ana has felt only a tenuous connection to the girl she once was. She thinks of the shores of Terelita, and its water-logged library, and her mother dragging a fishing net across the beach, but cannot remember if these are memories or scenes from a novel she once read. Her father was the first mate on a squid vessel. Ana wanted to be a nurse.

Now, she is an orphan and that outweighs her other qualities by far.

"Hello?" Ana whispers. The container of baby powder in her left hand releases a white cloud. Half gets sucked into Ana's lungs. The rest is pulled into the cage. For an instant, Ana sees a hunched figure outlined by the whorl of dust. The hair atop Ana's head stiffens, like lightning has seeped through the ceiling. Thunder rattles the keys of Beatrice's typewriter.

"What are you doing?" Beatrice asks, from the doorway.

Beatrice watches Ana cough while rain drips from their splintered ceiling.

Beatrice disappears for hours and returns with black dirt trapped in the lines of her palm. Beatrice speaks in her sleep, a garbled language that sounds like a cassette tape running backwards. Beatrice panics at the sight of visitors on the lawn and pushes her fists against her eyes, counting backwards from fourteen.

Lupe regards Beatrice's habits with the superior amusement of one watching an animal prance on their hind legs. Lupe often accompanies Francisco to the witches' market on the foothills of the mountains, has attended French immersion school at the colonies, can navigate international airports on instinct alone.

"I worry about her," Lupe tells Ana, watching Beatrice bite into an unpeeled orange.

"No, you don't," Ana says. Ana speaks little, but is unafraid of honesty. During her first week at St. Sofia's, Ana had bent herself into a triangle and cried on the Turkish rug in the sitting room. She had cried while the nursemaid brought her tea and lemon wedges on a rusting tray. She had cried while the other girls assembled themselves around her, nudging her torso with their slippers. There is nothing left to hide from anyone.

Lupe sips Italian espresso, while Ana struggles with the twist top on the bottle of cola. Ana distrusts Lupe's deliberate movements, the planned blinks that snap her eyelids.

"Mm, you're right. But she is fascinating, isn't she?"

The children at St. Sofia's are all mutants, in their own respects. Garbine's left eye is clouded by an opaque white film. Henrietta does everything in sets of four, and arrives to breakfast panting, exhausted from her ordeal with the staircase. Ana never sleeps more than half the night, feeling her bed tip like a sailboat taking a nosedive into the ocean.

Ana follows Beatrice once, as she trudges barefoot through the old hunting trails in the jungle behind St. Sofia's. It is early dusk. The light filtering through the canopy is bruise-green. Jungle rats scamper from Beatrice's path.

Ana watches from behind a tree as Beatrice enters an open field, covered by a layer of flattened yellow grass. At the field's center is a dark ring, like a fire had once burned there with uncanny precision. Beatrice gathers her skirts and collapses at its edge, dropping a fist into the ground.

"Why did you leave us here?" Beatrice sobs. Ana cannot avert her eyes. Her knees, elbows, and cheeks flush. She has never witnessed something so private, but her feet have dried into the mud and refuse to lift.

Beatrice stills, tipping her face towards the sky. She remains motionless until the light shifts westward. Ana eventually grows tired of shaking plump, red ants from between her toes. Predators rattle branches in the canopy above. She leaves Beatrice there, watching the sky for the sign of something that does not arrive.

Day one-hundred-two, the cage is rattling, Ana writes.
 Day one-hundred-three, the cage is rattling.
 Day one-hundred-four, the cage is… strained.
Ana does not know how else to describe it. The cage creaks through the night, like an old skeleton climbing from its coffin. Beatrice leaves it covered more often than not, but breaks appear in the fabric – thin slits

in rows of six.

Ana is familiar with invisible dangers. The shallow reefs of her childhood are booby-trapped by jellyfish and ornery crabs. Poison seeps from innocuous kelp on the shoreline. There is something restless in the room, something ready to wriggle from its hiding place and lash out.

It's really no surprise when the thing in the cage escapes.

"No no no no no," Beatrice mutters, when Ana wakes to find her hovering over the cage with her palms pressed against her cheeks. There is dried blood on Beatrice's elbow. She smells of dirt, hormones, and vinegar.

"She got out," Beatrice says, without first asking if Ana is awake. Ana supposes it is obvious enough. Ana can feel her own eyes glowing, radiant, like satellites burning in an empty sky.

"*What* got out?" Ana says, into her pillowcase. A patch of cold saliva spreads across her cheek. The room is quiet, aside from the rhythmic slap of palm fronds against the window.

"I was supposed to keep her safe," Beatrice answers.

The cats disappear. All at once, like they've been sucked up through the chimneys. The mice sense their opportunity and seize previously lost territories. Then they are gone too, and the scratching in the walls goes silent. Lupe is the first to notice the canned food in the cupboards has vanished. Ana finds her staring at a tin of Heinz beans, gouged open and rolled to a stop against the dining room table.

Ana turns to see Beatrice at the edge of the room. Rain shadows slip across her face. For a moment, Ana is thrilled by their gruesome secret. She plucks a bean from the carpet, crushing it between her thumb and index finger.

"What is it?" Ana says, once Lupe has disappeared to find a maid. The dining room is lit by a tray of forgotten tea lights, flickering in a pond of wax. Ana reaches for Beatrice's most vulnerable points, capturing her by the wrist and neck.

"I don't know," Beatrice says. Her pupils are swollen, inching into the whites of her eyes.

"Well, where did it come from?" Ana presses her fingers into the skin of Beatrice's wrist, and feels Beatrice's pulse answering back. Beatrice's heartbeat is sluggish, giving one throb for each five Ana feels against her breastplate.

"Francisco gave her to me. He told me to take care of her. I don't—"

"Where is Francisco?" Ana asks, realizing she hasn't seen him for days. There is an old, misfiled memory of him stirring the red sludge of old tea, but the narrative ends there. Gabriel sometimes wanders the hallways with the expression of a tourist who has lost his map, but Gabriel does not speak, other than in curt commands to the nursemaids.

"Where is he, Beatrice?"

"He gave me the cage to watch. He said to keep it shut." Ana's hand tightens around the fabric of Beatrice's collar.

Dolores, Fernanda, and Garbine are gone by the following morning. When they don't arrive at breakfast, Ana climbs to their rooms and finds empty sets of pajamas stretched atop their beds. A draft fills Garbine's bathrobe with air, and it drifts across the room.

The great lesson of orphanhood is that nothing is certain. The other children ignore the empty chairs around the dining table, accustomed to the notion that people sometimes drop away without warning. Lupe steals a honey-filled waffle from Dolores's untouched plate and chews with her mouth open, teeth knocking against her fork.

Across the table, Beatrice watches for movement in her peripheral vision. Beatrice must realize it too, Ana thinks. The silence of the orphanage has become deliberate. There is something crouched in the darkness, nostrils broad and working. Gabriel has a letter opener tucked into his belt, as he appears to disperse the maids from the kitchen. They fan out across the building, locking the windows and doors.

Something is watching them.

That afternoon, Lupe leaves with Gabriel in a checkered taxi. Ana watches them through the window. They huddle beneath a black umbrella, while the car hydroplanes across the driveway. Gabriel stacks their suitcases into the trunk and suddenly, the orphans are alone. Ana watches the steam of her breath, spreading like moth wings against the windowpane. A tattered seagull flaps uselessly in the rain.

Elena and Josefine are gone by that afternoon. Ana finds evidence of their sudden disappearance – a teacup filled with swirling liquid, an open book with no fold to mark the reader's page. There is a shred of Josefine's paisley skirt swinging from a chandelier, but aside from this, the rooms reveal nothing of the orphan's whereabouts.

Beatrice reenters from the garden, wearing yellow galoshes and a stiff raincoat.

She drops her cap on an antler of the stuffed deer head on the wall.

"I've looked everywhere," Beatrice says, shaking the rain out of her hair.

Droplets catch the light like chunks of star matter, exploding. She seems unconcerned by their sudden isolation. Her limbs bounce as she drops into an armchair.

"What does it look like?" Ana asks, uncertain of her phrasing. She does not yet have the vocabulary for this situation. Ana watches Beatrice cracking her toes against the Turkish rug.

"It looks like—" Beatrice begins, and pauses. She lifts an arm, and Ana watches her shadow swing up the wall. Ana wishes she would drop it. She is uneasy with half-finished motions, car rides, doorways, what exists in the in-betweens. Beatrice herself is an intermediary between two worlds, neither of which Ana understands.

"It looks a bit like me."

Ana doesn't have an answer for that.

Ana doesn't sleep.

They sit together in their lit bedroom, listening for the scuttle of paws against the floor. Beatrice eventually sags into her desk chair, snoring unevenly. Aside from this, the orphanage is silent. The whirr of industrial dryers in the basement is missing. There are no schizophrenic snippets of conversation from cycling television channels in the next room.

Beatrice's snorts finally subside, and Ana can hear her stomach digesting the last stale biscuits they'd found in the pantry.

The orphanage gives a final exhalation, and Ana feels her chin drop. Everything is wrong this evening. The sky across the curtains is a precise shade of meat-pink. The wind runs in reverse, sucking leaves and dismantled newspapers into the darkness. The empty birdcage waits, latch open.

"Beatrice?" Ana says, suddenly terrified of each pause between thoughts. She searches for the pocketknife, buried beneath scraps of homework on the desk. It has a jigged bone handle, inscribed with the monogram *FR*. Beatrice had stolen it from Francisco's desk drawer, but Ana does not know if the dark speck along the blade appeared before or after that.

"Wake up," Ana says, but Beatrice doesn't stir. A blade of drool hangs from the corner of her mouth. Her breath smells faintly of lemon drops.

Across the room, a closet door swings open.

The taste of rust spreads across the roof of Ana's mouth. Every bruise on her shins throb simultaneously. Ana stands up. She walks to the room's edge.

One of Beatrice's socks, damp and knotted, rolls across the floor. It comes to a stop against Ana's big toe. Ana stares down at the palm trees printed on the fabric. *Hello?* she doesn't say, reluctant to snap the thin layer of silence.

Something rushes past Ana's leg. The muscles of her chest seize, causing a violent hiccup. For a moment, Ana thinks she catches sight of an extra shadow, darting across the wall.

And then, something bites her ankle.

Ana wakes later, Beatrice standing over her. They are both covered in what-is-most-definitely blood. Beatrice looks elated, displaying a length of yellow teeth. Her hair is gathered into four bulging knots.

"Finally!" Beatrice says, "I thought you might be dead."

"Why didn't you call an ambulance?"

Beatrice looks confused at that.

"What would it matter if you were already dead? Besides, look! I caught her."

Beatrice gestures towards the birdcage. Ana waits for the images in each eye to connect, but she blinks and the room divides into halves. Eventually, she understands the cage door has been closed again. There is duct tape tightly wrapped around the lock.

"She won't go out anymore," Beatrice continues, "I gave her a good talking to. She was just bored."

"Bored?" Ana repeats, using the bed to pull herself upright. The noise bouncing between her ears is that of a screaming teakettle. Ana blinks the flakes out of her eyes. "It ate nine orphans."

The birdcage is still, but in Ana's vision the room fractures again. A swarm of disconnected particles drift around her head.

"I'm sure she didn't mean to," Beatrice says, but Ana is already weightless, floating onto the unmade bed.

When Ana wakes again, both Gabriel and Francisco are in the room. Ana's skin has been cleaned, but her shirt is stiff and fused to the hair of her arms. Beatrice is close. Ana cannot see her, but hears Beatrice's toes tapping against the chair ledge.

"You were very irresponsible," Francisco is saying. "You know how your sister can be."

"Don't take her back," Beatrice says. Ana tries to slow her breathing, but is sure her pulse is audible when her blood jumpstarts. Francisco does not answer immediately, and for a moment Ana is certain she's been found out. The room smells sour, hormonal. A bottle of pills rattles in someone's pocket.

"What are we going to tell Lupe? She assumes the other children are visiting the library at Sanbal," Gabriel says.

"Tell her we've sent the girls to the orphanage in Bolata. Tell her we didn't have the funds to continue such a large program."

"She'll never believe it."

"Well, she's not going to believe they've been – either."

Ana is quite sure what was supposed to have filled the break in Francisco's sentence, and the missing word leaves an echoing ping behind it. Through the slit in Ana's eyelids, she sees Francisco scratching the outline of a pentagram, tattooed on his inner biceps. Outside, the crickets give half-a-chirp and fall quiet, as if suddenly aware of an impoliteness.

Beatrice responds with a hum of frustration.

"You know your sister can't stay here."

"Where are you going to take her?" Beatrice says. Ana can nearly hear the sound of Beatrice's fingernails, bending back against the armrest. There is a tone in Beatrice's voice that reminds Ana of the way a cord must feel, tightening around a neck.

"Somewhere where she can be safe."

In two weeks, Ana's wounds blossom into scabs. The summer ripens fully and the cats return, ribs shimmering beneath their coats. The deer head mounted above the fireplace blinks into wakefulness. Trains climb over the hills, carrying women in broad sunhats towards the coast.

Beatrice has stopped speaking again. She waits in the place where the cage once stood, but now her eyes veer in opposite directions, as if staring into two places at once. Neither one mentions this spring's Incident, because no words have the gravity and magnitude required. Ana wanders the estate, entering rooms and forgetting why. The sight of Garbine's pink slippers tucked beneath a bare bedframe still fills Ana with dread.

"*Who* was it?" Ana says, once she realizes she has been asking the wrong question for embarrassingly long. Beatrice is eating a bowl of cream, topped by over-ripened strawberries. The pink of a blooming cold sore lingers at the corner of her mouth.

"It doesn't matter. She didn't belong here. I don't think I do either, but my body is all wrong."

Beatrice's face is filled with such desperate honesty that Ana can't bear to question her further. Across the hall, a new room has been clean and furnished. Ana will be moving in tomorrow, and she will finally be free of Beatrice and the grooves the birdcage has left in the floorboards.

"Hers wasn't right either."

"No," Beatrice says, with a certain finality. Beatrice, however, offers the next and last tidbit herself.

"We share a birthday," Beatrice says.

For some reason, this makes Ana feel as though she has tripped and fallen forward out of her body.

In late summer, even when the heat seems to embalm the room in damp pressure, Ana sleeps with the windows closed. The twilight chorus of starlings falls silent in June. She has not seen a chipmunk since mid-July. There is no correlation, Ana tells herself, without believing it.

Everything is connected, in its own sinewy way. Sometimes, Ana watches Lupe staring into the cold blue light of the refrigerator, and imagines the parallel trajectories of their lives. Beatrice's line runs perpendicular, emerging from distant space and meant to intersect with theirs' for only an instant.

Ana does not yet know that she will be dead within four summers. At this moment, the universe is vibrant with possibility. There are monsters tucked into the folds of space. Beatrice spouts prophecy in her sleep, reciting dates while her spine twists beneath the comforter.

Their days are green, white, then pink again. Dogwood petals stain the windowpanes. Some nights, Ana wakes searching for the empty birdcage and finds nothing.

Chains appear around the chapel door, but like all things, they settle into the landscape of quiet mysteries. Ana does not question the new fences around the property or the howls that roll across the hills at night. The grand lesson of St. Sofia's is that some answers should be guarded, locked away, protected from themselves.

Some answers will devour you.

Cedar Lake

Ekaterina Sedia

At certain age, one just doesn't want to be bothered with persistent daily humiliations – for God's sake, in one's late forties one can certainly do without condescending glances from the Graduate Admissions deans and insinuations that perhaps one was out of school for way too long, and that maybe one would be better off taking some classes in a community college first. You know, just a suggestion. If you have your heart set on a graduate degree, you can certainly try your luck elsewhere.

At least this is what Alison remembered him saying – after the first "I'm sorry" her ears rang and her cheeks burned as if she was a child, humiliation and hurt never dulling with age, unlike everything else. She rose from the chair in the dean's office, awkwardly, focusing on lifting her hips out of the deep gray plush without getting them stuck between the polished curving armrests. Her feet were heavy and she felt herself wobbling, waddling out of the office with all her rejected middle-aged indignity.

"Community Colleges are really better suited for non-traditional students," he called after her, into the aquarium dusk of the hallways meeting at strange angles, with secretaries' desks wedged at the junctions, making the standard office cubicles seem private and cozy. This place was an epitome of indignity, and Alison hurried outside, to where the pillars supported the awning that didn't quite reach the entrance.

Non-traditional student indeed. The very name was soaked with the same hateful condescension, the same devaluing of her life: her children, her staying at home to raise them was nothing more but her failure to live up to the dean's image of what a student was supposed to be like. It certainly didn't include Alison – middle-aged, fuming, and waddling away from this place, as quickly as her sore feet would carry her. She cried in the car before driving off the parking lot and heading for the New Jersey Turnpike, and she cried on the Turnpike, all the way from Exit 9 to Exit 7A. As she headed east on route 195, she thought that perhaps a community college would be closer, and probably easier, and maybe it wasn't such a bad idea to ease into things rather than going for the graduate school right away. After all, it was her tendency to plunge into new endeavors full bore that stopped all her attempts at regular exercise short, in a burst of pain and nagging injuries.

By the time she arrived home, house so quiet and shady and cool, her tears had dried. There was a brochure for summer courses at Galloway Community College in her mailbox, and she took it as a sign.

The campus wasn't much: nestled deep in the Pine Barrens, it was sandy and dry, with occasional oaks towering above the scraggly pines. Acorns crunched underfoot on the graveled paths, as Alison looped her way around and around the main building, her shirt getting soaked with slow sweat. Black flies clung and got into her nostrils, and the wet, suffocating air smelled of molten pine resin. It was the flies that finally chased her inside.

Unlike graduate schools, community colleges were not about humiliation. It was empty inside, the hallways hollowed out by the absences – like a mouth with a tongue cruelly cut out, Alison thought. Didn't they use to cut out people's tongues back in the old days? She found the admissions office with no problems, no deans in sight, and they took her information and issued her a computer password.

Before she knew it, she was in the computer lab, choosing her classes, under benignly indifferent supervision of a junior faculty member. Then they sent her to the bursar's office, where they took her credit card and never suggested she should go elsewhere.

"Baby steps," she said under her breath as she left the air-conditioned building. "Let's see what this place is all about."

The crunchy gravel paths turned to sand as they led her away from the building, and the canopy closed over her, protectively. Soon, the path dipped, the soil grew wet and silver-green with sphagnum, and pines gave rise to Atlantic white cedars, their roots entangled in sinewy knots bulging out of thin soil, the bases of their trunks even more enormous as they flared into ruddy buttresses. The path became a wooden bridge almost touching the tea-colored surface of the cedar swamp.

Alison liked cedar swamps, with their hummocks and dark pools of still water, their peculiar smell of resin and decay, wet organic soil and sun. The air always stood still there, trapped between the giant trunks and shockingly slender, feathered branches, and no sound penetrated those darkened places.

Alison gulped amber-colored air as she awkwardly left the wooden bridge, slipped and landed on her hands and knees, butt in the air. She got up quickly, even though there was no one there to see her, and wiped the muck off her hands on her chinos. They were getting too small anyway, cutting pointedly into the soft spot above her hipbones. Mud splattered her sneakers, and she grabbed a handful of sphagnum moss to clean her hands and shoes. It was so absorbent, it always held many times its weight in moisture. They used to use it for wounds, Alison remembered, back in the old days. It would absorb so much blood, staunch its flow, and it was sterile to boot. She lived in the Pine Barrens long enough to have learned a ton of things like this: about the bog iron and the Revolutionary war, ghost towns, the Jersey devil, the endangered species, the controversies surrounding the Pinelands Commission.

She had recovered from her awkwardness and carefully found her way to a drier spot, where she could step from one hummock to the next until she came to the shore of the largest of these pools – water golden-brown with tannins, pure and acidic, and so still it seemed a dark mirror splayed carelessly between the trees. The cedar buttresses swept upward around her, shielding and yet encircling, gentle and threatening like a little too tight, too long embrace.

She sat down, her back resting against russet, smooth bark, because it was better to be held dangerously than not being held at all.

Jim was happy about the community college; the tuition was much less than a graduate school would be, especially full-time. Part-time community college they could handle, he said, and he didn't quite say the other part but Alison knew that he was thinking it: *maybe you'll just get this out of your system, give up, and not bug me about more school, expensive and useless, and it's too late for you anyway.*

When you're married for so long and raise kids and worry about money, a lot of things have to go unsaid, Alison knew. Otherwise, there would be arguing and possibly crying, choking into the pillow with shrieking, helpless sobs, and hoping that he would find you and try to comfort you, while also hoping that he wouldn't. With Jonathan, the youngest out of the house, not talking was becoming more difficult – the children were the mediums through which they had communicated, and now it was awkward, as she imagined it would be between two immaterial ghosts trying to discuss something of import. So they just said hello when he got home from work, and she barely looked up from the skillet of Hamburger Helper. She could not wait for the classes to start, so that she could be out too, to come home and be greeted as if she mattered enough for that. And sometimes she fantasized about living alone.

In September, the campus suddenly filled with people. It felt as if they had always been there, invisible, and come September, they simply materialized, mid-stride, these young apparitions in jeans and sweats and sundresses, with hair bleached by the sun during months spent at the shore or just outside. Alison wanted to fuss over them, and it was strange to mingle with these aliens her kids' age, as if she belonged there.

Her first class, Anthropology, ended early, and she was glad for a break that would let her escape. Her feet found their way to the cedar swamp, and in what she knew would become another ritual, she stepped off the wooden bridge and found her way to the hidden spot among the buttresses.

No one else was there, of course – exploring the swamps was never a common activity, and even those who did rarely left the secure wooden slats for the wobbly, sopping ground that undulated with every step in some places, and threatened to open under one's feet treacherously. It was her place now, and she stretched and surveyed the dark waters laid flat and matte before her.

There was rustling then – in the trees around her, first in their branches, but then it traveled down the trunks, as if an army of squirrels scrabbled down the bark. But there was no movement and no obvious life – just the noise, growing cracklier and louder until Alison hunched close to the ground, whimpering, her hands over her face. And yet, inside her, through the terror and confusion, one thought swam to the surface: *at least something is changing.*

And then the noise descended to the ground, sunk into it and quieted, as if extinguished by soft, wet moss and soppy muck. Alison dared to look up eventually, and just then, all around her, the cedar buttresses creaked and swung open in a blur of rust-colored uneven flanges, like the doors of a cuckoo clock in Alison's childhood home. But instead of the noisy, inane bird, the things that came forth were difficult to recognize – or even admit to their existence.

The shape of them was like that of toddlers – protruding bellies, pudgy unsure legs, large dolphin foreheads. They moved out of the concealing trunks in a slow stumble, their joints creaking, their blind, mute faces covered in cedar bark, their twig fingers spreading too wide, as if there was no bone stopping them.

I am mad, Alison thought. *Why would there be bone if they're made of wood?*

They were silent, apart from slight creaking, just above hearing, and even then the wind's rustling all but overwhelmed it. They moved slowly, flickering, and on some level below thinking, below perception, Alison recognized that they moved toward her. The realization blinded her – and the figures around her disappeared in a white panicky flash, as she struggled to her feet, numb and prickling from sitting too long, and ran.

She composed herself in her car, still shaking, but the terror already draining out of her heart, and its emptiness starting to fill in with ideas and suppositions to make it all tolerable, because otherwise... She didn't even dare to imagine what would it be like, to bear the brunt of the full realization any longer. Instead she said to herself: it was a nightmare, heat, hallucination, night terror, waking dream. Beavers splitting the trees and building a dam down the creek, the way sun filtered through the branches and reflected in the dark water. And under this barrage of unconvincing comfort, the cedar babies kept toddling on toward her, mute and blind, and changing with every step – flickering in and out of her.

When Alison was young, she used to have a recurring dream – a fantasy she played out in her hypnogogic states, until it melted into sleep. There were tiny people living under her bed, their lives consumed by trying to get to her pillow. Sometimes, she dangled her hand off the bed and smiled to herself imagining them jumping up, trying to grab onto her fingers, getting on each others' shoulders – so tiny and funny and deformed. Then she yanked her hand away, fearful, for she knew with certainty only sleepy children know that if they managed to get a hold of her, they would quickly run the length of her arm and shoulder, jump off onto her pillow and whisper something in her ear. Something so terrible and forbidden that she would die the moment she heard it, her heart unable to bear such weight, and then the repetitive noise of the cuckoo clock downstairs would freeze her with terror at the sudden sound, somehow validating all her fears.

Now, much older, she dreamed of the cedar babies – this is what she nicknamed them – aggregating silently around her bed, with dry electric flickers running along their limb-arms as they waddled and toddled, and she could not find her voice to scream, to call Jim for help, as he was sleeping just a few feet away. She woke up then, a weight on her chest and her sheets soaked with sweat, her face and neck burning, cinder-hot, her mouth flooded with acid saliva, and lay awake, wondering if the episode on campus was a thing like that – a dream, a heavy weight of nightmare and childhood obsession.

It was the middle of October – first midterms, when she gathered enough resolve to go back to the swamp. Her classes were progressing as well as could be expected; her secret fantasy of being a great student – the kind that blew away her professors who then would write little encouraging notes on her papers and tests never came true – as usually the fate of such fantasies. Instead, she got okay grades, and her papers came back with few encouraging notes and a ton of corrections and squiggly lines, mapping out how her words, arguments, and paragraphs should be rearranged to flow better and to make sense. Her professor of anthropology, Dr. Meikel, the one Alison liked best because she was young and competent, wore Banana Republic suits and bit off her words with careful conviction, invited Alison to examine her own frames of references and cultural assumptions. Alison tried her hardest on the exam, and still left the classroom early, unsatisfied and afraid of failing.

She strolled reluctantly across the lawn, now a patchwork of yellow and red, to the path almost invisible and slippery under the fallen leaves. Her heart was so loud in her chest that she thought if the terrible noise ever returned, she wouldn't be able to hear it this time. Whatever came, she was prepared. It took all of her willpower to sit down under the dark cedars, instead of leaning against the trunk, legs tense, ready to sprint away at the first sign of danger.

Time went slowly in this swamp – trickled like lazy heavy cedar waters, dark with decayed leaves. The air grew crisp and cool enough to prickle the inside of her nostrils. Then the sun started to set and the darkness grew imperceptibly yet quickly, and when the long cedar shadows fell on her, surrounded her like a loose fist around a butterfly, she stood up and ran. She imagined the cedars splitting behind her back and releasing their terrible contents, and ran faster as her imagination dug its spurs into her sides. When she reached the lawn and the college buildings, blue with falling darkness, there was a stitch in her side and her mouth was dry and burning, her lungs prickled raw by cold air. She dared to look back, and there was no one chasing her, just the trees closing over the path, already lost in darkness.

Jim was home when she got there. He sat in his chair, and she felt the prickling of guilt at wasting time instead of cooking dinner. Jim was so used to her making it every day that she wondered if he even understood, or if he just sat there, vaguely wondering why this night felt different and why he was hungry.

"Hon?" she said.

He stirred, looked up. "Long day, huh?"

"Library." She was already in the kitchen. "You want a burger?"

"Sure." He sounded relieved. "I was worried about you."

She slapped two preformed beef patties onto the blackened corrugated surface of the George Foreman grill. "No need to worry," she said. "It's just community college."

"That's not what I meant." There was a click of the remote, and the newscasters filled the living room with their well-rehearsed empathy for the world.

"Me neither," she muttered, quite confident that her voice would be obscured by the TV prattle and the sizzling of meat. She thought a bit and added thick slices of bacon and a few weeping, crunchy onion rings that immediately wilted and caramelized. It was a very good grill, she thought, and dug through the bread bin looking for suitable buns.

Jim liked hamburgers, hotdogs – all that easy food that cooked quickly on the grill. He didn't mind an occasional pizza delivery and cheered up at the sight of Chinese takeout. It almost seemed like all her effort in the kitchen all these years had been a waste, and she would've been chagrined at the thought if it didn't give her more time to spend away from home – at the library, she would say, the very repetition of the lie giving her voice growing conviction, or with a study group. Anthropology wasn't too bad, but she was also taking Introductory Chemistry, and that was a bear, since she hadn't had any chemistry since high school. This was usually as far as she would get with the talk of school before Jim turned on the TV. That would've been upsetting too, but it cut the need for more elaborate lies. Sometimes she wondered if he suspected anything – not her waiting for some unlikely event in the swamp, but maybe something else, something more mundane. Maybe he was jealous and thought that she had had an affair – but he clearly didn't, and his lack of concern hurt a little, as if it was so impossible that she could have an affair (not that she actually would). Then she thought how she never questioned him when he was late from work, and worried needlessly, because he hadn't been late for dinner in years.

She did manage to study, amidst all this silent resentments and fruitless waiting, pulling a solid B- in Chemistry and an A in Anthropology. She called her youngest, Jonathan, and he emailed her links to his Facebook photo galleries where she posted all the pictures he took of Massachusetts woods and the brilliant oranges and scarlets. Of course she was proud of him – how could she not be? – and surprised that he commiserated about his classes with her, a sudden closeness that sprung out of the absence. She wondered if she missed him enough. She was glad he was coming home for Thanksgiving.

By the end of November, the swamp had hardened and the moss turned white and stiff. Alison had to wear gloves and winter boots just to last a couple of hours after the classes, until the sun set – and the colder it was getting, the earlier the sun set, as if to spare her. The day before Thanksgiving it disappeared early enough for her to do some shopping for the next day, and as she drove to the store her mind still lingered on the elusive Cedar Babies.

Why did they come to her that day? And why did they hide ever since? Were they offended that she'd run, was it one of those fairytale one chance only things? Was all the nonsense she told herself back then true, and she just imagined the whole thing? And if she didn't believe it to be true, why did she go back? Why was she no longer scared but rather pulled to the swamp, growing more desperate by the day? These were all questions that swirled in her mind but she refused to answer, because the answers seemed silly and partial, they didn't take into consideration her frames of reference. She only knew that the pull of the swamp was not letting go, and if she didn't see them soon, her heart would give out.

With only three of them home for Thanksgiving, she bought a turkey breast rather than the whole bird, potatoes and yams, cans of pineapple and cranberry sauce, marshmallows and fruit cups and toasted onions and green beans. Soup, bread, gravy, pans. A can of pumpkin filling in case she felt like baking tomorrow, and a pumpkin pie in case she didn't. An apple pie, because Jonathan hated pumpkin. She looked forward to spending the whole day in the warm kitchen, away from the frozen swamp, the small wooden bridge treacherous and slippery, the tree trunks that turned gray with hoar.

By the time she got home, Jonathan was already there, doing the laundry he drove all the way from Massachusetts, which seemed excessive to Alison. He hugged her, and she hugged back, his body larger and stranger than she remembered it. He forever resided in her memory as a baby, and it always took some adjustment when he was present in the flesh.

"You look good, mom," he said. "Glad to see the school isn't too hard on you."

She shook her head. "Hungry? I'll make you something."

"I'll grab a sandwich," he said. "Sure you'll be cooking enough tomorrow. Do you ever get a chance to rest?"

"Sometimes." She smiled, looking at him, so big, wedged crookedly between the basement wall and the washing machine.

"Are you still doing Black Friday sales?"

She smiled. "Of course."

"You're crazy, mom. Stuff will be there later, and the sales are just as good."

She shrugged. It was a good enough reason to get out of the house, away from Jim; after having spent a whole day cooking and then eating, just having to be in the same space all day was exhausting. "I need to get your father a paintbrush, the basement wall's been peeling forever, and he still hasn't done anything about it. And you'll be home for Christmas too, right?"

He nodded. "I'll text you the link to my wish list if you want."

When he spoke like that, she felt like a dog, who understood human speech imperfectly, intuitively, and approximately. Then again, how else would one understand another being? Dr. Meikel certainly seemed doubtful of the possibility. "Can I get the things you want in the actual store though?"

"Sure, if you want to." He shrugged and peered inside the dryer, into the tangled blue mess of jeans and t-shirts Alison didn't understand either.

She thought of shopping as much-needed relief then, just being somewhere else, walking for miles across the smooth marbled floors, jostling in an early, irritable crowd, looking up and seeing a vaulted crystal ceiling that sparkled like rime-covered tree trunks. She cooked the next day and went to bed early so she would wake up at 5 am. Jonathan and Jim laughed and called her crazy, and she thought back at them, *if you only knew.*

She lay awake that night, staring into the ceiling obscured by thick, almost wintry darkness.

When Jim came to bed, falling asleep quickly, Alison listened to his soft breathing nearby. She imagined the ceiling splitting up like a boil, and the cedar babies, deformed and covered in slow sparks, descending upon her – raining down, to finally tell her their horrible truth. She realized that her arm was dangling off the bed and jerked it up in a heat wave of panic. She pressed her hand against her chest, between her breasts, habitually feeling for her sternum and the spread of the ribcage, her heartbeat a soft hammer under her palm. She got up before the alarm.

The morning was cold and the roads were slippery with ice, and Alison clutched the wheel until her hands went numb all the way to the shopping mall. This year, it didn't seem as crowded as usual – she found a parking spot in front of JCPenney, so close to the entrance that she didn't have to put her gloves on. She lingered over the sales racks until she felt like herself again, and then started to work her way toward the mall proper.

Somehow, she missed the exit and ended up in the children's clothing department. She hadn't shopped there for years: she hoped that Danny, married now, would soon have children, and then she would pick through the piles of delicately colored onesies and shirts with rounded collars; surely, they would let her see her grandchildren. They would have to.

Right now, she had no business looking at children's things, and yet she lingered, her fingers trailing thoughtlessly along the shelves with careful stacks of matching skirts, pants, jumpers, tops, with different animals on them. She picked up a pink top with an elephant on it, then a small pleated skirt, bright yellow. A blue sweater, a green pair of soft terry-cloth pants, striped t-shirts, delicate bonnets... she hoped she would have enough money in her Christmas fund left for Jonathan and Jim.

Near the checkout, she heard someone call her name, and tensed, the shopping basket swinging reflexively behind her back.

"Doing some shopping, Alison?" Dr. Meikel walked up to her, her coat swinging, one arm cradling a white and blue heavy-bellied vase. "I didn't realize you had little ones at home."

"I don't." The basket swung forward, defeated. "These are just for some friends. My kids are all grown. My youngest is a college freshman."

"That's nice." Dr. Meikel smiled politely, hugging her vase close. "Are they home for Thanksgiving?"

"Just my youngest."

There must've been something in her voice that made Dr. Meikel raise an eyebrow and nod curtly. "I'm sure you'll have a wonderful weekend. I'll see you Monday." She then disappeared from view in a flourish of her long coat in the direction of Intimates.

Belatedly, Alison regretted never asking Dr. Meikel any questions. It was out of respect – how could she ask someone like this anthropology professor about such personal things? – and she hoped that it wasn't interpreted as indifference. She didn't even know if Dr. Meikel had any children, but suspected not. There was something very single and upscale about that vase.

After the Thanksgiving weekend, winter stormed in early and hard, with freezing rain and winds. Alison could not sleep because the branches of the pin oak just outside rattled against the siding and knocked on the windows, and she thought of the freezing cedar babies, hidden deep within the trunks, their twig fingers frozen and brittle. And they wouldn't come out no matter how much she was pleading, and the folded baby clothes, hidden deep in the pantry, behind all the dry beans and cans of soup, were warm, sleeping, like a beating animal heart. She decided not to wait for Christmas.

Dr. Meikel gave her a raised eyebrow when Alison showed up in class with a large duffel bag, but didn't say anything. She was an anthropologist, and probably was used to the pose of a careful if sympathetic observer; Alison knew that she tried hard to understand her subjects' values. So of course she wouldn't ask any questions, not even when Alison flinched as Dr. Meikel handed back their papers. It was her first C in this class.

Afterward, she took her bag and headed for the swamp. The path was now barren of all the leaves, stiff and stark, ringing hollow under Alison's boots – Doc Martens Jonathan outgrew when he was fourteen. In the days that she hadn't been there, the forest had grown lighter, became hollow somehow – devoid of leaves, the oaks' black skeletons lay flat against the light sky, and the pines had grown pale. There was a hollow feeling in Alison's stomach too, as she slipped and stumbled her way to the edge of the creek. The buttresses of cedars reared up around her, in their usual still violence, and she sat down for just a little bit, to catch her breath. It was so different here now; even though the sun was hidden in the clouds, the quality of the shifting light told her that it was going to get dark soon, and she needed to hurry.

She laid out the clothes in a circle, in front of the cedar trees. The bright colors made the waters look even darker, and the fringe of ice, lighter. The lacy leaves of the cedars cast their barely visible trembling shade over her as she worked, assembling outfit after outfit: yellow with green, blue with red, stripes with purple. She didn't know who the cedar babies were and what they wanted from her, and maybe it didn't matter all that much. She just hoped that they could use these clothes, to protect them from the deathly winter. The only thing she could offer them.

The sun started to set, and it had to be enough.

Pinhole

Tantra Bensko

Wren Ferndale lived at the house at the end of the road at the top of the hill, where the black walnut trees dropped hard, wrinkled intimidating nuts. Sometimes, we were hungry if we were out playing for a long time. More often, we wanted to take photos using Terry Wilkerson's pinhole camera. We would leave the box she had made, with the hole, and no lens, set up just right facing the front yard, and leave it there for hours to capture the ghostly image of Wren playing around on the steps, the raked leaves, the stone terrace with the toads. Wren sure liked them. She'd climb around them and pet the toads, seemed to have a few of them she knew. One was really big and grey. The pinhole camera, the shutter open so long as it recorded the toads in the photographs, blurred their bodies because of the way their warty sides ballooned out and in with each breath. Terry was an expert, at least for her age: the photos were all beautiful. Soft and indistinct, not much color, but like a moving X-ray of another world.

And anything with Wren Ferndale involved got our group of girls speculating. Some of the girls weren't even neighbors but spent the night with us mostly to go through us to get a chance to stalk Wren. And the days of the photo shoots became legendary. Missing out on one of those could mean exclusion from the deepest secrets. We would point out moments in the photos of what had been happening when she stayed in one place long enough to burn onto the film with some definition. Our replays of the scenes in the photographs became fantastical, and sometimes we didn't know what was true anymore, especially when looking back on it. The things we'd play around with in our imagination, the game we made up about Wren, if some of the photos' scenes were real, and how much.

But this is how I remember it. I'm Marla Guinne.

Terry was a slender, narrow girl with an assertive butt who always had a tan no matter what time of year, which showed all around her little blue jean short tops, that brown skin set off by white teeth and long dark brown hair. She got an idea suddenly, jutting off the couch chest first, with so much energy, and that hoarse voice, so that anything she said I wanted to agree with it. I wanted her to realize what an ally I could be. I knew I'd never be enough of a go-getter for anyone to take much notice of me, except for me being neighbors with Terry, who had the pinhole camera, and lived only a few houses down the hill from Wren.

Her idea was this: "Hey, I know. Let's sneak something into Wren's yard overnight, someplace she likes to go."

I suggested, "Maybe by the swing? She likes to sit in the swing, you know," I said to Susie, who, being new, hadn't been at the sepia photo shoot where in one of them, Wren's sandy hair flew up in the air with light behind it, as she was suspended in the air with no chain showing, all of it distorted as if laid on top of a ball. Really strange image. You could see the whole swing as she went down and back up, but she was caught most at the moment at the top where it hovered before going back down. The set was framed in black at Terry's house. That gave it a Gothic ghostly look.

"We could count on getting a good clear close up."

I got excited by an idea I knew might make Terry give me some more credibility as an active member: "I know where we could watch her from. There's that ridge by the swing set where, if we get on the other side of the ridge from her, and attach a string to the shutter flap, you could get some short enough exposures by being at close enough range to get some spectacular shots. If we tug hard enough we could pull the whole camera to us. Especially if we put it on something flat to slide along the ground, so we don't ruin it. We wouldn't have to wait for her to leave before grabbing the camera." I could see the whole thing, though I wasn't sure about the details, as I hadn't progressed to the inner circle enough to know how the camera worked very well, or how delicate it was. But I knew the shutter part would work, anyway. I was enflamed by that idea.

"What should we put there? Where would we get it, whatever it is?"

"Do you have anything at your house you don't want? Or in the yard?"

Terry looked around and everything I saw became a possible object of mischief. We were all looking but some more daintily than others. Most things around us in the living room were her parents'. We'd finished the hot chocolate her mother had brought in for us anyway. We didn't have anything against them, so we didn't want to take anything from plain view. We explored the attic first, climbing up the ladder and pulling the chain for the bare light bulb.

Terry's brother had put some things up there that were pretty fun to imagine in a photo with Wren. A big chess set. A taxidermied owl. A chair in the shape of a mushroom. I made notes about them in a square pad covered in leather and sewed with strips along the sides, and with a strap. I made sure they could see I was the scribe. I made a map of where each one was in the attic, and drew it. It would help us in our club meeting about which one to take, to assess the relative size and ease of getting it down the steps, and accessing whatever we chose efficiently.

And, it had the chance of inclusion in the collage about the Wren game. I thought it seemed perfect for it. Then, as I thought about it longer, I decided it would probably not make it into the game at all. It wasn't all that fitting, because the other drawings that got put in the shuffle were more directly about Wren. But at least Terry saw how well I could draw.

Then, we grabbed some bananas from the bowl and looked in the basement. It had a giant spider web made out of string covering one corner, left over from the great Halloween party. Why take it down? I was proud to be invited to that one. I went to it as Wren, and I'm not sure if that was OK, because Angela was Wren too, and she'd been invited to more of the club meetings – I mean secret society meetings - than I had. I thought it would make everyone like me, but I should have known other people would have the idea and it would have to be planned out ahead of time at a meeting. They humored me and didn't read any minutes to me or tell me to take it off. They were friendly, but no one talked to me very long and no one offered to get together, just us, sometime.

I laughed hysterically, and ran over and rubbed my hand over the white sculpture standing in the corner. "This is *perfect*!" It stood the same height as me, a graceful swan on a pedestal, all of it hollow, made from a mold I guess. I don't know what out of.

One of the girls asked, "What about the spider web too? We could tie it to the trees, and she'd have to go through it to get to the sculpture."

"Or go around it."

"I think it would be too hard to take the spider web down later, and bring it back. But we could run in when she's not out there and grab the swan back. It's pretty lightweight," said Terry. I liked picturing Terry running, her tan skin dark against the white swan. I think she reminded all of us of a boy a little bit. She was taller than us too, and spoke more loudly, with authority. I assumed she'd be the one who would get to sneak in and grab the swan while we all watch over the hillside and silently cheer her on, even though I came up with the idea. But considering I'd get to watch my swan – well, technically, her swan, but my idea – our co-idea – and her strong legs running, in my direction, I didn't mind.

Strange thing about pinhole cameras of any kind. How they turn everything upside down.

Susie asked, "So, is Wren just normal, but you had to pick someone interesting to take pictures of someplace as close to Terry as possible? And since she's our age, and goes to a different school, we happen to be spending all this time making the game about her?"

"She's special," said Terry.

Angela said, "You play the game, you know, with the pictures, drawings and everything being shuffled, and we pick some of them for that day's adventure without looking and put them in order. And assign girls to represent different things, play different roles, and chose what around us will represent the different things in Wren's life, lining up the day's obstacles and goals and all of that. Then we act it all out. There are tests, but you don't know what they are until each game is over. Terry makes the rules."

The first secret Terry had told me after I passed my first initiation I thought was mediocre: Wren didn't go to a different school. She didn't go to a school. That seemed really amazing at first, something we could all fantasize about, a girl not going to school at all! But then, I decided maybe she was home-schooled. I figured the only way Terry knew more about her than we did was that she spied more. We only got together on weekends for the game, but she went over there any time she wanted, like if she was playing hooky. So maybe she just happened to see her staying at home too. Maybe she just had a contagious rash that day. I felt sorry for Susie, just going to get that secret if she succeeded in the initiation over the weekend. I gave her a sympathetic look.

"Terry came up with the whole thing by herself. It's brilliant," exclaimed another girl. "It's like acting training. I want to be an actress. I feel like one day, a recommendation from Terry will go a long way in the entertainment field."

"I like to write, and draw, direct, produce, do scenery, make-up, costuming, - oh, and act too," said Terry.

"So, anyway," continued Angela, "you get to be part of the photography sessions. Those are all part of the game, and provide the base material for the game to continue into the initiations, when all the pictures get shuffled up and chosen. It's like Tarot cards that you act out. Then, in the meetings, we decide where to go from there. And Terry then devises the next game, for a day when we can all get together for it, whoever she invites. It's very complicated. It can take a long time between initiations. Some of us have higher levels of initiation than other ones. Sometimes you know if a girl is in the same level as you and sometimes you kind of don't. You have to figure it out."

I jumped in. "You might get to pass through different levels of the society if you do well enough in the game, like when you're setting up the photo shoot, and sneaking around, and stuff, and then when we're acting it all out. Each level you get to go up in the society if you pass the initiation, you learn something secret about Wren. Only people on that level can talk about it." By telling her that and looking at her solemnly, I associated myself with them. I made a gleam in my eye and nodded down to her. I was glad I was taller than Susie, and knew better than to sleep in big curlers that made my hair flip up at the bottom all the way around like one crazy thing. Uh. This was important. It was a secret society. Whatever the main inner secret for the top level seemed like it must be so esoteric that it wrenched open the fabric of the universe to know it. Wren had some power that meant the world was not limited to what we had always believed.

And Terry knew the secret. We weren't allowed to know whom else she had given the top level to, if anyone, but we suspected no one else knew. Everyone still seemed normal, and wouldn't be once they knew just how strange life could be, surely. Only Terry seemed sometimes almost possessed, her hair shining in the dawn light when we set the cameras near Wren Ferndale's house, as she ran almost like a horse with such sinewy muscles, almost faster than a girl could go. Sometimes I wished she were a guy. She was never sleepy, or tired and bloated after eating. Her stomach never stuck out even if she slouched. I wondered if any of her perfection came from knowing the secrets.

"Secrets like she thinks a neighbor guy is cute, or like she's a spider-witch who spins a web of night and eats neighbor guys?"

"We can't tell you," Angela said. "But the game is fun in any case, and the photos are out-of-this-world beautiful. And we can never think of anything else much fun to do. Who doesn't like to spy on someone?"

"And gossip."

"It's not gossip. It's power secrets." Angela's eyes looked like agates, jaded with knowledge beyond her years, from the game, the sun filtering into the irises, her lids at just the angle to show us how life-changing the secrets were.

Well, maybe they got to be power secrets later in the game, the higher up levels of things about Wren. The second secret was a good one: Wren lived alone. That surely meant she was supernatural.

No normal little girl could be allowed to do that, or manage it on her own. None of us ever saw any cars there, or adults go in or out. But the house was lit up and the yard was mowed, and it was an expensive place that was paid for somehow. She obviously had enough to eat. How could she do it?

I thought maybe a sickly mother or father lived there who couldn't drive, but took care of the bills.

But Terry said no. And when she said it, she lowered her voice in an intimate way to me, and I shivered. I was one of them, as long as I believed.

I marveled over how much time it must take Terry to turn all the ideas, drawings, maps, props, and everything into a serious initiation into the next level. How did she manage to do that and play on all the sports teams, like Rugby, Field Hockey, and Softball? And how did she have time to study Wren? What would happen to her leadership if any of the other neighbor girls started spying on Wren alone, and came up with special things about her, ourselves? I lived close enough I could possibly do that sometime. I mulled that over. Terry would probably hate that.

But I wanted to see if the third secret was true: Wren could turn the pages of a book with her mind.

I was suspicious that maybe Terry had seen her reading in the wind was all. Not bothering to turn the pages, because the wind did, or maybe she wasn't even reading, but in a daze, so just didn't care what page it was on, especially if it was a picture book. And if she never went to school, how could she read? And if she liked to read, why not go to school? And the biggest thing was – this wouldn't work well for a secret if all of us might at any time see her do that, while we were playing the game. She might any day come out and read in the sunshine, turning the pages.

If Terry was making things like that up, I thought, she was the strange little girl, not Wren. She seemed so normal, though, got good enough grades but not over-the-top good, and the boys noticed her at school, more than they did me, yet. My mother said to just give it time, and they'd like me as much as they did her, when my breasts grew out. My mother pointed to hers and showed me what genetics I had to look forward to. Gross.

I wanted more. That was just a teaser for the much bigger fourth secret, Terry said, seeing how it agitated me. And this week, if I did everything well that Terry was judging for in the initiation, I would learn it. Good. I'd never be as far along with the secrets as some of the girls, but I was glad to be a lot farther than Susie. She might not even get the first secret that weekend. She didn't look especially smart with that golden hair that was so shiny, so brushed.

We went to sleep fast so we could wake up very early and situate ourselves unnoticed at Wren's house. Girl-guests going to bed early always pleased Terry's parents. That was another normal thing about Terry. She had both a mother and father, and neither one was a stepparent. Their house was clean, and Terry didn't have much in her room that was weird other than the kinds of things we all did, like Creeply Crawlies we'd made when we were younger, pouring liquid plastic in molds to make spiders and scorpions, all kinds of bugs. She liked to draw monsters, but we all did that.

That night, I had two dreams that I remember. In the first one, we were watching over the edge of the hill after we'd gotten all the photographs and Wren had gone inside for a while. Terry ran down to pick up the statue. Just as she was lifting it up, Wren came out of the house and called out to her. Terry set it back down and waited. They talked, but I couldn't tell what they were saying. It seemed like maybe they were going to be friends. Wren just acted normal, like any other girl, except kind of like a girl talking to a guy. And so did Terry. After a while, they started kissing by the swan. They sat down on its back together entangled.

I was shocked, probably even more than the other girls. That was the final secret: Terry was in love with Wren. Wren was just a normal girl. It was all about having an obsession. I started to cry. There were no supernatural abilities that rent the universe. The secret society was based on our leader liking someone else more than she liked us. Definitely more than she would ever like me. I woke up crying.

In the second dream, I was chosen to run down and get the swan to bring it back. I was proud they would all be watching, and that I was strong enough to carry it. I was starting back toward the girls, and it was really heavy. I wasn't sure I'd be able to get it back. What was I going to do if it kept getting heavier? If I couldn't get it back, I'd never be invited back, or learn more levels of secrets. I had to drag it, and I knew she might follow the draglines and figure it out.

Then, the door opened in the house. At first I thought it must have been one of Wren's parents, and that really scared me. But as I looked longer, I could see it was her instead. She came over to me and talked. She was mystified, sure, but still, a normal girl just the random object of our game, with no special powers. I didn't know if I should tell her about the other girls, so I just said I had lent it to her, that it was mine, and I wanted to make her happy for an hour or so. We laughed, and seemed like we were going to be good friends. I thought either she had no powers and would make a fun girl to go finding frog friends with – or she was supernatural and would show me what she could do, herself.

I said goodbye with a promise to visit later, and carried the swan over the hill no problem. It had become light. I could even run skip with it. When I got to the girls, Terry pulled me aside by jerking my shoulder and hissed in my ear: "She's mine. I've watched her all this time. I made up the game. Her house is closer to mine than it is to yours."

"Why can't we share her and just all be friends?"

"You've earned the right to the big secret, and it is this: it's possible to kill an opponent in love through an act of will if you focus the death ray. And you are my rival: she apparently likes you. Mark my words. You'd better not talk to her again. Watch out if you know what's good for you. If you value your life." And she pushed me.

So, I figured out that Terry loved Wren. I wanted her to love me. I stood up on top of the hill, where I could see Wren sitting in the swing, spinning it around one direction, then the other, letting go of the tight coil as it unwound. I rolled the swan statue down the hill toward her to flatten her, my opponent to Terry's attention, but the swan broke into pieces before it killed her. So, I held out my hands and sent the death ray to her, and Wren fell over dead. Terry would be all mine.

But of course, Terry hated me. She sent the death ray at me, and I turned weak and my arms hurt, I was shaking, I couldn't breathe, and no words came out. I woke up gasping.

I didn't know if I could ever feel like Terry cared about me after those dreams. My mother joked about me going through the typical girl-crush phase before I started dating boys, and I knew she was right, but I never liked to admit it.

I just felt like all the life-force was pulled out of me by that dream. It seemed so real. I felt like I did when I got dehydrated on a summer afternoon when I forgot to drink water all day. Puny. It wasn't the first time I'd dreamed about Wren, and I started to wonder if she could get into people's dreams and mess with their heads. Terry too. Maybe that's how Terry told us the fourth secret. In dreams. Maybe Terry really had weird powers. Maybe that's why they were such a good match for each other. They could live together and do creepy things to other girls and laugh about how interested we all were in them, more than we were in our own lives, forever.

I stared glumly at Terry over cereal in the morning. I slumped over the bowl, hardly able to hold my head up except with my hand. It tasted stale. Everything was stale – the air, my clothes, dust on the counter from yesterday, being a girl, the game. "I want to be the one to retrieve the statue," I said. "I figured out it's the thing to use, and also where we should sit, and where to put it, and how we could pull the shutter with the string. I even attached the string to the flap on your camera."

She seemed shaken by my glare and said it would be OK. I didn't even feel happy about it. I just felt heavy. I didn't even want to go, really. I didn't care.

But then, she sneaked some chocolate coffee candy for us from her parents' canister and I was ready to go. We all were.

We realized that one person couldn't really carry the swan alone, as it was too unwieldy and heavy.

Some of the girls and I stuck it in Wren's yard by the swing set, which was a pretty long way away from her house on the other side of some tall trees, by some snow drifts that hadn't fully melted, up against the vegetable garden gate. It would be amazing with the black and white film. It would make a truly gorgeous surreal photograph, especially if Wren wore something pretty instead of a bulky coat. I hoped the temperature would rise fast before she came out for her morning's frolic.

Terry won awards with her pinhole camera photos of other things, and I figured she really wished she could show the ones of Wren, especially one like that, at the shows. But it wouldn't be legal. It didn't qualify as street photography on someone's land, and she'd have to get her to sign a model release. I thought maybe one day once we outgrew the game, Terry and she would get to be regular friends and she could do that. But not if Wren was as weird as she implied she was. Not hardly . . . unless they both had powers, and fell in love and neither one bothered to talk to me.

I started watching Terry more closely. How did she know these things about Wren? What if she was telepathic? I was horrified, thinking she might now how much she meant to me. I covered my thoughts with invisible hands. What if Wren was telepathic too, and they talked all the time, laughed and joked about us. Wren would be just humoring us, knowing we were spying on her, and slowly revealing only one bit of her weird at a time, and only to Terry, so her beloved could have a good time amazing her stupid little friends, us. Then, at least, I hoped she would help us believe it by proving all the things Terry told us, as we watched. Maybe that would happen that day, I thought. I hoped, and yet I didn't.

We scrambled over the ridge and waited. When Wren came out of her house, she was wearing a long, flared, fitted jacket with big buttons, which gave us great relief. No furry square winter coat at all. Even her cap would work in the composition. When she saw the swan, she exclaimed, at first called to it that she wouldn't hurt it, thinking it was real, though over-sized. Maybe she was used to oversized things. Maybe she was like Alice, I thought. Then, she looked around and crept toward it, started to touch it with a fingertip gingerly, pulled back, and finally took the chance. She ran her hand along the smooth surface, as I had done, and smiled. It did feel good. She sat on it, and leaned up against its neck, and that's when Terry pulled the cord on the shutter flap. It looked like Wren was in love with a real swan. Very poetic.

Wren stayed in that position long enough for Terry to get the long exposure she needed. We held our breath. I tried to will her to stay still. I sent my energy to her and encapsulated her, holding her within it as if she were a statue herself, repeating "still, still, don't move," and pressing her in place with my esoteric hands. She stayed there so long I started to wonder if I had real powers. Maybe Wren, Terry, and I could all be witchy friends if I developed my abilities sometime in the future. She started to move away, and Terry closed the flap with the cord, and the photo was done. It would be the best one ever, unless some errant light got in and ruined it. Usually when a little got it, that just made it better.

It's so weird how our eyes see everything upside down and our brain fixes it for us. What else can it do?

I was starting to really like Wren after seeing her with the swan. She was delicate, and loving, wispy, and graceful. Terry wasn't any of those things, more of a tom boy who liked to have her way. What if it was really Wren I wanted? I started to not care as much what Terry thought about me, if I would ever become her right-hand girl, and rise in the ranks of the secret society. I wanted to touch Wren's skin the way she touched the swan, for her to nuzzle my neck so sweetly, with her eyes closed like that. I felt bad for the first time that we were invading her privacy. She had a right to play in her own yard by herself without being watched. And now, we were messing with her mind. She would miss that swan when it disappeared. I kind of wanted to steal it from Terry and give it to Wren. I felt terrible I had killed her in my dream just because Terry loved her. I loved her. I turned away from the other girls, as we lay on the other side of the ridge, with our heads barely peeking over, as we watched. I didn't want to watch any more. Besides, what if she happened to look in our direction? We were close enough she might make out a row of foreheads. I made one less forehead.

It was all silly. Juvenile. I was growing up. I decided maybe I'd just walk over one day and knock on her door and say, "Hello, I live in the neighborhood and thought you might like to get to know each other. Would you like some berries?" And I would open my basket for her where I had gathered them and put them in there with a nice cloth. That's how normal people acted. They made friends in regular ways. Why not? She was my age. She might really enjoy some company. I never saw her with friends. I wondered what her life was like. If she was truly a witchy person, I wanted to know before risking going to her house. I'd hold out for the fourth secret, and if it seemed flimsy, I'd visit her. Now, *that* would challenge Terry's authority and maybe get me kicked out, but on the other hand, if I did it right, I could bring back bigger secrets and the games would get even better. People would want to know all about my experiences. If I told them. It made my stomach hurt to think about betraying Wren's trust in that way.

But it's not like I could tell Wren about what the girls did. And how could I be friends with her if I didn't talk about such a big thing as that? But if they all did something bad to me, of course, then, it would be OK to tell.

I wanted to see in her house. I felt blood rising. On impulse, I slid down the ridge a little ways, still hidden, and ran around to the other side of her house. While she was spending the morning outside like she always seemed to do, watching the cardinals, singing, swinging, I would be spying inside her house. I ran up to a window and looked in.

Everything was covered with incredible cloth, hanging from the ceiling to the floor, and the cloth was shiny and rich, with patterns to die for. They didn't just hang down straight, but more like a poem, the bottoms of the cloths coming into the room, curving. There were no straight lines anywhere. No one's house looks like that. All the walls made my heart want to burst with the beauty. I wondered how she could have reached up so high to attached them along the edges of the ceiling. Even the ceiling itself was covered, the cloth gracefully dipping down in the center. The lighting was golden, unreal.

How could anyone keep the cloth so clean and gleaming? It seemed it would accumulate dust terribly.

Especially considering the fire in the fireplace. I marveled over how strong she must be to chop such big pieces of wood. I saw rifles next to it, and a pot hanging over the fire, probably full of something like rabbit stew.

I wondered if she'd been given a gigantic inheritance, and if no one liked her enough to take over raising her. We didn't really need much actual raising at our age. We were pretty grown up. I thought about how I would like to live on my own too, without parents or siblings, in a house with hanging cloth everywhere. I could shoot my meat and raise vegetables in the garden and pick the fruits from the trees, have cherry trees and walnuts and pears like she did. I would can food for the winter. I wouldn't need to drive anywhere. My parents wouldn't care if I disappeared and did something like that.

I ran around to the door, and found she had left it unlocked when she went into the yard. Of course, I went in. I took off my boots first, and hid them inside the hedges by the door. I was taking a chance by believing Terry that no one else lived there. I could be in a lot of trouble if her father came at me with a rifle. Or Wren, who seemed to be a good enough shot to kill small moving animals. I didn't turn around to wave at the secret society, who must have all been watching with their mouths open. I giggled thinking about how they would be so shocked that I, the one that they never thought much about, was bold enough to just walk into Wren's house. I'd be a legend. No one would ever stop talking about it, but only amongst ourselves, because everyone would get in trouble if anyone else found out.

We were all trespassing after all. I could do anything at Wren's house and none of them would ever alert any authorities, or parents or anyone, because they needed to save their own skins.

I wondered if Terry would hate me or promote me. I could be the co-conspirator with her. It was a very good game in any case, and I wanted to share in the glory. But also, I just didn't care. I was thrilled it was even more magical in her house than I had imagined. It wasn't scary-looking at all in there, except that I was intruding, and could be killed or yelled at. And I could lose all my friends, and not make this new one, and so be all alone with just my family, and they didn't think much more about me than the other girls did. I was an after-thought wherever I went. Except, now, I was the girl who entered Wren's house. Nothing about my personality would ever be the same. I could be a hero, if I brought back the real secrets to the society.

I walked quietly into the kitchen, and saw rows and rows stacked up of apricot jam in glass jars with the sunlight from the window behind them making them glow, all with no dust. What little girl takes that much time to dust? Maybe that was one of her super powers? Fat toads leapt around over everything. Her little friends had to pee, and she had to spend a lot of time cleaning that up. Unless . . .

The kitchen was warmed with an iron stove, and that was set up for cooking on top of it. I noticed the place was lit with candles stuck into iron things that stuck well out from the walls. There was no electricity. I poked into the bathroom, and saw it had a trap door for a toilet. The bathtub had hose leading into it. I looked out the window beside it, which it ran through with a little hole cut into the side, and saw a water-catchment and piles of snow that had been shoveled up around. She truly could survive there alone, and maybe with simple industriousness. I longed to live there with her and help her with the chores more than anything I'd ever wanted – even more than I had wanted to be taken seriously by Terry.

I heard raucous, desperate whistles and caws like birds that had migrated that time of year, coming from over the ridge. I knew it was the girls trying to warn me Wren was coming in. But what could I do? I couldn't go out the door she was coming in. I ran to the living room and hid behind one of the tall shimmering red cloths. It felt marvelous against my cheeks, but I was having trouble breathing. I put my hands by my face to hold the cloth a little away from it, but I knew it must look very odd, if she would happen to look in my direction, the way the cloth stuck out, especially with hands pressing against it. My heart was beating so hard I wondered if it was moving the cloth back and forth.

I figured if I made it back alive, a returning hero, I should win enough points in the game to get more than just one secret this time. I could even be set up as someone who had the secrets that the other girls had to gain, slowly. I hoped Terry would see it the same as me, that I had become almost equal to her through this life-threatening ritual, though she did invent the entertaining game to begin with, and discover a unique neighbor that none of us would have ever known existed. But I should at least be higher in status than any of the other girls. I was annoyed it didn't matter as much to me, after seeing the wondrous intensity of Wren's house, and what a self-sustaining life was like. Someone that no one much cared about, just like me, could go off on her own and apparently not be noticed and live a magical life of her own, like this. I had no idea such a thing could be possible. A community wasn't really necessary. Just a vision. And money. She must have a lot of that. I wondered where it was, and if I could steal some. I hated myself for that.

The door closed, and I heard light footsteps. Wren hummed as she went to the fireplace, and sang as she pushed around the logs, and lifted new ones into the fire. She sang about how lucky she was that someone cared enough about her to bring her a swan, how she loved that person, or angel, or jinn or astral swan, who had heard her silent wishes, her prayers, her songs about wanting a swan so very, very much, how maybe she wasn't as alone as she thought, that she didn't have to cry any more. She sang that maybe it was a sign she would have a real swan come into her life and be her friend, or be her lover, or maybe she had a swan-angel looking out for her. I heard her footsteps turn to dancing.

I was that weird being that had answered her wishes. I was the telepathic one with powers. True, someone else might have seen the swan statue and thought it would be ideal too. But maybe not. Maybe someone else would have latched onto something else in the basement just as good, and put that in her yard. I was sad about it being taken back to Terry's house. They might even be grabbing it as she sang about it, though they might be too enthralled by wondering about whether Wren was going to kill me or make me raise into the air. I couldn't stand her feeling so happy and then disappointed. She would feel like it was a cruel joke.

While she was in the kitchen, I slid out from behind the cloth, and stood in a position as best I could that mimicked a swan, in the middle of the room. I made a sound like a swan the best I could, though I wasn't sure I was getting it right at all. It sounded kind of sick. I heard the sounds in the kitchen stop, and she ran in and stood there.

"I am Esoteric Swan," I said, without moving. "I heard your wishes and answered them. Let's go bring the swan into the house now. It belongs here, where I am now standing." I was so glad I was wearing all white. I lengthened my neck, and looked divine.

She said nothing, nothing at all, but kept turning to look at me, forgetting to close her mouth. We went into the yard, where the swan was thankfully still standing, and though I saw the foreheads over the ridge in my peripheral vision, I didn't look over at them. I stole Terry's statue. We carried it into Wren's house. We put it on the matt and scooted it across to get the muddy snow off, and then placed it where I had stood. I was imagining how I had taken on more meaning in her life than probably anything else had, that she was wondering just how magic I was, what other powers I possessed, wanting to know my secrets. I could leave without saying anything at all. No way would the girls risk going into her house to take the swan back. Terry's family probably had forgotten they even had it anyway. She sure wasn't going to tell the police. But my place in the society was probably done. I probably couldn't be forgiven for stealing from Terry, ruining the plan, being such an upstart as to overthrow the ranks.

I stood in front of it, my nose touching its beak, mimicking its pose exactly, as if I were its reverse shadow, its astral symmetry, the living embodiment of what it represented, its soul. I didn't move, but slowly released a swan song with all of my longing, my love, my aloneness, and it grew louder and louder, taking over the house with a type of sound I had no idea I could make.

"Are . . . are you my Esoteric Swan come to live with me?" she whispered with a croak. "Is the statue like an engagement ring?"

"Yes," I said. "You are correct, Wren Ferndale. It is I, at last. And we will live together here, always. I love you."

From Strangers

Ephiny Gale

Several years ago, the mansion and its grounds were at the peak of their splendour. Now the girl is nine or ten, and forbidden from entering the garden due to its disrepair.

Tonight is the first night she has been left to her own devices, unattended while her parents sit by lamplight at the other end of the house. If she ties a knot in the end of her white dress, she can slip out through the broken window overlooking the abandoned koi pond.

Between the flowers and the weeds, picking her way across the stones half-buried in the mud, the girl makes her way towards the topiary maze. She has a vague memory of being younger, and running through the sunlit, manicured hedges, when life was clean and simple.

The girl halts at the maze's entry, poised on tiptoes, and slowly lets her heels sink to the ground.

Before her, a strange young woman perches on a stone column. The woman's legs are pale as moonlight, and above them her dress looks like the star-spangled sky, like the night itself has flowed down to wrap around her skin. But it's the woman's neck that the girl's eyes settle on, where approximately four dozen teeth are strung on a silver chain.

Some of them look like the girl's baby teeth.

"No need to be frightened of me," says the woman. When she opens her mouth, the teeth inside it are largely pointy and assorted, like they've been picked at random from a variety of omnivorous and carnivorous animals. "It's wise to be frightened of other things; the world is a generally frightening place to live. But you needn't waste your fright on me specifically."

Once upon a time, a princess married a king, and they lived happily ever —

"Your dress," says the girl.

"You like it?"

"I've never… I've never seen anything like it."

The woman smiles gently, keeping her lips pressed closed. "A present from my father," she says. She uncrosses her moonlit legs and reaches into a hidden pocket at her waist. Her arm disappears to the elbow before resurfacing, and clutched in her hand are a variety of wrapped candies.

The girl watches, unblinking. The woman's free hand sorts through the wrappers: shiny, glossy, circles and rectangles and cylinders, striped and checked, ruby reds and royal purples and liquid-looking golds. Her fingers stop at a small, aquamarine wrapper. She drops the rest of the candies back into her pocket and pulls the aquamarine foil off with a single tug of both hands.

"Want to try?" asks the woman. She tears the crimson, sugar-coated candy in half and pops part past her lips. A slight wind whips up, and instantly the twigs in her hair and the mud encrusted on her shoes drop away.

The girl reaches for the other half. It fizzes in her mouth like a raspberry soda. It melts over her tongue like butter in a pan. She feels the fizz race through every inch of her body, cleaning her thoroughly inside and out.

When she gasps, the grass stains on her dress are gone, the mud flecks on her stockings have disappeared. The girl is spotless.

"Be more careful on your way back," says the woman. "You wouldn't want your parents to know."

She drops down from the column, graceful as a cat, and vanishes inside the maze.

Once upon a time, a king married the most beautiful maiden in the land. And when she died young, she made him promise to never marry anyone less beautiful.

And they had a daughter.

The second time the girl sneaks away, her parents are sitting back-to-back in front of the fire, clutching glasses of brandy. Her mother has fallen asleep and is starting to drool, and her father dare not move for fear of waking his wife. The girl is safe.

She races through the garden, full-to-bursting with joy and anticipation, and cannot remember the last time running was so exhilarating. She has chosen a brown dress and brown shoes, deliberately, so that the weeds and twigs leave minimal marks.

But there is no strange woman waiting for her at the start of the maze. So she steps inside.

Inside the maze, the weeds are thicker than ever, and flowers and vines blossom in colours and shapes she's never seen before. Beetles, metallic and luminous, dart over moonlit lilies, their bodies shining topaz, lime and sapphire under their flickering wings. They remind her of the candies in the woman's palm. She fights the urge to pluck a beetle from the air and see if it tastes as sugary as it looks.

She finds the woman half-way through the maze on the edge of a dried-up well. The woman's dress is so silver, the girl feels as if the moon itself has fallen down to Earth.

The girl wants to leap into its arms and have her hair stroked and eat candy until it seeps out her pores.

Once upon a time, a princess was courted by an unwanted suitor, so she made the following impossible demands:

Three dresses: one as gold as the sun; one as silver as the moon; one as sparkling as the stars. And a heavy fur coat, made from the fur of a thousand different animals.

But her suitor sent out all the king's men, and they brought her the impossible dresses, and they brought her the impossible coat...

So she ran away.

"There are many sorts of candy," says the woman. "Candy to heal wounds, candy to keep you awake, to make you big, small, hideous, pretty... Let me know the sort that you would like, and if it is in my power, I will give it to you."

The girl is silent for a few moments. "Candy to fix things?"

"What sorts of things?"

"To fix the house, the garden. To make the sun come out again. To make my parents happy."

The woman smiles with just a hint of teeth. "Ah," she says. "That last one I can do." She ferrets around in her pockets for a spherical candy wrapped in orange and gold silk. The silk is tied at either end with tiny purple ribbons.

The girls moves to take it, and immediately a small cloud of gem-coloured beetles fly off her clothes. She laughs, and the woman takes her free hand through the last of their dissipating wings.

"Have them each eat half," says the woman, her teeth entirely too close. "It won't last as long as you want it to, but happiness never does."

The girl, feeling brave, asks, "What happened to…" She gestures to the woman's morbid necklace.

"That's the result of my favourite kind of candy: the kind that pulls your teeth." The woman grins, and then turns serious. "And while I wear them, no-one can ever touch me again if I don't want them to."

Once upon a time, a princess was found sleeping in a tree hollow in a coat of a thousand furs. The king's men threw her over their shoulders and took her back to their castle, where she was still just as beautiful as the king's dead wife.

They were married in the fall.

When the girl's parents eat the candy, everything changes. Her mother sells all of her jewellery, even her wedding ring, and they stock the cupboards with food, and the girl and her mother read together, tucked into bed with full stomachs. Her father comes home from work and hoists the girl onto his shoulders, kisses his wife, and they begin to fix the house – the draft under the front door, the leak in the kitchen roof, the rotting floorboards in the study. The girl makes sure the broken window is fixed last.

But they never get that far. The candy wears off after a week and a half, and her mother cries for three days over her wedding ring, and her father loses the job he's just been promoted to. And soon after, when her parents just can't get out of bed anymore, the girl ducks back through the broken glass and into the garden.

She's distracted, and takes the wrong path, and runs into the half-decomposed corpse of her once-white cat. It's covered with several flies and one single gem-coloured beetle.

After that, she finds the woman easily: in the very centre of the maze, standing in a dress of sunshine and honey and spun gold.

"How are you always here?" asks the girl.

"I'm only here when I'm expecting you," says the woman, and opens her arms to bathe the girl in sunlight.

Once upon a time, after her brief honeymoon, a young queen was locked in her room at sunrise. She cried no tears. She'd had the choice between posing as an anonymous, soot-covered scullery maid and becoming an unnatural queen, and she'd chosen the latter.

The day was warm and stifling. She took the mirror off the wall and laid it on the carpet. She reclined on the cold, finger-smudged glass in her dress of silver moonlight.

The mirror rippled.

And she passed straight through.

"I'm not here much anymore," says the woman. "There's another world. A better world. Time is different there. I experience the future there more than the present. And in the future…" She pauses to kiss the girl on the forehead. "You're already there."

The girl's eyes widen comically. "I'm there?"

"You are. You can come back with me now, if you like." She fishes in her pocket for a candy wrapped in white. "All you have to do is swallow this."

Once upon a time, a queen fell through a mirror onto a chessboard, and the white knights and bishops and pawns had been waiting for her. They offered her candy to dissolve the base of her teeth, which came out with a firm tug, and helped to string them around her neck like armour.

The girl examines the candy thoroughly. The outer wrapper is clear and shiny, and the inner wrapper is a dull milky white.

"You can think about it," says the woman, "and you don't have to come at all. But I know life can get miserable for girls your age, and in my experience it doesn't get much better. So you have this," she closes the girl's hand around the candy, "if you decide you want to leave."

Once upon a time, the white queen climbed back through the looking glass, walked through her bedroom door (now unlocked), and descended into the basement to the room where her father's men had slaughtered a thousand breeds of animal.

She picked thirty-two teeth from where they lay scattered in the dried blood of the palace floor. There would be a candy to make them stick in her mouth – a candy to make them her own.

The woman wraps the coat of a thousand furs around the girl's shoulders. "I wouldn't want you to get cold," she says.

"Will it be cold there?"

"Not especially. But the short trip there might be."

The girl unwraps the candy carefully, methodically, like opening a present. Inside, the candy is in the shape of a bunny rabbit, and when she squeezes its tiny white body it bounces back into shape like rubber.

"Go on," says the woman, pulling another white candy from her pocket. "I'll be right behind you."

The girl places it onto her tongue, experiencing an instant sense of vertigo. The ground beneath her rumbles gently, and then there is nothing under her feet but air.

More than falling, she has the sensation of being propelled down the hole. The smell of wet soil invades her nostrils. Fleshy worms and plant roots protrude from all sides.

Before the maze slips completely from view, she watches the woman swallow her own piece of candy, and she follows her down into the earth.

Once upon a time, the queen spied a child — a child who looked so much like herself as a girl, when her mother had died.

She went home to her chess pieces, and mourned because her future did not contain this child. This child that she could shelter and save, as she had not been.

But she wanted it so badly, she felt the future change. Her reality shifted. She saw herself on the chessboard, embracing the girl, who was warm in the coat of a thousand furs.

She saw the girl in a thousand places in this world, exploring and having a childhood. And the queen grinned with her thirty-two teeth.

D'arcy Gray and the Midnight Mailman

Ian MacAllister-McDonald

There were three robin eggs in the nest in the tree behind the house, and then they hatched and then there were three baby robins. I went out to check on them and see if the babies had opened their eyes yet, and when I got onto the back porch I saw the momma and papa flying and shrieking like they were trying to scare the devil. Only it wasn't the devil, it was a hawk sitting on at the end of the clothesline, looking big and black and terrible.

I told Sister Mary-Anne and she went out with the broom and swatted it away, but the next morning one of the babies was gone, and the morning after that the other two babies were gone, and then the momma and the poppa robin were gone also. I asked Sister Mary-Anne if she thought the robins would lay more eggs in the nest and she said she didn't think so. That's when D'arcy Gray and me got the idea to kill the hawk.

"We should get a sling shot," said D'arcy.

"That's a weapon. I don't think the Sister's would let us get one of those," I said.

"Who said anything about asking," D'arcy said. "It's a stick and a piece of rubber tubing. We can make it ourselves."

"What if we get caught?"

"Look, do you want to kill this damn hawk or not?" D'arcy said.

I shrugged, "Yeah."

"Okay then," she said.

"So where do we get one," I said.

And D'arcy, very cool-like, said "I know a guy."

There are twenty-three girls at St. Therese's Home For Girls, and D'arcy's thirteen which makes her the oldest by two years. I'm nine and have never been adopted.

D'arcy's been adopted four times but keeps getting sent back because she likes to do bad things like lie and steal and sneak out with boys. The last time was the worst though. It was so bad that even D'arcy didn't want to talk about it. I had to find out from Missy Specks who heard about it from two of the Sisters talking in the hall.

Missy came to me after she heard, all huffing and red faced. "She drowned a baby," she said and pushed her glasses up with the back of her thumb. "You remember those folks who adopted her? Yeah, well they adopted her, see, because they couldn't have a baby of their own, see, but then they *did* have a baby anyway. And so they said maybe they'd give D'arcy back." Missy was still huffing and puffing and her cheeks was so red you almost couldn't see the freckles on 'em. "And so D'arcy took the baby and tried to put it down the well." I asked what she meant by tried to and Missy Specks said "Well she didn't do it. They caught her."

"So she didn't drown the baby, then?" I said. Missy gave me a look like I'd just ruined her story.

Sister Mary-Anne says D'arcy's a devil's child and that were it not for the love of Jesus wouldn't nobody love her. And when Sister Mary-Anne says a thing like that D'arcy will usually say something smart like "Ain't that sweet for Jesus," and Sister Mary-Anne will whip her with the switch. Then when Sister Mary-Anne walks away, D'arcy will rub her skin where it smarts, and smile real excited-like and say "You see how mad she got?" And then she'll start laughing.

Later when I asked D'arcy about the baby story, she just said "Oh shoot, that wasn't how it went at all."

"How'd it go then," I said.

"You don't listen to them," she said. "They just like to make up stories about me." And I have to say, I think that's partly true too. I don't think D'arcy's so bad, I just think she likes to do bad things. When I told Missy Specks that, she said "What's the difference?" And even though I couldn't say, I still think there is one.

D'arcy said why she needed the hair, but I still didn't get it even after she said it. "I gotta send away for the slingshot," she said. "The hair's postage."

I told her that didn't make any sense.

"Well, that's the way it is," she said and took out the scissors.

"Why can't it be your hair," I said.

"Because I said so," she said.

The next morning I put my hair down so the Sister's couldn't see the place in the back where D'arcy had cut out a hunk. I didn't like the idea of walking around with a bunch of my hair missing, and I kept waiting for one of the Sisters to come up and say "Penny, why's your hair down? Put it up." And when I put it up, they'd see the place where D'arcy had cut it off and I'd start to cry. But nobody noticed, and so by lunch I wasn't thinking about it anymore.

Then at lunch D'arcy gave me a tug. "Hey Penny," she said, and looked down at her lap. I stopped filing my nails and looked down too. D'arcy uncovered her hands to show me a length of elastic tubing coiled beneath her palms like a baby corn snake.

"What's that?" I said.

"It's the thing that goes with this," she said, and made her fingers into a Y. I gasped. "Where'd you get it," I said.

"Shhh!" she said. And then whispered "I told you, I sent away for it."

"But where?" I said.

And she said, "Meet me in cellar during break. I wanna make a slingshot."

In the cellar I asked again where she got the elastic but D'arcy didn't tell me. Every time I'd ask, she'd say gimme the glue, or pass the rope, or hold this tight please, and then I'd hold the elastic to this Y-shaped stick that D'arcy had found in the yard.

We'd just about finished with the slingshot when Sister Sara opened the door to the cellar and caught us.

Sister Sara looked at D'arcy, and I hoped she'd ask her first, but she didn't ask her at all.

Instead she turned to me and said "Penny, something you wanna tell me?"

D'arcy's a magical liar and there are times I wish I could lie as well as she can – not that I want to lie all the time, but it'd just be nice to do it sometimes when you're in a tight spot. But that's not me, and I've never been good at lying. When I said "We found it," all quiet and staring at my feet, all it took was for Sister Sara to say my name again, and my lip started shaking and my heart started kicking, and in no time at all I was telling the whole stupid story about the hawk and the baby robins and how it wasn't fair a damn hawk should be able to swoop down and steal those babies and just get away with it like that. And I started to cry. And I said why didn't God help those poor little baby robins. And Sister Sara took me in her great fat arms and patted my cheek and looked at me and said, "You know that hawk needs to eat too. It's probably got babies at home and it's just trying to feed those babies."

"But why the robins," I said.

"That hawk's just doing what it knows to do," Sister Sara said.

And then D'arcy said "How come that excuse don't work for me?" But she said it real quiet, and I don't think Sister Sara heard.

The next day I went to D'arcy in the yard. She was leaning over the fence and looking down the road. There wasn't nothing there but she went on looking, like she was expecting something.

"Hi," I said.

"Go away," she said. "I'm not talking to you."

"What?" I said.

"I'm not talking to you," she said again.

And I just stood there because I didn't know what to say and D'arcy didn't even look at me. So I turned and went back to the yard and I cried. Sister Mary-Anne saw me and said what's the matter, and I told her D'arcy didn't want to talk to me. And Sister Mary-Anne said "You don't worry about D'arcy. Go play with Missy Specks." And then she said "Missy won't be around much longer."

We call her Missy Specks on account she's got thick glasses that make her eyes look like big, black marbles. She's fat with red hair that she wears like Pippi Longstockings and freckles all over her face. D'arcy said she's the kind of girl that won't never get adopted because if you're a Momma and can pick between a pretty girl and fat girl with freckles, why wouldn't you pick the pretty girl?

That's why D'arcy's been adopted four times. She has the prettiest eyes you've ever seen. I mean, every part of her is beautiful, but when parents come looking, they always remark about D'arcy's eyes. "Those are the prettiest eyes I've ever seen," they'll say, and then they'll adopt her.

There's another girl here who all the girls just call Wheels on account her legs don't work and she moves around in a wheelchair. Sometimes she'll hop out of her chair and walk around on her hands, with her legs just sorta dragging behind her. She can move quite fast and it's a scary thing to see her come after you.

"Wheels won't never get adopted either," D'arcy said. "But she can't help that because she's just a dumb cripple. Missy Specks is fat because she stuffs her face, which means she can help that."

"She can't help the glasses," I said when D'arcy said that.

"I bet she can," she said back.

"She can't help the freckles," I said.

And D'arcy just said, "You like Missy Specks?"

And I said, "She's not so bad."

And D'arcy just rolled her beautiful eyes and said, "Well ain't that sweet for Missy Specks."

Sometimes I worry I won't never get adopted. I'm not a cripple and I don't have glasses, but I'm not near as pretty as D'arcy either. The Sisters tell me I'm a beautiful girl and it's just a matter of time. But they say that to all the girls. When I asked D'arcy if she thought I'd get adopted one of these days, she said "You're a beautiful girl and it's just a matter of time!" and then she laughed.

Someone once told me I have pretty hands, so I keep a nail file with me to make sure they stay that way.

I sure would like to have a family one of these days.

When I went over to play with Missy Specks, she was digging a hole in the ground with a shovel and putting all the dirt over on one side.

"I'm being adopted," she said, pushing her glasses up with the back of her thumb. I kept waiting to see what she was gonna put in the hole, but she didn't seem to be thinking of that, she just kept digging. She told me all about her new Momma and Poppa. I'd seen the ones she'd talked about when they came through to look at all the girls.

They were a man and a woman, both round with red hair and glasses. The man had a mustache and a floppy brown hat, and the woman had a dress with palm trees all over it. When they left a bunch of the girls laughed and made fun, but I think they were still a bit jealous when they heard Missy was gonna go with them.

It's a funny thing because most times when a girl's adopted she gets very quiet and then she cries and all the other girls get very jealous even though that girl's crying. But Missy Specks didn't cry at all, she just went on talking about how she's gonna have her own bedroom and all her own toys, and she's gonna get to go on trips because the Poppa does business in Florida, and she's gonna eat crabs and coconuts and learn how to surf.

"And I'm gonna come back here someday and I'll be tall and skinny and my skin will be all brown because of the beach and the surfing, and you won't even recognize me," she said. "I'll come back here and none of you won't even recognize me."

Later that night when all the girls were asleep, D'arcy came to my bed. "Alright, wake up," she said. "We have work to do."

"I thought you weren't talking to me," I said.

"Not talking to you? What do you call this?" she said.

"You said you weren't talking to me."

"I had to say that so they wouldn't think we were working together. It's part of the secret plan to kill the—"

"But they took our slingshot."

"Forget the slingshot. That was a dumb idea. I have a new plan." "What's the new plan," I said.

And D'arcy said "Come with me and I'll show you."

They keep the doors locked at night, so D'arcy jimmied a window in the first floor bathroom and we climbed out.

When we got around front D'arcy said "Stay here," and sprinted to the mailbox at the end of the drive. But I didn't like staying so I sprinted too.

"What are you doing? Go back," she said, and took a little tin container out of her pocket. I could hear Something Hard rattling around inside.

"What is that?" I said.

"Nothing, just go back," she said, and stuffed the tin container into the mailbox. "Would you scram, he's gonna be here any second."

"Who is?" I said.

D'arcy started to say something then stopped, then stiffened and looked up the road. Then she said "He's coming," and sprinted back towards the house and hid in the bushes, and I hid with her.

I looked up to where the drive meets the road. The man was tall and dark and thin, like the shadow of a skeleton ambling upright through the night. He had an empty-looking satchel thrown over his shoulder which bounced against him as he walked. When he got to the mailbox, he opened the front and took out the tin container that D'arcy had left; he took off the lid and dumped The Hard Thing into his hand, felt its weight a moment, then popped it into his mouth and swallowed.

"What was in the tin?" I whispered.

D'arcy said "Shh!"

Then the man reached into his satchel and took out a package, a box wrapped in brown paper and twine, and put it inside the mailbox. He put up the little red flag then stood there a moment, all skinny and crooked and peering. His head turned like he was scanning the darkness, then stopped when it got to our bush. He cocked his head to one side and took a step towards us. I wanted to say something or ask something or scream but D'arcy clapped a hand over my mouth. And the man stared at our bush and we stared back, and my breathing was loud and wheezy through D'arcy's fingers, which made her clamp tighter. The man stood there stick-still, and looking curious, and hungry and - in a way - terrified of us. And the terror in him made the terror in me bubble and froth.

He stood and stared a moment longer, then turned casual-like and shuffled off down the road, disappearing into the darkness.

D'arcy slapped me on the back, "C'mon. Let's get it."

Back inside, D'arcy went into the boys' bathroom. Since all the Sisters are girls, and all the girls are girls, the boys' bathroom is really just for visitors, so hardly anyone ever goes in there. I said "Who was that guy? What did you put in the mailbox? Why did he eat it? What did he give you? What's in the package D'arcy? Hunh? What's in the package?"

D'arcy removed the twine and brown paper, and opened the box. "This," she said, and showed me inside the box.

Inside the box was a pistol, like the kind you see on cowboy shows. And beside that was another, smaller box with bullets in it.

And I gasped. "What are you gonna do with it?" I said.

"Kill robins," D'arcy said.

"I thought we were gonna kill the hawks."

"Oh, right," D'arcy said. "That's what I meant. Hawks."

And then I said, "Who was that guy?"

"Who'd it look like," she said. "It was the mailman."

"Mr. Kreeger delivers the mail here. That wasn't Mr. Kreeger." And then I said "And he definitely doesn't deliver the mail at night."

"Well, you're right about that. It definitely wasn't Mr. Kreeger," D'arcy said, running a finger along the smooth, steel barrel of the gun.

"Is it a new system?" I said.

"No," D'arcy said. "It's a very old system." She lifted the gun out of the box and aimed it into space, closing one eye and tightening her finger around the trigger. And then she said "Damn near *ancient*, the way I heard it."

And then I said something else.

And D'arcy said "Hunh?" And kinda shook her head and put the pistol back in the box.

So I said it again, "What was the thing you put in the mailbox? Y'know. The thing in the tin he took out and ate?"

And D'arcy smiled like she knew a secret she didn't want to tell and said very quietly, like it was the most obvious thing in the world. She said: "Postage."

Later that night I had a dream about Wheels. I was in the hallway and she was at the far end by the kitchen, and she was walking on her hands after me, only not how she normally does, with her legs dragging on the floor behind her. In the dream her legs were up in the air, dangling low and lazy and over her head like a Scorpion's tail. And she was just walking towards me like that, very slowly, and her legs were swaying like dead things, and I could see the tops of her feet. At first I tried to be polite and I said "Hi wheels," and went to go into another room.

But all the doors was locked and I couldn't get through, and she just kept coming towards me. I tried more doors but they were all locked. And so I said, "Hey wheels you know about any doors that aren't locked?" just trying to make her talk to me. But she didn't say anything. And so I said, "Hey look, I think I'm gonna go now." And when I stepped to one side to go around, she stepped to that same side, making so I couldn't pass. And when I stepped to the other side, she stepped that way too. And she moved closer so that her feet were just about touching my face, and I said, "Don't touch me with your feet Wheels." But she wasn't listening. She was staring up at me, neck crooked and bent and mouth hanging open, and legs swaying, and she kept on coming. And I could see the tops of her feet because they were just next to my face, and her legs were swaying. And she was staring. And her mouth was hanging open. And her legs were swaying.

And that's when I heard the screaming. And that's when I woke up.

And about two seconds later I realized that the person screaming wasn't me.

Wheels was screaming and all the girls ran to her bed.

There was blood on her sheets and blood on the floor, and some blood on the walls and ceiling even, and when Sister Mary-Anne ripped back the sheet we all saw why: Wheels' left foot was missing it's little toe, like it had been clipped off with pinking sheers. Wheels saw this with the rest of us and even though she couldn't feel it, she saw it, and she screamed and screamed and screamed.

The Sisters spent all afternoon looking, but didn't nobody find it, and eventually they brought in Doctor Bob to stitch her up, minus the toe.

The police came too and asked some questions and poked around and said they didn't know how so much blood could come from such a small cut. They said it was a mystery and then left. And the Sisters clucked about how there's no justice for the weak, and were FDR any sorta man at all he'd do something about it. Then they left too.

It was Missy Specks who saw the hedge clippers poking out from under D'arcy's mattress. And she ran and told the Sisters, who ran and told the police, and the police came back and that's how they found the gun.

I watched them take D'arcy away and my heart was beating and pounding and wailing because I knew they were gonna take her down to the police station and D'arcy would probably say about how I helped her get the gun, even though I still didn't know how I helped. But she'd tell 'em anyway and because I'm a lousy liar I'd start to cry and say what happened and then they'd put me in jail and then no parents would ever wanna adopt me.

I spent all the rest of that night and the next day and the next night waiting for the police to come knock at the door and say "We need to take Penny to jail, please." And they'd come and take me to jail.

But that didn't happen.

Instead, two days later, D'arcy came back. They set up a bed for her in the boiler room at the far end of the basement, with a lock on the door. The Sisters told everyone D'arcy was just staying for one night and that none of us were to talk to her. We all said "Yes Ma'am," but then when everyone had gone to sleep I went down anyway.

There was a little square hole in the top of the door with chicken wire stapled across it. I found an apple box in the corner and set it up, and on my tiptoes peaked through at D'arcy sitting on her bed, head down, playing with her fingers. There was a plate of food on the floor, but it looked like no one had touched it. It looked just like a jail cell.

I started to say something, but before I could, D'arcy said, "All this over a damn toe. I don't know why she wants the stupid thing. Not like she's doing pirouettes anyhow."

"D'arcy?" I said.

"She didn't even wake up when I took it. How's that hurting a girl?"

"D'arcy," I said again.

"Yeah. What?" she said, still not looking up.

"It's me," I said.

"I know who it is," she said. "What do you want?"

"I just wanted to see how you were doing," I said.

And D'arcy laughed, which surprised me; just kicked her head back and let out one loud Ha! "You know you really stink at lying," she said.

And I didn't say anything because she was right.

"You want to know if I told about how you helped me get the gun. That's what you want to know."

I started to talk.

"Tomorrow they're gonna come and take me away," she said.

"To jail?" I said.

"To the Center For Juvenile Delinquency," she said.

"What's that?" I said.

"It's like jail for kids," she said. "I'm gonna go until I'm 18, and when I'm 18 they're gonna see if I have to go to real jail. I'm not sure about that yet." D'arcy got up and dragged her bed over to the door then stood on it so she was looking through the chicken wire. "But they told me all about juvy," she said.

"Who told you?"

"The other girl in the jail. Where do you think I've been sleeping the last two nights? She's been there three times already," she said. "She said I'm gonna get a room just like this one here, and I'll share it with three other girls. And they told me how the girls there are all ages, and how the older girls like to beat up the younger girls. And how the older girls like to do things to the younger girls—"

"What kinda things," I said.

"Sinful things," she said.

I felt the skin on my back crawl. "I think she was just trying to scare you," I said.

D'arcy shook her head and chuckled. "So what do you say, wanna go with me?"

"Did you tell the police that I helped you with the gun?" I said, and I knew I was starting to cry.

"You wanna go and have a bunch of older girls do weird things to you too? I only got five years there, but you you'd get a lot longer since you're younger than me."

"Did you tell them!"

D'arcy hopped off the bed and stepped away from the door, smiling that smile of hers.

"I didn't really help you," I said. "Not really. I didn't even know what you were doing. I just followed you, that's all."

"Uh-huh," said D'arcy. "Tell it to the judge, honey."

"So you didn't tell them?" I said.

"No," she said. "Not yet."

I started to talk.

"But I could," she said. "Any time, I could tell them what really happened, and when they ask you, you'll start crying and saying yes yes yes to everything they wanna know. Only way you're getting out of this is if they don't ever know enough to ask."

I closed my lips.

D'arcy folded her arms and stared at me, still smiling.

"What do you want?" I said.

"Do you have your nail file," she said. I said yes.

"Give it to me," she said.

I gave it to her.

The eyes didn't come out in perfect round marbles. They came out like jelly, soft and purple and not really even looking like eyes at all. Definitely not the beautiful eyes that got D'arcy adopted four times. D'arcy put her pillow in her mouth to keep from screaming, but she didn't wind up screaming. Instead she sorta gasped and the pillow fell out. But her hands were cool like they belonged to someone else who'd done this a hundred times. They worked the nail file in quick little circles, until finally the first eye just kinda slimed out. She didn't take a break for the second eye, but started right away on it. The second eye came out quicker than the first, and when both eyes were out, D'arcy carried them to the door and fed them through the chicken wire, plopping them warm and soft into my hands.

"Postage," she said.

Now the eyes are in the mailbox and I'm in the bushes. My hands are bloody and the moon is full and everyone in the house is asleep. Everyone but D'arcy that is. And as I crouch and wait and hold my breath, I think that if my hair got D'arcy a slingshot, and a little toe got her a gun, what will two eyes get her? What's the value of postage? The size of the thing, or the pain in losing it?

Then I think about how tomorrow is the day when Missy Specks' new parents are supposed to come and adopt her. The man with the mustache and floppy brown hat, and the woman with the goofy palm tree dress, both fat and red and freckled just like Missy. And I think that when they get here Sister Sara will probably take them aside and mention how Missy caught the bad guy, caught D'arcy. And how that makes her sort of a hero around this place, and how they should be very proud to be adopting such a good and clever child. And then the new parents will probably smile and hug Missy and say how much they love her.

And while I think these thoughts I start to cry, because I could go to Sister Sara right now, wake her up, and say what I did. But I know I won't.

I'm too scared and a lousy liar and would probably go to jail-for-kids.

And then I start to cry, because I think that even if everything goes right–
   – if D'arcy does what she said
   – if she keeps our secret
   – if she goes away
   – if she never tells a soul
   – if I never again make mischief
   – if parents come
   – if, like me, they are not pretty but not ugly either
   – if they see me and like my beautiful hands
   – if they sign the papers
   – if they take me home
   – if all this happens and everything goes perfect, that still makes me Not A Hero. And when parents do adopt me they'll have no idea they're really adopting a liar hiding in the bushes with blood on her hands. And every time they say "I love you," they'll be saying it to the wrong person.

And I cry.

And I cry.

And I cry.

And then I stop.

The man is standing beside the mailbox at the end of the drive, and he's looking at me. He's skinny and crooked and dark dark dark, and his satchel hangs empty-like, and he's staring dead at me. And I think if I don't move and don't breathe, then he won't see me and he'll leave his package and go away and all this will be over soon.

But then he raises a hand and gestures *come here* with one finger. And because hiding is like lying, and I'm a lousy liar, I do. I go to him.

As I get closer I keep waiting for the man to get less dark, less shadowy; for my eyes to adjust, but they never do. I stop a few feet away. The man keeps looking at me. I can't see his face, but I can kind of imagine it, and like before it's curious and hungry and, in a way, terrified. And it's that last part that worries me. He's a man in the night delivering guns for toes, what does he have to be scared of?

Then slowly, the man reaches inside his satchel and takes out a clipboard with a blank sheet of paper and a pen on it. He takes the pen and writes *sign here* followed by an X.

He hands me the pen and I sign.

I feel the ground shift beneath my feet. Not much. Just a little. Like the world's tiniest earthquake.

The man returns the pen and clipboard to inside his satchel, then takes out a package. It's very small and very light and, once again, wrapped in brown paper and twine. I wonder what on Earth D'arcy could want with something so small. A box of matches? Some sugar packets? A poem? I can't think of much else. Except it doesn't feel like it has anything inside. I lift it up to my ear and start to shake it, but when I do the man reaches out and grabs my wrist, and waves a finger at me: *No no.*

Then he lets go and opens up the mailbox. He takes out the eyes and, like paste, wipes them onto his tongue, not even weighing them this time. And once he's swallowed them down his dry and ageless throat, he re-closes the lid, lowers the little red flag and continues down the road.

I stand and watch him for what feels like only minutes, but then I hear birds and see light coming up over the trees and know that hours have passed.

If I'm going to give D'arcy her package I need to do it before the Sister's wake up. If not, I should just run. In either case I need to do it soon.

D'arcy's going to be upset if she cut out her eyes for nothing.

The Sister's will be upset if D'arcy gets her package. I can't say how I know this, but I do.

And as I think about this a robin flies down and lands on the grass a few feet away. It has a bright red belly which means it's a boy, and I can't tell if it's the papa robin from before, but he kind of looks like it. I stare and watch him hop around the grass for a few seconds, and he looks beautiful and innocent and I find myself wanting to pick him up and squeeze him. Then the robin darts it's beak into the dirt and pulls up a worm. The worm wriggles and writhes and stretches out of the ground. Its bottom half seems to get caught on something, and its body goes taut, then rips in half. Its guts spill out and this seems to delight the robin who dances around for a second, eats one half quickly, then picks up the other and flies away with it. It vanishes in the direction of darkness and, suddenly, I know exactly what I'm going to do.

Pretty Jennie Greenteeth

Leife Shallcross

Felmere is about as old as a house can be, and there are all sorts of queer corners and cupboards and stairs that go odd places. Papa tells us stories about it; of how Queen Elizabeth visited when she was but a girl, and of escaping priests and Loyalist Cavaliers hiding in our cellar many hundreds of years ago. And other stories, about things in the woods outside the house that are even older still. I don't know if Princess Elizabeth was ever really here. But I know some of the other stories are true.

Harriet says she doesn't believe the stories. She says it is naughty to go into the woods, and worries about getting a scolding. Emily isn't sure. She doesn't like to go, for the trees and the noises frighten her. Still, when I say we must go, they follow me out, down the dark path to Jennie's corner, and they each bring the treasures they have gathered up since last time.

Harriet almost always gives something she has made, and Emily something she has found. I usually bring something I have stolen.

Once in Summer, once in Autumn and once in Spring (but never in Winter), we all stand on the edge of the water and watch the little ripples arrowing towards us, and we all say our rhyme together and cast our treasures in.

I might not be good like Harriet or pretty like Emily, but I know about the secret of Felmere Woods. I have seen the mossy bones lying hidden in the undergrowth. I know what to do to keep us safe.

It was Bessie who told us about Cousin John, when she was putting our hair in rags the night before he arrived.

Harriet sat still and was good, of course, for Harriet is always good. Emily endured, because Emily loves to have her golden hair in curls. I fidgeted and complained, for I cannot help it.

"Will you sit still, Miss Charlotte!" Bessie said, her voice all tired like it gets when she speaks so. "You must look your best tomorrow, for it's your Cousin John who will be master here when your father goes to heaven, so it's to your advantage to make a good impression!"

"Papa never said!" said Harriet, her soft brown eyes surprised. Bessie pursed her lips. "Well, that's the face of it," she said curtly. "Like as not, he'll marry one of you three into the bargain. So you'd best be minded to get on with him."

"What about Cousin Richard?" asked Emily, extracting her thumb from her mouth. "Will he be master too?"

"Not unless something untoward happens to your Cousin John," said Bessie, yanking at my hair.

"Ow, Bessie!" I protested, fidgeting again.

"There can only be one master at Felmere," said Harriet to Emily. "Don't be silly, Emmie."

After Bessie had put out our candles, Harriet and I sneaked into Emily's bed in the nursery, as we always did when there was something we three needed to discuss. We didn't need candles to find our way. We could have done it blindfolded, walking backwards.

"What do you think he'll be like?" asked Harriet. "Which one?" I grumbled. "There's two of them."

"Cousin John, of course," she said.

"Who knows," I said, scratching my head where my hair itched. Bessie always made my rags too tight.

"Do we have to marry him?" asked Emily.

"Only one of us, Emmie," said Harriet. "And not until we've grown.'"

"Will you marry him, Hattie?" asked Emily.

Harriet and I looked at each other. In the dark, with just the firelight, you can hardly see the dark red stain on Harriet's face.

"Perhaps," said Harriet doubtfully.

She doesn't think she'll ever get married, on account of the stain.

"Not me," I said. "I'm never getting married."

"Oh, Charlotte," said Harriet, looking exasperated.

"I'm not," I said stubbornly. "One of you two will have to do it."

The carriage arrived after luncheon. We all got bustled out to the front steps to stand there in our next-to-best clothes. Harriet and Emily's curls were smooth and glossy and gleamed in the sun. Mine were all askew, from scratching at them, Bessie said.

There were two carriages, with one for servants. The first one was a large carriage, much grander than ours. With four horses. The wheels crunched on the gravel and the driver shouted "Whoah!" and the horses stamped and snorted. Right then, I would hardly have been surprised if the King and Queen had got out of it.

This is what happened.

Thomas, the footman, went and opened the door. A lady in a very grand dress and a hat with feathers got out. She looked at all of us, but when she saw Harriet, her eyes got a shocked look in them. That was the lady that used to be Aunt Felton. She is Mrs Wroxham now, on account of marrying Mr Wroxham.

Then a man got out. That was Mr Wroxham. He looked around at us and when he saw Harriet he looked away again quickly.

Cousin John got out next. He was a tall boy, with strong shoulders and fair, wavy hair that flopped over his forehead. He looked straight at Harriet and stared. He stared and stared and then he smiled. It wasn't a friendly smile.

By now, even the part of Harriet's face that isn't stained was red, and I could feel my fingers had all curled up tight in hard fists.

I forget, sometimes, that Harriet looks odd to people who don't know her.

Last of all, Cousin Richard got out of the carriage. He was thinner and darker than Cousin John. He looked at each of us. When he saw Harriet, he got a tiny frown on his forehead, but then he looked her straight in the eye. And smiled a real smile.

In church, the Reverend is always preaching on about it not being our place to judge.

But I could not help it. I judged each of them by how they looked at Hattie that first day.

It was an awkward sort of day. We sat in the salon for most of the afternoon, listening to Mrs Wroxham talk about Cousin John. He did not seem at all abashed by this, but just lounged in his chair, staring around the room and at us. Every now and then Mrs Wroxham would remember to be interested in us and ask Papa a question. And sometimes she would talk about Cousin Richard.

I learned from Mrs Wroxham that Cousin Richard's chief virtue is that he is clever, whereas Cousin John is good at all things.

I began to be glad we don't usually have guests at Felmere.

After dinner, we sat in the salon again. But this time Papa told us we might play some games. So Harriet went to get out the letters so we might play anagrams. At first, it seemed as though Cousin John thought he was too old for such childish pursuits. He is fourteen, after all, a full two years older than Harriet and Cousin Richard and very superior with it. Then Mrs Wroxham said something to him behind her fan and he slouched over to join us. There was a small kerfuffle when we went to sit at the table. To begin with, it looked as though Cousin John might be placed by Harriet. But then, when he saw where he was to sit, he moved away and put himself between Emily and I, leaving Cousin Richard to sit by Harriet.

It was not an enjoyable game. Cousin John cheated.

I will be truthful and say that, though I know it's very wicked, I sometimes cheat. But only ever to win. And only if I will not get caught.

John cheated so that he might make cruel words like 'stain' and 'red' and 'mark' and lay them out for Hattie to see. He did not care who saw him cheat. He pulled Emily's hair and called her a tattletale when she told him he must not peek, or keep letters back. When I caught him looking at Emily's cards and gave him my hardest stare, he just laughed at me.

Later, when we sneaked into the nursery again, I got mad at Harriet when she said she did not care about it. I heard how her voice hitched when she said it, but she wouldn't admit Cousin John was a rum cull and told me not to use such nasty cant. I got in a huff and went away to hide in the library. But the fire was low there, so when my feet got cold, I decided to go to bed. That was how I came to overhear Mr and Mrs Wroxham talking.

It was not quite my fault I should have heard them, for Mrs Wroxham had left her door ajar, and I was walking slowly on account of my cold feet.

"It's quite bad, isn't it?" I heard her say.

"Bad? It's shocking!" he responded. "How is a man supposed to kiss a face like that?"

"No, I doubt she'll ever marry," said my aunt. "How tiresome. I suppose John will be expected to keep her, then."

There was a murmur from Mr Wroxham.

"Yes, well, maiden aunts do have their uses, I suppose," she said. "There are the other two, of course. I have no opinion of the middle one. Such a surly child! The youngest is very pretty and biddable, I think."

I was mostly just furious they would be so unkind about Harriet. But at the same time, I was secretly pleased she did not think of me marrying John.

I did not realise about Emily until later.

The next day was worse. At breakfast we found out that Mrs Wroxham did not customarily rise before noon, and must have her breakfast carried up to her like an invalid. But not before ten o'clock.

Mr Wroxham breakfasted with us, and was very hearty. He spoke to Papa about such things as fishing and shooting. When John came down, I felt sure he would choose to go with Papa and Mr Wroxham. But he didn't.

He looked about, and came to sit by me.

"Is there any strawberry jam?" he asked. He was staring straight at Harriet. She was looking down at her plate most determinedly. John saw me watching him and smiled.

"There it is," he said. I hate his smile.

"I say, Cousin Charlotte," he said. "This house must be bully for hide-and-go-seek."

"Oh, it is!" said Emily excitedly, for she loves to play hidey.

"Well, then," said John. "Let us have a game of it after breakfast." That was when Richard came into the breakfast room.

"A game of what?" he asked. He was frowning at his brother.

"Hide-and-go-seek," said John, still smiling. Richard did not take his eyes off John.

"They're only girls, John," said Richard quietly.

I could not help myself.

"You won't beat us at hide-and-go-seek!" I said angrily. "We know all the best places!"

You see, it was my fault.

"Really?" asked John. His smile had grown even more smug.

"I tell you what, Cousin Charlotte," John said, "I bet I shall find you first."

"You won't," I said, folding my arms. Even Papa laughed now.

"If you find Charlotte first," he said to John, "I shall give you a guinea. Our Charlotte is the very devil at hidey when she doesn't want to be found."

"Thank you, sir," said John politely. But when he looked back at me, he smiled again.

It's true what Papa said. Emmie might love playing hidey most because she is youngest, but I am best at it. Emmie is too afraid of dark places, and Hattie does not like dust.

John began counting in the breakfast room and I went straight to my favourite place. There is a cupboard under the stairs, where our house-keeper, Mrs Plumstead, keeps all sorts of odds and ends. There is a space at the back, behind the shelves. I must crawl in under the lowest shelf, but then I can sit up. I keep some books there and a tin for biscuits. I also have a candle in a jar, and a flint, so I can read. John would never know it was there unless someone told him, and that would have been very disloyal.

I lit my candle and made myself comfortable. He did not find me.

I did not come out until I heard Harriet calling for me to come quickly, for Emily had been taken ill. We went to the nursery. Emily was sitting in Bessie's lap, whimpering in a way that made me think of a hurt animal. Bessie was holding a bucket.

I came in behind Harriet, thinking Bessie might give me a scolding for being dusty.

But Bessie did not even look at me. She was rubbing Emmie's back in an anxious sort of way and saying "There, my lamb, better out than in," in a low, coaxing voice.

Emmie was sick into the bucket, though it didn't sound like much came out. Bessie glanced down at it, and away quickly.

"Why is she sick, Bessie?" I asked.

"Gone and eaten something that didn't agree with her, the daft child," said Bessie shortly. "But it's not like her," she added in a worried voice. Emmie gave another little sobbing moan and Bessie's mouth pulled down at the corners.

When I got a chance, I looked in the bucket. At the bottom, in a puddle of foamy spit, was a long, pink, squashed-looking worm, and some spiky shapes that made me think of beetles' legs.

Bessie did not let us tarry long in the nursery, but sent us away to sew our samplers in the salon. On the way I told Hattie about the bucket, and she made a face like she was going to be sick, too.

"Why would she eat those things?" she asked.

I did not answer, for I had my own thoughts about why, but I did not know how to tell them.

"Where did she hide?" I asked. Hattie's face twisted up like she was going to cry.

"I don't know," she whispered. "I saw her run off towards the schoolroom, but I went with Cousin Richard to show him where to hide."

I felt sick at my own stupidity.

We should not have left Emmie alone.

I do not like sewing. Instead, I sat in the window seat and looked out over the garden, across to the other side of the field to where the woods began. I was thinking about Emily hiding in the schoolroom, and what is on our nature table there.

Suddenly, there was a great ruckus from downstairs. We heard a shout and a crash.

Both Harriet and I dropped our samplers and ran out into the hall. This is what we saw.

Down in the entrance hall Richard and John were fighting. John had his arm locked around Richard's neck. John's shirt was all pulled awry, and his hair was messed up.

Richard's nose was bleeding and dripping onto the floor in great, bloody blots. He was crying, too, and yelling something. But it was hard to understand his words on account of John choking him. They stumbled across the tiles together and crashed into a wall, knocking over the umbrella stand. Hattie had gone very pale, making the crimson of her birthmark stand out very bright.

I heard another shout and running footsteps. Thomas came running and so did Mrs Plumstead and together they pulled our cousins apart. To begin with, Richard and John both glared at each other angrily while Mrs Plumstead scolded them. But then John looked up and saw us watching, and he got a satisfied look on his face. Richard glanced up, too. But he just looked more mortified than ever. He kept looking down at the blood on his hands and trying to wipe it off. He may as well not have, for there were streaks of it over his face also, and drips of it all down his shirt.

After that, Richard and John were sent to their rooms in disgrace for the rest of the afternoon. I did not want to sit inside any longer, so after luncheon I made Harriet come outdoors with me. I wanted to find some tadpoles, which Hattie doesn't like, but I told her we could also try to catch some butterflies for Emily, and perhaps pick some flowers for her press.

We caught three pretty white ones that we put in a jar. Harriet thought they would look well with some sprigs of lavender, so I fetched some, and also some pink rosebuds I saw growing. They were very charming together, and that made Harriet smile. She likes pretty things. Then Harriet was content to sit under a tree and admire them while I got my tadpoles. They were very shy that day and I had to be quite patient and careful and wait for them to swim into the jar.

When I finally had them, I lay on the edge of the brook for a while. There was so much to look at. I watched an enormous green dragonfly skimming over the rippling surface. Then I looked into the water at everything underneath. I like the way the water stretches and bends things, so you are never quite sure what you are looking at. When I rolled over, I could see, not far off on the edge of the field, the dark green of the trees of Felmere Woods.

Harriet and I went in to visit Emily and try to cheer her before we went to bed, but she just huddled under the bedclothes, very quiet and pale, and said hardly a word. I wanted to ask her if John had done something horrible, but she cried if Bessie left her side for even a moment and Bessie was very strict that we should not upset her. We left her the jar of butterflies to look at.

The next day I heard Bessie talking to Mrs Plumstead on the landing. Bessie said Emily was refusing to eat.

"She's such a wee scrap of a thing," said Mrs Plumstead worriedly. "She must eat or she'll be naught but skin and bone in a day or two."

This made me think of Jennie's corner, and the mouldering bones scattered amongst the ferns. I know some of them are from the joints of meat I have stolen from the kitchen.

They are nasty, grey, gnawed-looking things. I did not want Emmie to turn into bones.

Then I heard Emmie begin to cry again in the nursery. Bessie heard her too, for she put Emily's tray into Mrs Plumstead's hands and hurried away.

I followed Bessie to the nursery. Emily was being sick again.

"But you haven't eaten anything!" cried out Bessie, despairing. Then she let out a frightened shriek. Emily had missed the pail and there was a horrible puddle on the floor. In the puddle were lots of little brown blobs. Some of them were still wriggling.

I spent the morning in disgrace. I even got a whipping from Mrs Plumstead and a stern talking-to from Papa for yelling at Bessie. I was still very angry with her for leaving Emily alone.

But not as angry as I was with John.

Still, being in disgrace gave me time to think. And then some time to make up a new rhyme. It also meant I was alone upstairs. Mrs Plumstead had locked my bedroom door, but it is an old lock and very loose. I have long been able to unlatch it with a hairpin or two.

When I was sure there was no one about, I went into Mrs Wroxham's room to find a likely treasure. I found what I wanted almost straight away, in a box on her dressing table. It was a brooch; oval in shape, set around the edge with diamonds and little gold scrolls. It was quite large – large enough to cover most of my palm when I held it. The diamonds were all around the edge of a picture of a boy. If you didn't know him, you might think him quite well-looking, I suppose. But I wanted to put a bodkin through his face, even though in this portrait he was much younger than now. Perhaps as young as me.

After luncheon, Mrs Plumstead said I might join the others again. She said they were outside, but she must have meant Harriet and Cousin Richard, for as I walked past the salon, I looked in and saw John. He was stretched out on the sopha, lazily turning a jar over in his hands. It had three pale butterflies inside it.

I stopped in the doorway. He looked up to see me, then cast me a sly sideways glance.

As I watched, he opened the jar and put his hand inside to snatch up a butterfly. He held up the butterfly, flapping helplessly, to show me. Then, as I watched, he took hold of its other wing and quickly pulled the poor creature apart. He let it fall, and the torn wings fluttered down like little, ragged scraps of paper.

I do not have the words to tell what I felt at that moment. But I put my hand in my pocket and clutched my fingers about my new treasure.

"I am not afraid of you," I told him. He looked at me for a short while.

"No," he said, raising one of his eyebrows. "I don't believe you are." We looked at each other some more.

"Mother thinks I should marry one of you, when you are grown," he said. "Not Harriet, of course." He gave a theatrical shudder. In my pocket, the rough edge of diamonds dug into my fingertips.

"I like Emily," he went on, his eyes intent upon me. "She cries quietly." I looked back at him stonily. My index finger found the point of the pin. "But, we are so alike, we two," he said. "I think I shall marry you, Charlotte." I turned and walked away.

I had not taken many steps before I realised he had come after me. I wanted to run. But I took a deep breath and was careful, and kept walking at the same pace.

"Where are you going, Cousin Charlotte?" he called to me, his footsteps quick behind me. I did not answer. I waited until he had caught up with me.

"I asked where you are going!" he said. I do not think he is used to his questions being ignored. I waited a moment; as he drew breath to speak again, I said "I am going for a walk in the woods."

"The woods?" he asked. He was walking beside me now, too close.

"Yes," I said. I stepped easily past him into the narrow corridor that leads to our back door. I did not stop to get my hat. He followed me out.

"Are you allowed in the woods?" he asked. His voice was mocking now. He must have known I was not. I could not imagine Papa failing to tell Mr and Mrs Wroxham that on no account must the children be allowed to wander into the woods.

"No," I said.

"Aren't you afraid?" he asked, slyly.

"No," I said.

"Perhaps I shall tell Uncle Felton," he said. "You've already had one whipping today."

I stopped.

I turned to look at him.

"Are *you* afraid?" I asked him.

He laughed, pushing his blonde hair out of his eyes. "I'm not afraid of going anywhere you go," he said.

I jumped the brook and hurried across the field. I didn't show him where to step, but he came close behind me. At one point I fancied I heard someone call my name and I looked back. I could see two tiny figures standing by the swing under the big yew tree in our garden. Harriet and Richard. I hoped no one else had seen us.

Once we were under the trees, I followed the main path until I came to the place where you have to step off. As I did so, he caught hold of my hair and pulled it sharply. I stopped and turned my head a little. My heart was pounding.

"Where are we going, Cousin Charlotte?" he asked. There was something cruel and hard in his voice. "If you try and lose me, I shall be very angry with you."

"I want to show you something," I said – which was true.

"What?" he said. I understood the hard note in his voice now. It was fear. Not a lot, just a tiny bit. But I do not think Cousin John was used to feeling fear.

"It's a secret," I said. "But, you must know about it, if you're to be master here one day." All of that was true, too.

He let go of my hair.

"Very well then," he said. "Show me." I gave him my very sweetest smile.

The further along the dark path we went, the quieter the woods became. Then we heard the gurgle of water. The ground began to get very mossy, and then we came to the edge of the stream. This is not the same as the bright brook from which I catch tadpoles where it tumbles out in the sun. It is a different watercourse entirely.

"Where is this?" asked John. His voice was hushed, like the air around us.

"Jennie's Corner," I said. "See where the stream makes a pool?" I pointed. He followed my finger to the hollow of dark water. A mossy log lay half submerged, and a few leaves floated upon the surface. But it was mirror-still. He looked at me and frowned.

"This is the secret of Felmere Woods," I explained. "In that pool lives Jennie Greenteeth. Any children that live here must come and bring her gifts and say their rhyme, unless they want her to eat them."

At this, John laughed out loud.

"I didn't think you such a baby as that, Cousin Charlotte," he said contemptuously.

But he was watching the water. I shrugged.

"It doesn't matter what you think," I said.

"Go on, then," he said, smirking. He put his hands in his pockets and leaned against a tree. "Say your rhyme."

I looked at him, then I looked at the water. There were no ripples. Harriet and Emily and I had been here not so long ago, after all.

"Pretty Jennie Greenteeth, underneath the water," I called loudly. "Sweet Jennie Greenteeth, I'm the Master's daughter."

"I can't say that," objected John. I frowned him silent.

"Gentle Jennie Greenteeth, I'll give treasures to thee," I chanted, "if you'll spare me, Jennie Greenteeth. Don't take me!"

John laughed.

There was a soft splash from somewhere close by.

John straightened up and took his hands from his pockets.

"What rhyme must I say?" he said, trying to sound disdainful. But I could see his eyes darting about.

"Well," I said, pretending to think. I stepped towards the water. "How about...Pretty Jennie Greenteeth –"

"Is she pretty?" he asked. I frowned at him again.

"I'll wager she's hideous," he said.

"Say it after me," I said. I stepped onto the mossy log.

"Pretty Jennie Greenteeth, down in the water dark," I said. John said it after me and took a few steps towards the edge of the water.

"One day I'll be master, up at Felmere Park," I said.

As he repeated the line, his foot kicked something and he looked down. I looked down too. A long, slender bone with knobbled, chewed-upon ends lay at his feet.

"Gentle Jennie Greenteeth," I said, "I'll give treasures to thee, if you'll spare me, Jennie Greenteeth. Don't take me!"

He said the last line, but I was glad to hear his voice quaver as he said it.

"Now what?" he asked.

"You must give her a treasure," I said.

"But you didn't!" he pointed out.

I took a few steps backwards upon the log and pulled my hand from my pocket. I held it up where he could see.

He frowned at first, then his brow darkened. "You stole that!" he said angrily.

From the corner of my eye I saw a little ripple begin, over at the far edge of the pool. I began to mutter my new rhyme. My other new rhyme.

Pretty Jennie Greenteeth, underneath the water...

"Give it back!" he demanded. I held my arm out straight, the horrible brooch between my thumb and finger. He came right to the edge. But I was far enough along the log now that he could not reach me.

Sweet Jennie Greenteeth, I'm the Master's daughter...

"Charlotte!" he said.

The ripples were moving faster.

I think perhaps he saw them at the same time he realised I really meant it about the brooch.

Gentle Jennie Greenteeth, I'll give you diamonds and gold...

He looked at me, then he looked at the ripples, then he looked at the brooch.

If you'll take him, Jennie Greenteeth, and drown him 'til he's cold!

He lunged. I dropped it.

The water erupted around me in a green and white fountain. I am not ashamed to say I screamed and ran.

I have no clear memory of what happened.

That is what I tell them, no matter how many times they ask me. I have told them I wanted to show John an old game we three played and he slipped.

Neither Harriet nor Emily have asked me any questions.

Mrs Wroxham near went mad with grief, and that was *before* they found him. After that, Papa had to call in the doctor. I know about what they found. It was wicked to listen, and I know I was supposed to be resting in bed like Emily, but I have determined that little girls are most likely never to find out anything interesting unless they eavesdrop. So I know that when they found him, he was still wearing his clothes, but all the flesh had been eaten from his bones.

I will admit I do feel sick when I think about that.

And I have since dreamed, several times, that I am there by the pool and the bones in the undergrowth cry out and talk to me. I do not like those dreams.

But then I remember the butterfly, and how he said Emmie cried quietly.

And I am not sorry at all.

Where Summer Ends

Colette Aburime

Whenever Farah pressed her toes to the earth, she fancied that hers were the only ones to have ever touched the land. Grass that twined through her toes felt new with every step, the glide of soles across soil a wonderment that made her heart break pattern. With her gaze on the forest, Farah twisted her hands into her dress, a sun-spotted speck in eyelet white. Under the trees, she could spread her petals like the hesitant bud she'd become, only bold enough to flower in the shadows.

The forest ran deep, flaky beech tree trunks mingling in close-knit packs. Breezes seasoned the air, and as the draft picked up, brittle gusts disrobed the branches of their honey red skins. The scent of dry earth curled over the grass and Farah perched on her toes, counted the seconds before she could wait no longer and had to part her mouth to swallow the spiced air.

It took three.

When that wind pressed cool hands to her cheeks, arms and legs, Farah forcefully stiffened against the cold. She couldn't tremble when Mother watched from the porch.

After the incident, Mom always watched. She was the fly on the wall, too high to swat. The itch at Farah's shoulders that, in all her newly discovered flexibility, she couldn't reach.

Mother and daughter lived in a thumbnail-sized home in the palm of Golden Dells, Illinois. The house was planted among grasslands, valleys scooped out in all directions with bumpy peaks sprawling between dives. Farah was glad to have hills for neighbors, glad to have left the city; you never notice how loud it is until you're flooded in silence.

"You should come inside," Mom called. Her voice was a scratch that frayed the threads of Farah's nerves. "The cider's ready. Sharp and sweet, just how you like it. We'll heat some for breakfast, warm you right up."

"I'm not cold."

Mom didn't know the chill was not the kind to make one sneeze and sniff. This chill could heal, licked at one's wound and sealed up the skin. A *tsk tsk* sound merged with the wind, and Farah couldn't tell if it was rustling leaves or Mom flicking her teeth with her tongue. Deciding it was her mother's disapproving hum, a warm burble of irritation rivaled Farah's healing cold.

She didn't turn around, but knew Mom's expression. Her forehead, dimpled between the eyes as she stroked her pale hair, milk across narrow collarbones. The gaze scorching coals prodding Farah's back, burning invisibly at her skin. Treetops anxiously swayed, shedding more auburn skin. Farah tightened with anticipation. *Coming,* she assured, swaying with them. She lifted her feet toward the golden-drenched forest, just steps away.

"Don't go."

Slow as the long hand ticks, Farah curved to face her protestor. Mom hovered at the edge of the porch. Picking at the railing, her fingernails shed slivers of white paint across the grass.

"It's been too many weeks, now. It's time you attended classes."

Farah's feet flattened to the earth. She should've known that's all she'd have to say. Should've never turned around.

"But I do—"

"All of your classes." Mom's finger lifted. "Every day. And without these period-long bathroom breaks I keep hearing about."

So she couldn't trust them at this school, either. Only talking when they shouldn't, never when they should.

"One can't help nature."

Mom stared at Farah from that dark-eyed abyss of heat. "Don't you want to make friends?"

Farah shrugged.

"Well, what about the open dress code," she tried again. "Must be nice not having a uniform anymore. All that white and gold was tiring... and tacky."

The words were meant to tempt a smile. Farah was not tempted. Mom's loathing of the Pride Lake Academy uniforms was a relapsing tease since Farah began her freshmen year. A year ago she might've laughed. A year ago she'd done a lot of things. Mute, Farah's body angled towards the forest. Mom rocked her slight form against the house's faded wound-red door. It creaked against the weight.

"I never liked those woods," she said. "It's strange that you'd rather spend all day in there instead of building new bonds... you had so many friends… And talking. Remember when we used to do that?"

Farah's toes clutched the crusted dirt, blood thickening, throbbing.

"There's nothing to talk about."

The porch whined as her mother padded down the steps, scraping through trembling blades of grass until she stood right at Farah's neck. Both averaged the same height, and next to her, Farah looked like the less fortunate friend. Skin, always fawn, had burnt and freckled under the summer sun. Even at the cusp of autumn, an uneven tan clung to her skin like burrs. So unlike the smooth ochre of her mother, which the sun had richened to a blessing. Their eyes shared no likeness either, the daughter's cooled ash to a mother's hot coals, a clear night in contrast to downcast skies.

Mom clasped Farah's shoulder, easing her around.

"There's a lot to talk about, Farah. You can't run away forever, doing who knows what in that forest."

"I'm dancing." She bit down hard on the words. "Just like you taught me. Please point to my sin."

Mom's stare softened, but she shook her head, jaw tensed.

"And I'm fine with that, but there's space in the parlor to dance. It's where I practiced as a child. Staying out in that forest day and night, now, that's not safe. Do you think I'm asleep when you tiptoe past me well after midnight?"

Farah did not think that. After plucking the day's hours away under the trees, only drawn in for meals and to wash, she'd slide into the house through the front room, her only option with no other entrances to their creaky hand-me-down home. And every night Mom was laid out on the couch, blanketed like a burrito, perched eyelids milky slits catching the moonlight. But it was the breathing that poured a light on her faux sleep.

Widened nostrils, breath held and released on a circle of air. The dancer's breath.

"Teach me," Farah uttered. It was a conversation they'd had countless times. Hardly even a compromise, home school. Mom worked from her laptop anyway, and Farah would show for her classes. Maybe. Mostly.

Just agree.

Mom's hand embraced her shoulder and Farah bristled, knew she would not. "I'd love that, Farah, but you know they won't allow it. And it's for good reason. Isolation is not the key. It's self-punishment. Containment." Her mother waved the hand not confining Farah at the trees. "There's no health in that."

Farah curled her toes through the dirt, balled her fists into her dress. Her mother was nothing more than a state-funded mouthpiece, spewing all she'd read from the books the county tossed them, and nonsense she'd ingested from lawyers and shrinks. Farah warned her about listening to them. These people had no cures, just invoices. What did they know of health?

"Farah."

She stared at the tip of her mother's nose.

"We need to face what—" Mother stopped, cleared her throat. "He did. What they all did."

Farah was a twig, stiff and straight. "Don't," she whispered like a warning.

Her mother sighed as the wind groaned, tossing hair over both their faces. Mother milled the cream curtain that sheeted her lips and eyelids but Farah yanked hers and twisted, plucking hard enough to uproot. She let a sheet of strands fall to the wind.

Shoulders lurching in as a breath staggered out. Dragging in peppered air and strength.

"You're safe."

Farah eased back, stepping near freedom until her mother followed. Then her feet and fists were grounded ice and weight.

"You're hurt."

Shut up! Farah wished to scream, but held back by clutching her dress tighter. A shiver rocked her elbows. These words drained, stole her inner heat and exposed the wrong-cold to her body.

"Show me where." Mother had moved before her, blocked the forest, placed both hands on Farah's shoulders.

"Show me where it hurts, and we'll do all we can to mend it." Farah looked beyond her.

"I'm leaving."

Mother tightened her grip. Cloud soft finger pads with a brace of claws. The trembling began.

"No, you're not. Come inside. We'll drink cider and we'll talk. About those kids, about that ma—"

Farah spat on her mother's shoes. Open-toe sandals. Only gleamed down to make sure she had hit no grass. Did no dishonor to the earth. The rush of wind and blood through the ears buried Mother's shrill cry of rage or disgust or surprise. Then slowly, her head rose from feet to Farah, mouth and eyes full as the moon.

"All these years, you were blind." Farah's voice rose over the wind's bluster, whipping, excitable as her leaping chest. "Foolish you'd think I'd let you see now."

Mom held fast to Farah's shoulders, still no words to say. Only silence cracked from her tight lips, a stark bleak stare from new moon eyes. But then she did talk, a grating whisper against open sores.

"Why didn't you tell me?"

New heat rose in Farah's core, coiled to a tight ball. Nostrils flared, fabric twisted thin. Mom was nothing like the forest. Mom was nothing like the wind.

"Stupid!"

Mother jerked, the claws released her, and Farah ran.

Ran until the forest swept her up and shut its mouth behind her. Ran so hard her chest burned, throat whined for mercy. Ran to forget Mother and Man and only halted when she was in deep and those judging, blackened eyes could not reach. Still the words chased her, knocking at her heels with every stride.

"Why didn't you…" Why didn't I.

Wind poured into Farah's jaw between gasps. "Stupid!"

Bending hands to knees, Farah fought to regain her breath, eyes clutched shut to the thoughts that tried to slide into her mind. *Be gone, you. You're no memory, you're a lie. It never happened. They never happened. He never - stop.*

Air. Forest. This.

She knew only the grass's grip on her toes, the tree's breath against her hair.

Apply your salve. Don't tear the scar tissue. All is healed. After several dancer's breaths and planting her core into the present, Farah became free again, thoughts of an unreal reality dispelled.

"Forest," she slipped to her knees. "Needed you."

The forest greeted her with all its voices. Squirrels and coons and chipmunks prattling and gathering, the red-dipped Waxwings and stainglassed Blue Jay hiss and whine. Farah smirked up at the infinite ring of treetops, knowing they smiled back, though remained unseen. The critters lay low in the mornings, shy and shaking off slumber. Still animated tongues spoke of where they'd run and fly and hunt this impending day, an accented chatter she could almost understand. It was talk she could enjoy.

Farah hardly let her heart steady as she climbed on pounding feet and began her stretch. One hand framed a tree as she pointed her foot, curling the leg to the base of her thigh and drawing it out, bow straight. Farah eased into several more positions, the spandex beneath her dress clenching across her ribcage with each elongated body part. She inhaled the mild air and stretched until her limbs felt loose and fire-dipped.

"I'm going to start," she breathed, chin to the trees. Jays and Waxwings stay veiled, though their fluttering calls pierced the forest, whispering *one, two, go* in instrumental as constant as the wind. Farah arched into a curtsy, fingertips settled on her hips. The music was set. Time to dance.

Her arms waved like oceans as each foot pointed with tight precision. She performed with the lessons learned from her Mother, center stage in mind. It was unavoidable, thoughts of her being so entwined to the instruction, so Farah reached into her mind and scrubbed at the image till she blurred like a washed stain. More of a teacher. Less of a mother.

"Place even weight on all toes."

Farah did, imagining a familiarly unfamiliar woman pacing before her in the Chicago apartment. Her head bobbed with Farah's plunging movements.

"Sink between moves like a spoon into soup, we're not chopping onions, we're stirring hearts…"

They used to chop onions. Lots of them. And tomatoes and chilies and fresh jalapeños. The vibrant scents would expand over their yellowed unit, a pleasing burn to the nose and, when consumed, the lips and tongue.

Mom had kept a plot in the Pride Lake community garden and simply transported the plants upon moving to their Golden Dells home, once Mom and Abuelita's, now Farah and Mom's. As far as memories stretched, Farah recalled cooking Abuelita's salsa picante all through the late summers, every summer, even after her nana died.

There had been no salsa this summer.

The peppers sat in the garden. Long overdue for picking where they remained beside the porch. Cracked, sunburned, and edging rot. Still the scents wafted and incensed the yard, their decayed breaths fragrant in death.

Farah expanded her lungs and inhaled deep. The spice of the garden never reached her here. No matter how close she remained to the yard, the thick beeches shunned it out. Farah jerked a fist through her hair. She'd slowed in her dance but spun, awakening her focus as the wind flapped like wings at her ears. Enough of rotten peppers and mothers.

Air. Forest. This.

Like a lost bit of lace, Farah's dress floated about her legs and followed her twisting form through its travels. The birds shook through the trees, bathing leaves down from the sky in star-shaped streams. Farah raised her chin to meet the fall, awe drawn on her face, her breath a pounding drum. A creature broke from the bushes and leapt forward, fat, brown and glinting gold where it paused under a patch of light. It cradled an acorn under its chin, chuckled and nibbled. Black eyes gleamed at Farah.

"Better hold onto that," Farah teased as she pranced towards the creature, to which it squeaked and bounced through the trees. Farah giggled along as it led the way. The squirrel brought her to the place where tree fragments sheathed the ground, and she dived right into it. The twigs broke the skin of her soles and flayed her calloused flesh like a knife shedding butter. Stinging sensations hit her, sharp as undiluted wine as her blood painted the ashen branches with ruddy rust. With moisture in her eyes, Farah still danced, letting the spiked bits dig deeper into her soles. The squirrel was long gone.

"I'm healthy," she reminded the image under her eyelids, then twirled so hard her dress hem whipped her cheeks.

It was what she did until the white morning bled into flushed afternoon. Whirling, swirling, never breaking form. Farah didn't need people to talk to within this new town. Dance replaced friends, and conversation became a song that she sung with her body.

Farah had just completed a pirouette when she slammed to her knees, coughing as she stumbled to the ground. Her lungs pruned from fatigue and she lied there on fallen leaves, chest rising and falling. Swishing her arms across the foliage, she gathered them so they coated her head in a gold mane. The trees stretched up around her reminded Farah of childhood when her nose only leveled to adult kneecaps.

After her breathing relatively softened, Farah rose on untrusted legs. She dragged herself across the mossy floor and beyond the muddy creek until she reached the forest's heart. The apple tree waited. Its wide branches extended like an uncle's outstretched arms, welcoming; always too welcoming. Approaching with tripping steps, she plucked off a fat apple. She turned the fruit in her hands from under the blade of light she stood beneath. It gleamed like blood. Farah thought its beauty deserved another human eye.

She shunned a stray thought of Mother with a bite, the taste of tart juices sinking into her tongue. After the fruit settled into her belly, Farah swirled about the moss to test her strength. Still tripping and wobbling, she munched another apple, still weak. At the third try of strength, she was determined to keep dancing, pinwheeled in a circle. During the twirl, her knees flexed and she stumbled into the slushy brown pile. The wind carried a high pitched giggle, a squirrel's chuckle, coming from the apple tree.

"Ha ha," Farah said, smearing her mud-dampened hands on her dress. She scanned the tree for the hidden beast that mocked her, couldn't find it. "But you shouldn't laugh at me. You're nuts too."

Another giggle cut through the wind. Rougher this time. Farah's sensitivity sharpened to a fine needlepoint. Squirrels did not laugh like that. Wavering to her feet, Farah backed away from the apple tree. Movement echoed above her, crackling, like a foot over leaves. With each of Farah's backing steps, the crunches mirrored the pattern. Her foot connected to a log and she tripped back, plopping to the ground in a tangle of scraped and stinging limbs. A barking laugh called out. The branches trembled from the tree, apples plunging to the ground. Farah blinked, and it appeared, a face within the tree.

Monster.

That was the first thought. But as she stared harder, a different word slipped to mind. Angel. The androgynous face had deep, yawning cheekbones. Pupils shone like bits of silver glass and hair descended around the face, the rich honey of cider. The angel descended from the tree on a drift of wind, not falling but not quite floating, landing on its feet.

"Dance requires more strength than that." The angel had a shadowy voice, like smoke and fires, and wore a dress white as Farah's once was, before dirt and water smeared it. Farah folded her hands over her filthy lap and rose.

"I only tripped, that's all." She spoke slowly so her voice would not shake. One did not fear angels. "I could dance forever."

"Is that so?" The angel's smile could rob one's breath. "Let's touch on it."

It held out a hand, palm upwards. The skin bore no marks or blemish, not even at the creases of its fingers. Farah placed her own fingers to it, grimacing with waves of embarrassment from her muddied hands. She'd touched Angel's skin only for a second before it took it back.

"I'll prove you can't." The Angel winked one foggy gray eye, smirked, and darted away.

Farah spun on her feet and followed, hurtling where Angel had fled. Each step was a spin, toes pointed, legs straight. She followed the laughter like a trail of smoke, blood pumping in her veins. Once she thought she'd caught a whiff of simmering salsa, but it was gone before she could take another breath.

The dance and chase drew so long that the golden streaks of day pulled away, coloring the sky from a flush to a bruise. Heat, stored in her bones, seeped out with each stumbling spin. Tree branches grew fingernails that caught and scratched her skin. Then that giggle Farah stretched and gasped to follow cut off with a snap, and there was nothing but the crickets strum.

Farah grew confused, but kept at the dance. Good riddance to that — the snicker resounded suddenly, streaming from further trees.

"Testing me," she breathed out, hardly able to draw the words from her chest. Her body begged for pause and she bared tight teeth, refused to be weak as she thrust from the ground in a leap, airborne for several moments, longer than she thought possible. Cold breath gripped her arms, cloaking her shoulders, and she remembered all was possible when the wind carried you, spun you. Farah parted her lips and drank its strength like arid elixir. It hit her brain like a drink.

Then he was there and everything stopped. Her dance, her heart. Farah broke form for the first time since she'd lifted her foot in dance, stumbled and shook like on a plank in a storming ocean. He wore his white suit. So stark and bright while skin and hair sank in the dark. The nametag gleamed gold while Farah shrank pale and yellow.

How did he… why isn't he…

He took one step and she dropped. Soup at her knees, exhaustion and fear paralyzing venom in her blood. She cracked her mouth to scream but the wind gusted and brawled, stuffed long tendrils in her mouth, further and deeper till she gagged on its fingers. He watched with a grin, said words her brain received like static, took another step as Farah curled into herself, dress so muddy that even under the moonlight it remained a dull matte. The girl mumbled pleas to the dirt, her good dirt, begging it to pull her into its shadows and swallow her. The ground shifted beneath her calves and Farah sucked air in hope, but then a yellow stick of light flashed and fell down on her, smacked and burned her thigh with the feel of a thousand ants across flesh. And it didn't stop. It never stopped.

She cried out again but the wind drank her voice. She screeched louder, harder, gurgling the cold fire liquor in her throat. Her screams melted into whispers.

"A-Angel."

He mocked the words on his own lips.

Angel, angel, my pretty angel. Fallen angel. Quiet, angel.

"Mama!"

His shoulders leapt like startled hills, his shadowed head whipped to the dark, then he was gone.

He was gone.

Farah lay iced in shock. Wind pressed against her spine, holding her down between cold breath and hot earth. Her throat's hack and wheeze was every sound. The black forest did not crease or snore.

After what felt like passing centuries, Farah lifted her neck the pinch she could muster, noticed a pond spread out by her feet. The surface rippled and she saw it, Angel reflected in the pond. Just as Farah, Angel slumped on its side. Hiding like her, tired like her.

Both chests heaved heavily, and Angel's dress, once white, mirrored Farah's in filth. Farah twitched her lips up in a smiling effort. Angel returned the smile, triumph on a sunken face.

"You win," Farah said. Everything shook, voice and body.

Angel caressed her head, combing out the straggling bits of hair that remained.

Her hair was crisp and brown with patches of naked skull peering through.

"No one should dance forever," she whispered, and the shadowy voice bounced off the trees like intercom speakers.

Footsteps echoed overhead, stabbing the air. Farah couldn't understand them, and she glanced at Angel's face. The mouth gaped, looked to warn her. Farah's belly churched in panic. *He's back.* A form blocked her view. Legs clothed in dark fabric.

Deep male voices, muffled, squeezed into Farah's understanding slow as a stubborn tube of toothpaste.

Good thing she called for one final sweep.

Not a happy reunion.

What's she holding?

A goddamn rotten apple. Been eatin' it too.

Is it even alive?

She, Jones. It's a girl.

With a head too heavy for her shoulders, Farah was stuck gaping at the black kneecaps that shuffled around her, circled her. She trembled when light cracked over her face and flooded her sight.

Damn. Why'd she pull out her hair like that, Geo?

Five days is a long time to be lost.

A man's face entered her view, mouth set. "Farah? I'm Officer Geoffrey. Can you get up?"

Farah could make no sound or movement, and the officer lifted her as if she were just extra air to his arms. She burbled out a cry, sent movement commands to her limbs. They didn't listen. Her eyes were the only part strong enough to move and she sought out the pond that reflected Angel, only the officer's frame blocked it. Another male spoke into a crackling radio then called out to Officer Geoffrey, who shifted on his heel. Farah had no trust for these men in uniform. The past and present proved they were nothing.

Forever too little and always too late. Her exposed body burned. Her bones quivered in thin skin.

The movement unveiled Angel once more, and both their faces fell, meeting each other's gaze. Angel caught in some other officer's arms. From the higher distance, Farah could see more of Angel. Cuts spanned its body in deep successions, like the being had caught its arms, legs, and face on every branch in the forest.

We've called the mother, Geo. She's prepared. Let's bring her back now. Farah twitched, an effort to leap from the officer's arms, but she only had strength to blink, blinks that synchronized with Angel's. Then Angel's image crinkled and folded. Farah shuffled her lips together, called, *"Don't take her."*

Something chuckled, a squirrel skipped across the puddle, and just like that, Angel was gone.

We Have Always Lived in the Subdivision

Karen Munro

We were the first family in Cypress Villa. We bought the biggest lot, at the top of the subdivision where the farmhouse used to be. A big new house where a big old house once stood. A grab at the eternal, Father says. People like to pretend that things don't change.

Our neighbors are accountants and nurses and e-commerce managers. Their houses are smaller than ours, without the extra rooms and passageways and other little details that Father paid a fortune to have the builders add. They live in simple, normal houses sitting on solid ground.

On the street outside our house is an old walnut tree, a hundred feet tall. It was alive when we moved in, but now it's dead. Father said the bulldozers compacted its roots. Damien says it pined to death. A walnut pining – that's his idea of a joke.

It dropped its last walnuts the year we moved in. I gathered some and put them in the pink lunchbox that I ordered from one of Alda's catalogs. They stained everything – the box, my hands, my dress – with sticky sap, like tree tears. One last year of nuts, then it lost its leaves that fall and made no new ones in the spring.

We don't like to be crowded. We keep the front gate locked and we keep Damien in his room. This is our home, at least for now. Some of us don't go out at all, and never will again. I try to be careful, I try to stay out of trouble. I've made enough trouble, Father says. When I make a mistake, he looks at me with a certain expression – like a trickle of cold water down my arms. But he still lets me out.

I go at dusk, with the key to the front gate in my pocket. I'm not old enough to drive, so I walk. I walk down Cypress Court to Cypress Lane, and turn on Magnolia or Peach or Willow. Every little street loops back and rejoins the main way. You can walk all night if you want, on streets named after the trees they cut down to build the streets. Damien finds that funny.

I walk slowly, breathing the cool dew and the faint tang of cars on the freeway to the south. I glance in people's windows, at their dried floral arrangements, their carefully displayed pottery and their large-screen TVs. I can see a great deal from the sidewalk. I can see perfectly well at night.

Sometimes I stand on the street corners to listen. In their kitchens, on their telephones, in their showers, in their beds, they talk. The little details of their lives are like flowers that only bloom for a day. Swim meets and grocery lists and veterinarians' bills. Stories heard on the radio, debates over television shows. I drift closer, listening.

If I were Damien I would bedevil these houses horribly. If I were Sven I could amuse myself, telling people what to think and see and hear. If I were Father I would know every thought that passed through every mind, and none of them would interest me.

Because I'm me I only watch, and listen, and wish I knew why this absorbs me. I wish I knew what draws me across those nighttime lawns. While the zotting bats stop short in the air above me. While the family dog backs shivering to the end of its chain.

"I need a body," Damien says, leaning with ponderous drama against his easel, his arms draped around his canvas as if it were a lover. "A naked body with big floppy tits and a gut. I need *substance*."

"Tell Alda," says Sven, flipping a page. "Maybe she can order one."

Damien nuzzles his canvas. "I can't even remember what the real thing looks like anymore."

I say nothing. Damien stands at arm's length from his painting, holding its edges in both hands. The front of his shirt is smeared with dark reds and browns from having just embraced it. "This is shit," he says, and tips it off the easel.

Sven shrugs and goes back to the catalog he's reading. It's one of Alda's — the house is slippery with them. Their pages are windows to a thousand different worlds. Sad, plastic world of home medical supplies, chipper world of novelty socks, serene and moneyed world of sailboats. We all flip through them, except for Father. In certain moods I find them comforting. In others they madden me. Sven scolds me for throwing them in the trash — they have to be recycled, he says.

Damien sighs. "Shit," he says, paging through a sheaf of old drawings. "Shit. Shit." All of Damien's drawings are the same — squiggly pencil outlines of naked bodies, haphazard and out of proportion. It's true he has to work from memory, which isn't easy. But this is the compromise Father offered. Damien's real art isn't made with pencil and paper. It's messier and more fatal, and Father forbade it a long time ago. It wasn't possible anymore, not in a world with Internet and satellites and cell phones and millions of people shuttling around on freeways. I'm not sorry he had to give it up. I'm glad, actually. But I don't say it.

Instead I say, "I like this one," holding up a drawing of a stunted, sexless body with big hands.

"It's shit." He opens a folder and lets all the drawings inside slide to the floor. "I can't work like this. I can't *live* like this."

"Then don't live," I say softly.

Damien ignores me, still sorting through his drawings. Papers flutter to the floor, smeared and crumpled. A box of pastels falls. He has a palette knife from somewhere – I didn't see him pick it up. As I watch, he buries the point in a stack of drawings and slews them across the carpet.

His eyes, I notice, have gone blank and shiny. As I watch they gain focus and lose depth until they look like false eyes, painted on the skin of his eyelids.

This is why Damien lives in the attic, in a comfortable room with all the paint and paper he can use. When Damien was made, a piece was left out. Most of the time you'd never know it – he spins along charmingly enough, like one of those little windmills where the man chops wood. But every so often, when you're most comfortable and least prepared, your gaze wanders and you notice the little man has no head. He doesn't mind; he just keeps chopping and chopping, as long as the wind blows him.

"Sven," I say. He glances up, then stands. The room feels different with Sven standing.

"Come on, Nina," he says.

I slide off my chair. There's still a drawing in my hand, so I bend down and place it on the carpet.

"We'll be back when you're feeling better," Sven says. He is unfailingly polite.

"All right," Damien says, distracted.

"The door will be locked," Sven says. "When you feel better, you'll put a note beneath."

Damien says nothing. I go out into the hallway, and not until Sven has turned the deadbolts do I feel completely safe.

Damien's room is a nest in the attic, a cuckoo's patch in the leafless black limbs of the walnut tree. Alda's room, deep in the heart of the house, makes me think of an underwater grotto. It's dim and shadowed. Lazy currents of dust pass through the yellow circle of light beneath her desk lamp. Shelves of catalogs loom in the darkness like the rock walls of an undersea trench. I lie on a slick pile of catalogs on top of Alda's bed, imagining the weight of several hundred feet of water on my head.

"Do you think Father would let me take swimming lessons?" I ask, fingering the catalog beside my ear. It's an old one; I can tell from the dryness of the paper. She's been getting them for at least fifty years, and Sven never manages to recycle them all.

"Oh, I doubt that, dear." If the room is an underwater cavern, Alda herself is an old conger eel, bloated and worn as an overfilled inner tube, swaying gently in an invisible current. She sits at her desk, under the yellow lamp light. "Why do you ask?"

"No reason." On the corner of Ash and Linden, I listened to a girl no older than myself tell her father about learning to kickboard. They didn't teach swimming in my day. It wasn't something you did, unless you fell in a river and then it was even odds you sank.

There's the faintest whisper of a sound – Alda licking her big thumb and turning the page. "We're in the middle of the country. Nobody swims here."

"You don't know what people do." My tone is sharper than I intended. "I'm just thinking, that's all."

"Not about doing anything naughty, I hope."

I was out last night walking, she knows. And Alda is one of the oldest of us. She was done with the world a long time ago, she doesn't understand why I still go out at all. I should go to my own room, but when I'm alone I lie awake hearing people's conversations over again. The most ordinary little things – like kickboarding – wear grooves in me.

"How long do you think we're going to stay here?" I ask. Alda sighs. She puts her catalog aside and looks at me with her chin propped on her fist. The flesh of her cheeks is soft and heavy, and her knuckles sink into her skin.

"What's on your mind, Nina?"

I look back at my hands, folded on my belly. I have small pale hands, smooth and unlined. "I just wonder how long we'll be here."

"Until we have to move, child."

"I know." I pull a catalog out from under my shoulder and consider its cover. Homey, rustic world of wicker furniture.

"You're young," Alda says. "Things will look different when you get older." With one big hand, she turns another page.

I lift a page of the catalog and test it against my fingertip. After a couple of tries, I manage to make a paper cut. Blood stings out, then stops. I wipe it on the glossy paper.

"But all this stuff," I say. "All these things people buy, and do. Don't you wish you could actually do them, instead of just looking at them?"

There's a long silence. When I look over, Alda is sitting with a page half-turned, her expression abstracted, her small eyes fixed on something far away.

"No," she says at last, with a quick little shudder as if cold water has run down her arms.

"You're going out," Sven observes from the foot of the stairs, one foot lifted to start up, a tray for Damien balanced in his hands. A tea towel placed discreetly overtop.

"For a walk," I say.

Sven is diplomatic – he doesn't remind me of the rules. He only nods and goes up.

The rest of the house is so quiet that you would think it was empty. The little creaks and shifting sounds from the cellar notwithstanding. I close the front door and lock all of the locks.

Outside, the night air brushes my face as if it were glad to see me. I feel a spark of something that's close to happiness. The world – or at least the subdivision – is laid open before me. For this, even this small pleasure, I will always be alive.

At the foot of the path I turn to lock the gate, and look up at Damien's window. I wonder sometimes how long it will be before Father decides that I need my own cell. I know there are spares. They're probably already furnished, from Alda's catalogs.

I'm not precisely a danger, not like Damien. Even before Father found him, Damien lived half-submerged in some blood-red river in his own head. Father didn't make him that way. No more than he made me in love with this quiet subdivision, these tame and trusting dollhouses. I don't itch to open people up the way Damien does, but I long for them just the same. For their silliness, their fleetingness. Their company. And that is dangerous in its own way.

Maybe I'm missing a part, the same as Damien. Maybe that's what keeps me listening on street corners and peering through windows at people I will never know. It's what makes me do naughty things, as Alda would say. And like Damien, I can't stop myself.

I walk down to Cypress Villa Court, following the breeze on my face.

It's a quiet night – a Thursday. Thursday night means family people are tired. It means frozen pizzas and movies on TV. The dogs of Cypress Villa go unwalked on Thursday night, and the conversations are slow.

I was born after midnight, in the back room of a saloon filled with dirty men drunk on lager and whisky. I didn't see a house made of brick until I was already done for. Four bedrooms, two baths, a two-car garage, a golden courtesy of light leading from the sidewalk to the doorstep – these houses would have been like palaces to me, once upon a time.

I walk a familiar path, up Linden and down Yew. I finished up at nine, although I look younger compared to today's monstrous children. It could have been worse, I know. I could have come to a full stop. Like so many before and since. Instead I've been allowed to carry on, to linger like a tree that no longer bears leaves or fruit, a useless witness to the seasons.

A man stands on the front lawn of a house across the street. He has both his hands on top of his head, as if he's trying to hold onto his hat against a wind.

When I see him, I feel something like a cool shadow pass over me. Father's disapproval. I should turn and walk away. I stop where I am. If the man ignores me, I'll walk away.

He turns and sees me. "Are you a cuvvy?" he says. I don't understand that last word. I could still walk away, but it's my undoing – I don't understand what he's said to me. I step forward.

He's old, but age has curled him almost as small as me. He wears a light zippered jacket and a pair of checked wool trousers, baggy at the knees. On his head, clamped beneath his veined hands, is the kind of cap that boys used to wear, light and flat, with a jaunty snap brim. His cheeks are long and hollow. His knuckles are swollen.

I've never seen him before.

"I'm out for a walk," he says. He clears his throat and spits into the grass beside him. I should turn away.

"They moved the barn," he says.

"Yes," I say. I take a step forward, then another. Father's disapproval is at my back, behind my shoulder. I can ignore it, just a little.

The man rubs a hand along his cheek, producing a rasp of stubble. "Where's the cuvvy house gone?"

I step onto the lawn. My shoes sink into the grass as if into quicksand. Covey, he's saying. The farm house that was here, it belonged to a family named Covey. Sven told me once, on his way to Father's study, his arms filled with old yellow files.

"The Covey house," I tell the old man. "It's up at the top. All the streets lead there."

He gives me a furtive glance, and it all comes clear to me. He's someone's escaped memory patient. Someone's visiting father or grandfather, who shouldn't be let out alone.

I step into his musty cabinet smell. If I were Sven I would give him something to see when he looks at me. Not a pallid girl child, but a lush black-haired woman. Red lips, a welcoming smile. A grown body. Comfort and understanding.

He squints at me. A pallid girl child is what I am.

"It's too hard to tell you," I say, slipping my small, cold hand into his. "Let me take you there."

I'm careful to close the door behind us with only the smallest of clicks. The front hall is dim and the long red carpet, patterned with blue vines, muffles our footsteps. We stop at the coat rack, where Father's hat hangs on the top peg, covered in dust.

"You can leave your coat," I tell the old man. "Your hat too, if you want."

He makes no move to take off either his dirty old coat or his hat. He coughs, then looks for somewhere to spit. There's nowhere but the rug, so he swallows.

"Alda has tea," I say. "I'll make you some."

The kitchen counters are covered in catalogs and mouse traps. We've had mice ever since the weather got cold, and sometimes I hear the traps snap closed a dozen times in a night. I clear a chair and the old man sits, rubbing his hands down his thighs.

While the water heats I look in the refrigerator, careful to hold the door so he can't see what's inside. Sven's had a recent craving for bread cut thick and spread with butter, which seems like the kind of thing to offer a guest, but there's no sign of it now. I close the refrigerator. Sven's in the darkened doorway behind the old man, staring at me.

"They moved the barn," the old man says again. "No. It burned down."

"Probably." I watch from the corner of my eye as Sven fades back out of sight. "Before they built the subdivision."

"Of course," the old man says. "I used to live here. Oh, sixty years ago."

"How old are you?" I ask.

"I lived in town. This was all farmland." He looks over his shoulder, as if he might see through the walls and doors and time itself, all the way out to a small town long gone now, withered and razed like old corn. "This is the Covey farm. They've got all the land from here to— " He pauses, his hand hanging at arm's length, then dropping. He turns back to the table and strokes the cover of a catalog.

I bring him tea. He takes off his hat and lays it on the table. I can see where the blood flows across his skull, beneath the mottled skin.

I ask him again how old he is, if he has children, what work he did, but he seems to have forgotten how to talk. When the tea is gone he drags his hat off the table and settles it back on his head. He scrapes his chair back and stands.

"I have to go to the post office," he says. He takes a quarter from his pocket and leaves it on the table. Then he goes through the darkened doorway where Sven stood.

I hear his footsteps go into the short hallway, hesitant in the darkness. There's a pause. Then a metallic rattle. I hear his lungs make their deep, catarrhic rasp.

When I click on the light, I find him stooping before the old brass knob on the living room door. He pulls two things from his pocket: a pair of round-framed glasses, and the kind of multi-use hand tool I've seen in Alda's catalogs. He unfolds it, grubby and tarnished, and stoops to the doorknob again.

The knob has never worked. Sven tried fixing it once from the other side. He managed to take off the brass plate and unscrew the handle. After hours of fiddling and cursing, he put it all back on again and put the leftover parts in his toolkit. We don't use that door.

The knob comes off in the old man's hand. He pockets it and bends to the open post hole. I step closer behind him.

"Can you fix it?"

He makes a small, constant grunting, like an animal.

A minute or two later there's a click inside the hole. He produces the knob from his pocket and screws it in place. When he turns it, the door opens. In the living room, Sven is sitting on the red couch.

"This is the Covey house," the old man informs him. Sven nods. "They've got a couple hundred acres from here to town. Corn, mostly. Some cows."

Sven watches the old man go to the window and start fiddling with the latch. Then a certain kind of quiet falls over the room, and I turn to see Father in the doorway.

Sven stands up and puts his hands behind his back. Father ignores him. He ignores me. He sits in one of the two armchairs in front of the bookcase. He waits until the old man turns, then holds out his hand to the other chair. The old man crosses the room and sits.

"This is the Covey house," the old man says. He's got his folding tool in his hands, opening its little blades and scraping them with his thumbnail, one by one. But his eyes are on Father.

"That's so," says Father.

The old man squints. "You're Covey, I guess."

Father smiles. "Bad rains this year."

"Don't I know it." The old man looks back down at the little blade he's scraping. "John Bourne's got fifty acres in soy, out in the valley. All flooded."

"I'll send a couple of men over to help out."

"He won't take it. He's an idiot."

Father nods. They sit for a while.

"Grant Pease has some calves he's looking to sell," the old man says. "Black-head, look pretty good to me. Not breeding stock, just slaughter."

Father nods. "I'll think about that."

Then they just sit again, saying nothing. The old man wipes his thumbnail on his trouser leg and studies his tool blades.

I start to think about leaving. As soon as I think it, Father looks at me without moving his head. I stay put.

"Well," the old man says at last. He slips the tool into his pocket and stands. "I've got to get to the post office."

"Sure," says Father. Then: "Would you do me a favor?" The old man makes a perhaps sound in his throat.

"I've got a frozen lock upstairs," Father says. "In the attic. If you wouldn't mind taking a look."

The old man squints at the ceiling.

"Charge what you think is fair," Father says.

"Two dollars," the old man says. "That's if I fix it. If I can't do it, no charge." Father smiles.

The old man goes out into the front hall. We listen to his progress. A few times there's a pause, then the rattle of a doorknob. After the last one, the footsteps pause for a long while. Then they start to mount the stairs.

Father says, "Sven, I'd like you to unlock the cellar door."

"The cellar," Sven says.

"And then I'd like you to visit the neighbors," Father says. "Nina's guest is staying in a house on the corner of Willow and Yew. I'd like to be sure that no one saw them meet."

"Not likely," Sven says. "It's almost midnight."

"Please be thorough," Father says. "Take your time."

Sven looks at me, then goes out.

"Nina," says Father. "Sit."

I sit in the other armchair. The seat is still warm from the old man's body.

I know Father won't speak first. I consider what to say. "I don't see the point," I say at last.

Above us, the ceiling creaks. Father tilts his head, his eyes on me.

"I'm not trying to hurt anybody." I study my hands, lying in my lap, until they make me angry. So small and pale and unchanging. "It's hard, going on and on like this. I don't know how to do it."

Father says nothing. This is a conversation we've had before.

"That man knew you," I say, changing tack.

"He's an old man. He's confused."

"Did you live here before? Were you Covey?"

Father shifts slightly in his chair. "We go on because we can," he says. "That's all. You know that."

I think of my walks through the subdivision, the endless looping streets. The walks I've taken in other places, on other quiet streets, and the men and women and children I've brought home. Father has been clear about this. I don't know why I can't stop doing it.

"Will we have to move again?" I ask. We don't always, if Father decides it's safe to stay.

Father looks at me for a long moment.

"We start out in a straight line," he says. "But sooner or later things curve around us. It happens to everyone. And if you have enough time, a straight line will take you all the way around the world."

I don't understand Father. I wish I did. I wish I knew how to ask the right question, the one that would make him tell me everything. How to think, how to be. How to live in the world that's available to me – jaggedy world of pencil drawings, paper world of catalogs.

How to stop wandering out into the bigger world, the normal world, the one I'm not allowed to have.

But all I can think of is myself, going on and on, around and around, in a garret like Damien's. Or maybe a little black room in the bowels of the house. I imagine Alda in a chair outside my door, flicking pages and sighing.

I feel an urge to do something I haven't done in ages: to get down and sit on the carpet, with my head against Father's knee. I haven't done it in so long that the memory is faded and crumbling, like a photograph from the year of my birth.

"You're too old for that," Father says. "And besides, the old folks are expecting you. There are some things they want to... reinforce." Far above us, there's a thump.

"We're not really living," I say. "We're like the streets. They cut all the trees down and now they're just names. Not trees anymore."

Father looks at me with just the faintest touch of disappointment. "We'll go down together," he says. There's another thump from upstairs. He closes the curtain that the old man opened.

I don't know why I can't stop going out. But then, I don't know why I keep going on like this at all.

Maybe when I was made, a part was left out. Or maybe that's not the problem – it's that something was left in.

Some time later, I open the cellar door and step out. The house looks strange to me for a moment, as if during the time that I've been downstairs, a new house has built itself around me. My whole body feels different, leaden and old. I want to crawl under a quilt of Alda's catalogs and sleep, but I can't. I have work to do.

In the kitchen, the light is still on. The old man's hat has disappeared from the table. So has the quarter he left behind. His empty teacup has been washed, and sits in the draining rack. I go to dry it, and as I do, a mouse trap snaps shut behind me.

I put the cup away and go upstairs. When I get to Damien's door I stop and listen. "Yes," he says, inside.

His room is still littered with drawings: distorted red-and-brown bodies on crumpled paper. There's a glass on the windowsill, half-full of a brownish liquid. A sweet, narcotic smoke lingers in the air, veiling something else.

Damien lies on the messy, half-stripped mattress he uses for a bed. He looks normal again. Not blank, not missing. He studies me, upside-down.

"You should know better," he observes, then pushes over. "Come on." I crawl up into the space between his body and the wall.

"You can't just go inviting any old oddbody into the house." Damien drops his hand over the edge of the mattress, and I hear the rustle of a plastic bag. He mimics Father's deep, slow voice: "What would the old folks say?"

I close my eyes. A lighter clicks. When I open my eyes, Damien is holding a hand-rolled cigarette in front of my face. I take it. The smoke is harsh and sweet, and sometimes it works.

We lie in silence for a while, trading the cigarette back and forth. At last Damien exhales a long cone of smoke and stubs out the roach without offering it to me.

I haul myself out of the bed and go to Damien's desk. There's a sheaf of brand new drawings spread over the desktop, hasty looping scrawls that bear no resemblance to the human form. I pull one closer to study its gristled red and brown lines. They're still wet.

"I'm going to sleep," Damien says, rolling over to face the wall. "Turn out the light when you go."

I sit with the drawings a while longer, tracing the blurred lines with my fingertips.

After a while the patterns start to feel familiar. At last they become meaningless.

Damien is sleeping. I gather up the drawings and tuck them under my arm. Then I go to his bed, slip my hand beneath his pillow, and pull out the old man's round-framed glasses. Father has tried to break him of this habit, the keeping of mementoes, but it persists. I'm careful to lock the door behind me.

Downstairs, the sitting room is empty. I pile Damien's drawings in the hearth and light them with the butane clicker. When they've burnt I mix the ashes into the bucket. Sven will take them out tomorrow.

I take my coat from the stand, and drop the old man's round-rimmed glasses into my pocket.

Outside, I pause to look up. The branches of the walnut tree crisscross above me like an ornate iron cage.

It's a mile and a half up the freeway to the anonymous trash cans at the public rest stop. If anyone sees me and pulls over, concerned at the sight of such a young child alone at night, I won't talk to them. I won't look over into their dome-lit car, at their fast food wrappers and dangling air fresheners and blue-hued satellite radio stations. I won't even pause. I'll just keep walking until they give up and drive away, until they disappear over the next curve into darkness and forget I was ever there.

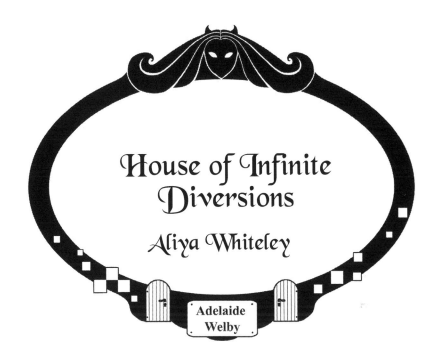

House of Infinite Diversions

Aliya Whiteley

Adelaide Welby

The House of Infinite Diversions lay down a side street in a small, affluent city. At first glance you might think it was a part of a long terrace of white Georgian family homes, with half-lidded, sleepy, sash-window eyes. In fact, it stood apart from the row, broken by an alley on either side that led into nettle-thick passageways and, beyond, a forest of a garden. The exterior was not quite white. It had a yellowish tint to it, rather like a tooth that is just succumbing to rot.

It was accepted that a certain amount of the girls who entered the House of Infinite Diversions would not return, and small plaques were affixed to a section of the thick wall that surrounded the city. One of these brass plaques – some polished to a warm sheen, and others turning to green in the rain – bore the name:

ADELAIDE WELBY

Her mentor, Mr Raphael, maintained her plaque. He visited it every Sunday with a rag and a tin of Brasso in hand, and he worried about what would happen when he departed this world. The short answer is – nothing. Nobody else cared.

But the long answer is – it's impossible to calculate how many lives we touch in our short time on this Earthly plane. And maybe Adelaide is still remembered in the most unlikely of circles, and a day is coming when Mr Raphael will find an ally for the polishing of the plaque, and the maintenance of a memory.

Not definitely. Just possibly.

Mr Raphael walked her to the front door and Adelaide tried to look suitably downcast. "Remember," he said, folding his hands over his waistcoat as if to cradle his hurting heart, "Don't be tempted to believe any promises. And keep on your guard at all times."

Adelaide put one of her hands on his clasped ones, and said, "Please don't worry so. You've taught me well."

"Yes, but is it enough?" he fretted.

How typical of him, Adelaide thought, *that I should have to spend my last moments before my greatest test reassuring him. As if he is the important one and this is nothing but a test of his teachings, and not of my character at all.* "Adieu," she said, knowing goodbye was a word that would prey on his mind.

"You're approaching womanhood already," said Mr Raphael humbly, looking over her white ruffled blouse and long black skirt. "You get to dismiss men with a single word. Adieu, you say, and I am meant to depart. No clinging to my presence for you. I see. I see." He kissed her left cheek, then her right, then hesitated over the left cheek again before walking away.

At last.

Adelaide rang the bell, and awaited entry.

Womanhood is not achieved upon a certain date. It's not a mark upon a calendar. Adelaide was twelve years old, and had been in Mr Raphael's care for six long years before she finally received her invitation to the House of Infinite Diversions, and she had gone beyond fear, expectation, or impatience in that time span. She had imagined every scenario that could stand between her and her freedom, and she had no doubt she would succeed where other women had failed. Her mind was already set on it.

And she need never see Mr Raphael again. Although she harboured a fancy of visiting him for tea every now and again, just so she could bask in his devotion for an hour or two, before it became annoying once more.

Adelaide's life was, in her eyes, laid out before her like a map, with each bend in the road visible. Here, in this house, was where the journey began. Just as soon as somebody answered the doorbell.

She rang it again – it was the kind that you press in with your finger – and heard the chime sound inside the house. Then silence.

It occurred to her that she had fulfilled her end of the bargain. She presented herself, as requested, at the house on the morning of the fifth of March. Just to be certain, Adelaide took out the thick, gilt-edged card from her leather backpack and read it once more. Yes, she simply had to be here. The card did not specifically mention entering the building. If she wished, she could leave now and start her new life as a grown-up woman of the city. She had done her civic duty, and no more could be asked of her.

She turned to go. And yet...

The thought came to her, flying in low like a wasp to a picnic, that she had been judged by the house and found wanting. Other girls had travelled beyond the door that remained shut in her face. They had undergone great peril of an unspecified sort, and she didn't even get to step inside.

Am I not worthy? she thought. Indignation rose inside her and burned her face.

She thought back over her training, but nothing had prepared her for the idea that she was a failure from the off. The feeling was deeply unpleasant. Unacceptably uncomfortable.

She turned back to the house and stared at it.

It had an unpleasant aspect, with curtainless windows that only revealed a darkness within, giving away nothing. And the door, now she looked properly at it, was not looking its best either. The blue paint was peeling, revealing a damp, grainy wood underneath, and the letterbox was unpolished. Could it be that the House of Infinite Diversions had fallen into disrepair? Surely somebody in the city would have noticed? And, if she was the first girl to come to the house and find it as a shell, how would she ever become a woman?

Fear gripped her. She leaned forward and rapped sharply on the wood. "Hello? Hello?" Without warning, the door swung back, and Adelaide found herself face to face with a grey-haired woman who displayed an unfriendly, downturned mouth.

"Oh," she said. "It's you."

"I, um, have a card," said Adelaide. She held it out, and the woman ignored it.

"Right, well, get on with it." She stepped back and Adelaide walked past her, into a hall of black and white tiles, from floor to ceiling, as unnerving as a giant chessboard upon which she had just been introduced as a piece.

The woman slammed the door, and brushed past her to stand on the first step of the curved staircase. "Get on with it, then," she said. She was dressed in light brown trousers and a pink woollen cardigan, over which she wore a blue-striped tabard with deep pockets. In one hand she held an old-fashioned feather duster. It came to Adelaide that this was no more than a cleaning lady, or some sort of caretaker.

"Get on with what?"

"Go where you like, wander about. Until you find it."

"Find what?"

"A diversion," the woman said, as if talking to a particularly annoying small child. She showed no sign of moving from the stairs, so Adelaide decided to stick to the downstairs part of the house. The hall held a number of closed doors, three on her left and four on her right that she could see immediately, although the corridor stretched on beyond that. None of the doors held any distinguishing features.

"Very well," she said. She picked a door on the right, and stood before it. Then she controlled her breathing, using a calming technique Mr Raphael had taught to her, and mentally ran through the relevant self-defence techniques for unwelcome surprises behind doors. A cough from the woman on the staircase sounded suspiciously like a suppressed laugh, but Adelaide ignored it.

She opened the door.

It was a darkened room, large and yet airless, with thick white carpet, and a bare bulb hanging from the ceiling. A long wooden table stood in the centre, with thick metal chains running along the length of it, and metal clasps at each end. Manacles, Adelaide realised with a shudder, and then her eyes took in the rest of the room properly. A trolley beside the table displayed knives, scalpels, pincers, pokers, hammers of differing sizes. The walls were adorned with more chains and manacles. A black vice and a rack with a wooden wheel for tightening, tightening. And, opposite her, a sarcophagus with ornate carvings, standing upright.

She stood very still, listening, looking, until she was certain she was alone. Even so, it took all of her courage to enter that room, and she did so only with the thought of arming herself against whatever madman had decorated the house in such a fashion. The trolley offered an array of possibilities; she crossed to it, and examined the instruments. They smelled, and the surfaces were thick with a dried residue of a brown substance that she really didn't want to name in her imagination. One of the smaller knives looked less well-used than the others, the blade still clean; she picked it up, wielded it, and felt a modicum of strength return to her. Mr Raphael had given her lessons in hand-to-hand combat, and even a crash course in the Filipino knife-fighting martial art of Eskrima. She wasn't an expert, but it was better than nothing.

"Blimey," said a voice behind her.

She whirled, readied herself; but it was only the cleaning woman, standing in the doorway, looking around the room with a mild interest, as if she had never seen its contents before.

"You're a wild one," she said.

"Who owns this house?" said Adelaide, softly. "Give me a description."

"The city owns it."

"The city condones this? The city allows..."

The woman smiled, a brief upturn of her mouth before it settled back into disapproval. "You're brave, but you're not quick, are you? And too imaginative for your own good. I tell you what – I'll give you a choice. You can leave the house now, and go on your merry way, or you can open the iron maiden and get to the bottom of all this."

"The – iron maiden?"

"Don't play dumb with me. I know you know what it is." She jerked her head at the sarcophagus. "It wouldn't be here if you didn't."

Adelaide felt the handle of the knife in her palm. She could stab this annoying cleaner in a heartbeat, but, of course, that was not what properly brought up young ladies did. They attacked and laid low the enemy. If only she knew who the enemy was.

"Keep your distance," she warned the woman, half-expecting some sort of trick. She'd read Hansel and Gretel – you get the witch to open the fire, and then you push her in. Or, in this case, you tell the girl to open the iron maiden and then give her a good shove before slamming the doors shut. "I wasn't born yesterday."

"Compared to whom?" retorted the woman.

Adelaide ignored her, and crossed to the iron maiden. It emanated a black, seething despair, a horror that was impossible to ignore. She reached out her hand to it and saw her fingers tremble as she brushed the metal casing. A long centre split revealed where it would swing open; she put her nails to the crack and pulled until the doors gave, and opened by a few inches.

A gush of blood, a torrent, spilling over her feet and soaking into the white carpet, turning it red, and there, inside the case, held up by the spikes that remained in the flesh, she saw a punctured body, and a face with open mouth and both eyes staring upwards at the giant metal protuberance that emerged from the centre of the forehead.

Adelaide knew her. It was the shock of looking in a mirror, seeing pain and blood when you thought you would be forever invincible. Seeing death.

"It's me," she said. She stepped back, clutched the table for support, dropped the knife. The woman came to stand behind her. "Yes, it's you. And me too."

Adelaide looked up into her face, scanned her features. "You..." Yes, she saw it – another mirror. Another version of herself, many years in the future. "I'm not going to leave this house, am I?"

"That's up to you. Shall we go into a different room? I'm not keen on this one." Adelaide felt her dry, insistent touch on her elbow, and allowed herself to be led from the room. Back in the hall, nothing had changed. Her blood-soaked feet walked on the black and white squares, leaving a red trail, and she chose another door at random. Behind this one lay a walled garden in midsummer, pretty in its untended wildness, with daisies and forget-me-nots springing up around the legs of a white painted bench that looked perfect for two.

Adelaide sat, and listened to a wood pigeon coo, as Old Adelaide sat beside her and patted her thigh in a regular rhythm. All her training had deserted her. She could think of nothing she could say or do. She never wanted to look at herself again.

"I prefer this side of our imagination," said Old Adelaide. "But you can't take the good and leave the bad, can you? Thoughts of beauty go hand in hand with cruelty. Climb the peaks and plumb the depths. Are you feeling calmer now? It wasn't real, you know. Look at your shoes."

They were spotless once more. Clean and shiny against the green blades of grass. "Why..." said Adelaide. She made an effort to bring her voice under control. "Why is this called the House of Infinite Diversions? This isn't diverting."

"Really? I'm exceedingly diverted. If it isn't, you have only yourself to blame." There was the flutter of wings, hushed and soft, and the wood pigeon was gone. A trickling sound replaced its cooing – there had to be a fountain nearby that had just started to flow.

The thought occurred to Adelaide that the garden looked familiar. Not from real life, but from a fantasy she had once harboured as a child, that Mr Raphael would one day take her to just such a place and leave her there, to grow wild and strong with the weeds. There would be no grown-ups: no parents who could desert her, or mentors who could tell her what to do. There would only be her, and the sun, and the birds and beasts of a quiet, walled patch of perfection, with fresh fruit picked from the trees to eat and water from a marble fountain to drink. And she knew then, that if she left her bench and pushed further into the garden she would find that marble fountain, and it would be every bit as beautiful as she had imagined.

"This shouldn't be called the House of Infinite Diversions," she whispered. "It should be called the House of Infinite Possibilities."

"Call it what you will," Old Adelaide told her. "It's entirely up to you. So. What do you think? Is there enough here to keep you busy forever? Enough doors that need opening? Or would you prefer to become a woman of the city?"

Adelaide thought about the idea that had once held such appeal for her. She could take an active part in the running of the city. She could get married and bear children; strong men to mentor and beautiful girls to grow into fine women like herself. As long as they did not lose their way and became excessively diverted.

At last the name of the house made sense to her. "I think," she said, "that I want to stay."

"You're sure? You could go and have a wonderfully normal and respectable life out there."

"I'm just beginning to realise that I'd rather be squelched by an iron maiden."

"I knew you'd say that," said Old Adelaide, with a touch of recognisable smugness. "Leave me here in this garden, and go and have a good old explore, and come back in a few decades or so. I'll be waiting."

Adelaide got up from the bench, took a long look around the delights of this most pleasant aspect of her imagination, and then left. There were so many doors to try.

Mr Raphael finishes polishing the plaque on the wall of the city, and puts away his rag and his can of Brasso. Nobody has ever approached him while he cares for that little rectangle of metal that bears her name, and he has never unburdened himself of the guilt he feels over her failure.

He loved Adelaide Welby so. He remembers how he sensed danger in her – a little too much enthusiasm for books, and the tendency to relate long, confusing dreams in the morning over breakfast. And yet she had wanted to be a good woman. He had seen that possibility within her, and he still couldn't quite believe that she had succumbed to the House of Infinite Diversions.

What moral rot had set in? What had she possibly been offered that could outweigh the pleasure of her civic duty?

He looks about, hopefully. Maybe someone is approaching, standing close by – someone who would love to hear a story of a talented girl, her fatal flaw, and her ultimate downfall. But there is nobody.

At least, nobody visible. We are here, Mr Raphael, we readers, we lovers of imagination.

The walls of the city do not contain us, or Adelaide Welby, or any of our number. And the maintenance of memory has nothing to do with the places where our names rest. We are remembered for as long as there are doors to open, and rooms to enter, with infinite diversions contained within.

Mr Raphael limps away, broken-hearted. The question is not who will remember us, but who will remember him.

Contributors

Ian MacAllister-McDonald

Ian MacAllister-McDonald is a playwright, filmmaker and educator from Portland, Maine. He holds an MFA in Playwriting from Brown University, where he also taught. He is the recipient of two Edward Albee Foundation Fellowships, a MacDowell Colony Fellowship, a Playwriting Grant from the National Endowment for the Arts, the Clauder Competition Gold Prize, The Visionary Playwrights Award from Theatre Masters, and most recently a Virginia Center for the Creative Arts Residency. He received a BA in English Literature from Loyola Marymount University, where he recently returned to teach.

Tim Jeffreys

Tim Jeffreys is the author of five collections of short stories, the most recent being 'From Elsewhere', and a couple of novellas, 'The Haunted Grove' and 'The Foundering'. Another novella, 'Voids', co-written with Martin Greaves will be published by Omnium Gatherum Media in early 2016. His short fiction has appeared in various international anthologies and magazines. He also edits and compiles the Dark Lane Anthologies where he gets to publish talented writers from all over the world. In his own work he incorporates elements of horror, fantasy, absurdist humour, science-fiction and anything else he wants to toss into the pot to create his own brand of weird fiction. Tim is also a talented artist and gained a university honours degree in Graphic Arts and Design in 2000.

Originally from Oldham, UK, Tim moved 'down south' over a decade ago and now lives in Bristol with his partner Isabel and two strange little girls of his own. He remains a northerner at heart, misses the rain, and, like most other writers he knows, dreams of one day giving up the day job. Visit him online at *www.timjeffreys.blogspot.co.uk*.

Annie Neugebauer

Annie Neugebauer (@*AnnieNeugebauer*) is a novelist, short story author, and award-winning poet. She has stories and poems appearing or forthcoming in over fifty venues, including Black Static, Fireside, DarkFuse, and Buzzy Mag. She's an active member of the Horror Writers Association, the webmaster for the Poetry Society of Texas, and a columnist for Writer Unboxed. She lives in Texas with her sweet husband and two diabolical cats. You can visit her at www.AnnieNeugebauer.com for blogs, creative works, free organizational tools for writers, and more.

Sierra July

Sierra is a University of Florida graduate, writer, and poet. Her fiction has appeared in T. Gene Davis's Speculative Blog, Perihelion Science Fiction, and SpeckLit, among other places. When she isn't reading or writing, she is dog training or studying new languages. So far she excels at Japanese, French, and German.
Sierra blogs at *talestotellinpassing.blogspot.com.*

Karen Munro

Karen Munro lives and writes stories in Portland, OR.
You can find her online at:*munrovian.com.*

Tantra Bensko

Tantra Bensko teaches fiction writing online with UCLA Extension Writing Program, Writers.com, Writers College, and her own Online Writing Academy. A couple of hundred of her short stories, nearly a hundred poems, and countless art pieces live in magazines and anthologies. A variety of publishers, such as ISMs Press and ELJ Publications have put out her books. She received her MA from Florida State and her MFA from Iowa. She now lives in Berkeley. She has also ranged across the country in a somewhat feral and miraculous manner. She is fascinated by the presence of mass social engineering and writes about it, including a Psychological Suspense series called The Agents of the Nevermind, including Glossolalia about a strange woman/girl discovering a crime at a poison company.

Leife Shallcross

Leife Shallcross lives at the bottom of Mount Ainslie in Canberra, Australia, with her family and a small, scruffy creature that snores. She reads fairy tales to her children at night, and then lies awake listening to trolls (or maybe possums) galloping over her tin roof. Her work has appeared in Aurealis and several Australian and international anthologies, including The End Has Come, edited by John Joseph Adams and Hugh Howey. She is actively involved in the Canberra Speculative Fiction Guild and is the current president. When writing is not consuming her spare time and energy, she plays the fiddle (badly). Leife can be found online at: *leifeshallcross.com* and on Twitter: *@leioss*.

Angela Rega

Angela Rega is a belly-dancing school librarian in love with folklore, fairy tales and furry creatures. She is a Sydney based writer and graduate of Clarion South. Her stories have appeared in publications including Crossed Genres, PS Publications and the Year's Best Australian Fantasy and Horror. She drinks way too much coffee, often falls in love with poetry and can't imagine not writing. She keeps a very small website here: *angierega.webs.com*

Aliya Whiteley

Aliya Whiteley lives in West Sussex, UK, and writes speculative fiction. She has been shortlisted for both the Shirley Jackson award and the James Tiptree Jr Award for her latest novella, The Beauty (published by Unsung Stories), and her stories have appeared in Strange Horizons, Interzone, Black Static, 3LBE, Kaleidotrope, and in many other places. She tweets most days as *@AliyaWhiteley*.

Terra LeMay

Terra LeMay was born on top of a volcano (in Hawaii). She tamed a wild mustang before she turned sixteen, and as an adult, she has held some unusual jobs — like training llamas and modeling in high-heeled shoes (though not at the same time!) Since 1999, she and her spouse have owned Epic Tattoo, an award-winning tattoo studio north of Atlanta, GA. It's across the street from a large book store. This was not an accident.

Terra's short fiction has appeared in Apex Magazine, Daily Science Fiction, InterGalactic Medicine Show, as well as other magazines and anthologies, in print and online.
You can find out more at: *terralemay.com*.

Rich Hawkins

Rich Hawkins hails from deep in the West Country, where a childhood of science fiction and horror films set him on the path to writing his own stories. He credits his love of horror and all things weird to his first viewing of John Carpenter's The Thing when, aged twelve, he crept downstairs late one night to watch it on ITV. He has a few short stories in various anthologies, and has written one novella, Black Star, Black Sun, released earlier this year. His debut novel The Last Plague has recently been nominated for a British Fantasy Award for Best Horror Novel.
He currently lives in Salisbury, Wiltshire, with his wife, their daughter and their pet dog Molly. They keep him sane. Mostly.
Find him at: *richwhawkins.blogspot.co.uk*

Megan Neumann

Megan Neumann is a speculative fiction writer living in Little Rock, Arkansas. Her stories have appeared in such publications as Crossed Genres, Daily Science Fiction, and Luna Station Quarterly. She is a member of the Central Arkansas Speculative Fiction Writers' Group and is particularly appreciative of their loving support and scathing critiques.

L. Lark

L. Lark is a writer and artist living in Portland, Oregon, who is prone to daydreaming and sunburns. She especially enjoys writing about ghosts, old houses, and all manners of eldritch abomination.
Links to her projects and publications may be found at: *l-lark.com*.

Jan Stinchcomb

Jan Stinchcomb's short stories have appeared in Necessary Fiction, A cappella Zoo, Happily Never After, Bohemia, Rose Red Review, Luna Station Quarterly, The Red Penny Papers, and PANK online, among other places. She reviews fairy tale inspired works for Luna Station Quarterly. Her novella, Find the Girl, is available from Main Street Rag. After two decades in Texas, she is back in California with her husband and daughters. Visit her at: *janstinchcomb.com.*

Ephiny Gale

Ephiny's fiction has been published in Daily Science Fiction, Aurealis, Postscripts to Darkness, The Future Fire, and Belladonna Publishing's acclaimed previous anthology, 'Black Apples.' She has also written several produced stage plays and musicals, including the sold-out How to Direct From Inside at La Mama and Shining Armour at The 1812 Theatre. Ephiny has a Masters in Arts Management, a red belt in taekwondo, an amazing partner and six imaginary whippets. She is currently working on both a short story collection and stage play collection. More at: *ephinygale.com.*

Colette Aburime

Colette Aburime is a creative writing and professional writing honors graduate from the University of Wisconsin - River Falls. She is the founder of writingwithcolor, a writing advice blog focused on diversity. When not found frolicking through the woods somewhere in Minnesota chasing after her latest bit of inspiration, Colette works on moderating her blog and cooking up concoctions that make her friends and family drool. Find her at: *writingwithcolor.tumblr.com*

Ekaterina Sedia

Ekaterina Sedia resides in the Pinelands of New Jersey. Her critically-acclaimed and award-nominated novels, The Secret History of Moscow, The Alchemy of Stone, The House of Discarded Dreams, and Heart of Iron, were published by Prime Books. Her short stories appeared in Analog, Baen's Universe, Subterranean, and Clarkesworld, as well as numerous anthologies, including Haunted Legends and Magic in the Mirrorstone. She is also the editor of the anthologies Paper Cities (World Fantasy Award winner), Running with the Pack, Bewere the Night, and Bloody Fabulous as well as The Mammoth Book of Gaslit Romance and Wilful Impropriety. Her short-story collection, Moscow But Dreaming, was released by Prime Books in December 2012. She also co-wrote a script for Yamasong: March of the Hollows, a fantasy feature-length puppet film voiced by Nathan Fillion, George Takei, Abigail Breslin, and Whoopi Goldberg to be released in 2016 by Dark Dunes Productions.

Calypso Kane

Calypso Kane is a semi-professional scribbler, expert hermit, and fan of sundry spooks and horrors. She's written for short story anthologies such as, Creature Stew, Her Dark Voice 2, The Odd and the Bizarre, and is all a-thrill to be part of Strange Little Girls.

Frances Pauli

Frances Pauli writes across multiple genres. Her work is speculative, full of the fantastic, and quite often romantic at its core. Whenever possible, she enjoys weaving in a little humor.

Once upon a time she was a visual artist, but she's since come to her senses. Now she fills her minuscule amount of free time with things like crocheting, belly-dancing, and abysmal ukulele playing.

Information about her writing, her series, and free webserials can be found at: *francespauli.com*

Printed in Great Britain
by Amazon

54216343R00118